# Dystopia

## The Long Road

# Copyrights

# Acknowledgements

Many helped bring this book to completion with words of encouragement, support and help. Many personal barriers impeded this work and there is so much I have to be grateful for.

I'd like to thank my friends and family who supported and encouraged me to write this book. A great friend Dickie Gales, who brought the accent of the character Dickie to life. Kelly Standish-Curry, who worked to help edit out the mishaps.

Jamie Waylein and Michelle Jodoin my lovely daughters who also served as the beta readers on this work.

Randy Mills a man who gives me space to write, encourages me to do so and cheers me on to bigger things. I love you Randy.

My children Chris and Jamie, who always believe in mommy even when she can't believe herself. I love you both and am truly blessed and thankful for such amazing children.

# Foreword

*"One of the darkest evils of our world is surely the unteachable wildness of the good."*
-H.G. Wells

This book took more than eighteen months to write, the first book fell out like word vomit yet this one I once described as bleeding through my fingertips. Part of the struggle was the ever changing landscape of the craziness that surrounds us. Keeping with the premise of the first book it was difficult not to include the struggles faced by many today.

The story of the friends that must make it to their family is one of struggles and strife, full of betrayal. A new understanding of the things people will do in bad situations. Often times I am reminded that the rule of law (ROL) only serves to keep the honest in line, once ROL disintegrates many of our friends and neighbors may turn to crime or even on the very friends they say they love.

The book continues the story of Matt and Destiny in a changed world. What would you do without your world of technology? Without fast food, fast internet and instant gratification? In a world where you question the source of every meal? Could you survive? Could you make it on a journey of more than nine hundred miles?

Like the first book, follow up to the story you will find a list of resources that I hope you will find as useful as I have. It is one thing to know of something, it is a whole different concept to put it into practical application.

I hope you enjoy The Long Road as much as I did in writing it, I hope you can identify with the characters and it sparks the questions in you that arose when writing it and that it encourages you to prepare.

DJ Cooper

# Table of Contents

*Dystopia* ................................................................*i*

Copyrights ..........................................................iii

Acknowledgements ...........................................iv

Foreword ..............................................................v

*Dystopia* ...............................................................*1*

*Chapter 1* ............................................................*3*

"Time is short" ....................................................3

*Chapter 2* ..........................................................*11*

"The time draws near" ....................................11

*Chapter 3* ..........................................................*18*

"Trouble in the wind" ......................................18

*Chapter 4* .........................................................*29*

"In the midst" ...................................................29

*Chapter 5* .........................................................*47*

"The End is now the Beginning" ........................................47

*Chapter 6*........................................................*55*

"Welcome Friends".........................................................55

*Chapter 7*........................................................*71*

"The Others " .................................................................71

*Chapter 8*........................................................*85*

"The Road" ....................................................................85

*Chapter 9*.......................................................*100*

"Out of the Fire" ............................................................100

*Chapter 10*......................................................*113*

"A changed landscape"...................................................113

*Chapter 11*......................................................*123*

In Darkness... Danger ...................................................123

*Chapter 12* .....................................................*141*

"The Storm" ......................................................141

*Chapter 13* ......................................................*155*

"Treachery" ......................................................155

*Chapter 14* ......................................................*175*

"Trouble Doubles" ......................................................175

*Chapter 15* ......................................................*185*

"Grief and Guilt" ......................................................185

*Chapter 16* ......................................................*204*

"The Camp" ......................................................204

*Chapter 17* ......................................................*218*

"In Darkness we move" ......................................................218

*Chapter 18* ......................................................*235*

"Wolf in sheep's clothing" ......................................................235

*Chapter 19* ......................................................*249*

"Luck can change" ......................................................249

*Chapter 20* ......................................................*258*

"Light at the end of the tunnel" ......................................................258

*Chapter 21* ......................................................*274*

"Unexpected friends" ........................................274

*Chapter 22* ................................................*286*

"The Relay" ...............................................286

*Chapter 23* ................................................*299*

"Overland" ................................................299

*Chapter 24* ................................................*316*

"Bittersweet arrival" ......................................316

*Chapter 25* ................................................*332*

"Sickness" .................................................332

*Chapter 26* ................................................*350*

"Reality of life now" ......................................350

Note from the Author .......................................1

Resources...................................................4

    Composting .............................................4

    Rain Water .............................................5

    Solar Hot Water ........................................6

    Wood Fired Hot Water....................................6

    Solar Panels ...........................................7

    Batteries...............................................7

    Solar Window Heaters ...................................7

    Morse Code..............................................8

    Bug out bags aka the BOB ...............................8

A.N.T.S .......................................................................................9

Cache ........................................................................................9

Canning and preserving ..............................................................9

Dakota pit or fire hole .............................................................10

Ham Radios ..............................................................................10

Videos .....................................................................................11

About the Author .....................................................................13

*Dystopia* ................................................................................*3*

*Chapter 1* ...............................................................................*5*

**"Dark days loom ominous"** .....................................................**5**

# Dystopia

The Long Road

# Chapter 1

## "Time is short"

*"If the day should ever come when we must go, if some day we are compelled to leave the scene of history, we will slam the door so hard that the universe will shake and mankind will stand back in stupefaction..."*
-Joseph Goebbles

*September 6th*

  John stood looking at the wood pile, wondering if what he had cut and split this year was going to get them through the winter. He thought, 'It is already this cold and it's only September, New England winters can be brutal.' Grabbing an armload for the old wood stove, he headed back inside.

  He loved a good fire in the mornings, but this early in the season, troubled him to be in need of a morning fire. Starting to cool off so soon meant the winter would be long and cold.

  John fancied himself quite the outdoorsman and decided he would try out his fire-starting skills by using his flint keychain. He began to strike the sparks at the paper he had all crumpled up and placed at the bottom of a pile of wood he stacked neatly in a tipi. Not really paying attention he started humming along to the song on the radio, then began to sing along. *"I'm not the one who's so far away, when I feel the snake bite enter my veins."* This was one of his favorite bands, he liked a heavier sound and *Godsmack* was definitely one of the bands that topped his list.

The phone let out the sound indicating a text just arrived.

Scowling as he got up to check it, "Damn phone, just when a good song comes on."

He walked over to where his phone sat on the charger mumbling, "First the fire won't start and now who the hell would be texting me at this hour?"

Turning back to the fire, giving up on his quest for flame free fire starting, he unceremoniously tossed a match into the stove. John felt edgy today as he went to check his phone. Seeing it was a text from Matt, all was forgiven and he checked it right away. Reading the text he raised his eyebrows,

"Hey there guy, you might want to check out the news."

*Bing, bing...* another text arrived

"You know me, I don't usually worry about news, but something is up with this."

John texted him back saying, "Hey guy, I'm checking it out now."

Aiming the remote and turning on the TV, John grabbed a cup of coffee and sat to tend this fire that still refused to start. Absently, he was looking to the TV from time to time.   One of the commercials caught his eye for lawn tractors drawing his attention to the screen.

Continuing to watch as the news returned, he caught sight of the ticker rolling across the bottom.  *"Ebola virus has been confirmed at hospitals in the following six U.S. cities.  New York, Atlanta, Las Vegas, Denver, Sacramento and Detroit… Please stay tuned for an official announcement."*

This piqued John's interest, and he decided he would wait and watch the announcement.  John rarely watched the news, except for the weather reports, because he felt like it was all propaganda. This new tidbit might prove entertaining, he thought. He figured he had a little time before the official announcement of this new *event*, which he was sure would raise some kind of cry for new laws or changes, 'they always do' he thought.  With September 11th right around the corner, he already expected something to draw attention away from it.

He didn't bother to wake Amy, knowing she was never interested in what she called his, "conspiracy theories."  While he sat waiting, he was contemplating what this could mean. Since it was bothering Matt, he was sure it was very important.

The *"Beep, Beep, Beep"* sounded on the TV indicating the news conference was beginning. He refilled his coffee for what he was sure would be another round of useless banter on this or that.  But, Matt wanted him to watch and he trusted his friend's instincts, so he watched.

Not long after the beeping, the announcement began; a spokesperson from the Centers for Disease control in Atlanta appeared for the camera and approached the podium. The announcer began to speak, *"Ladies and Gentlemen, Dr. Ralph Sorenson, incident manager for the CDC Ebola response."* A rather nervous looking and visibly uncomfortable man walked into view. A tiny little man, with a comb over and what looked like glasses from the 50's took the podium and began to speak.

*"Health officials have confirmed cases of Ebola within the U.S. Patients are being treated at undisclosed hospitals in the following cities; New York, Atlanta, Las Vegas, Denver, Sacramento and Detroit."*

There was a long pause as the weary spokesperson continued, *"Understand, we know how to stop Ebola. It won't be easy or fast, but working together with our U.S. government and international partners, we are doing it in Africa and can do so here, but it will take time."*

He paused for the murmuring to quiet and continued. *"Ebola is a deadly virus. It is spread through direct contact with the blood, secretions, and organs or thru other bodily fluids of those who are already infected. This is not an airborne virus, I repeat, it is not airborne! You cannot catch it from casual contact. Symptoms, which can begin anywhere from two to twenty-one days after infection, include fever, muscle pain, headache and a sore throat, these symptoms will then be followed by vomiting, diarrhea and rash. If anyone in these cities has been experiencing these symptoms, please report to the nearest health care facility as soon as possible. The CDC is sending workers to the affected cities to fight Ebola's spread, and while the number of CDC experts may change slightly from day to day. More than fifty CDC personnel are being sent to remain in these six cities continuously.*

*"Again, the CDC's public health experts in West Africa and here in the United States are working closely with our U.S. Government and international partners as part of this worldwide*

*emergency response to the Ebola outbreak. Our primary goal is to contain this disease and keep Americans safe, thank you for your vigilance and stay safe America."* He nodded to the announcer, turned and without looking back, exited the stage.

John laughed out loud saying, "Matt has sure lost it if he thinks this is news."

Although, he didn't want to admit that something struck him in how antiseptic it all was, and he thought it might be best to keep his ear to the ground. He was amazed at how little else about the whole Ebola thing was said. It seemed eerily absent from all the other channels. It was like a little blurb and then nothing else and this is what struck him as strange.

He was getting ready to shut off the TV when Amy came out of the bedroom saying, "What's this? You, watching the news?" Yawning, she whined, "it's cold in here, didn't you make a fire?"

John leapt from his seat; he had fallen into his own thoughts and completely forgotten about the fire. Clamoring over to it, he realized it was but a smoldering pile of newspaper ash; none of the wood was doing anything but smoking. In a flash he had a blaze going and Amy was snuggling next to the stove calling out for coffee.

John wondered sometimes how he and she had managed to stay together, they were nothing alike. She made fun of his theories every time he had anything that concerned him. Luckily he and Matt talked often and he could talk about anything with him. They had been friends for as long as John could remember. As he stood making more coffee, he reminded himself 'I need to call Matt and talk with him about all this.'

The rest of that day while Amy watched her shows on the TV, John made a quick inventory of the supplies on hand. He was still concerned about the early cold and worried more about if things went badly this winter that there would be many that would not be ready to brave it. He chopped more wood that day than many others. He didn't know if it was because of the news or just that those damn shows annoyed him.

Something about the news this morning was really beginning to eat at him and by dinner time he was completely into his own thoughts on everything that could go wrong. He decided that between now and the 11th he needed to do a few things and would start on them tomorrow. He didn't bother to tell Amy his thoughts because he knew she would just scoff at him.

# Chapter 2

## "The time draws near"

*"I do not believe in a fate that will fall on us no matter what we do, I believe in a fate that will fall on us if we do nothing."*
-Ronald Reagan

The days passed like a blur as John continued his inventory, his thoughts on the anniversary of September 11th. There always seemed to be some kind of threat on this anniversary. He wasn't sure if it was because of the day that the crazies came out of the woodwork or if there was something about it.

It was another cold day; he wished this cold front would pass. The thought of winter starting already was unnerving to say the least. Amy was already in complaint mode, constantly bitching about the fire. He wished she would get up and just put some wood in the stove instead of crying she was cold.

Sometimes he did wonder why they were together; she was a pretty woman with her nails always done beautifully. She had short blonde hair that sat on her shoulders and perpetually needing some kind of goo or ooze in it.

He on the other hand, was what his friends affectionately called, the "Grizzly Adams" type. Having scruffy hair and beard, he carried a few extra pounds. Which he swore Amy orchestrated with all her good cooking.

Some days he also wished she would live up to her threats to go and move to Florida to stay with her mother. But most days he loved her and wanted to keep her safe and warm.

Being the day before the anniversary of the fateful day the towers fell, he wanted to make sure his things were well organized.

He looked at this day as his annual inventory and prep check day. It was not that he actually thought there were any threats, but it made a good reason to make sure his house was in order before winter.

He checked his bug out bags and replaced anything going out of date on this day. Being prepared for an emergency was always very important to John, especially living in an environment where a day without heat during the winter could equal death. He had a "BOB" for Amy too, but he doubted she would ever carry it farther than down the long driveway. He began to go through the bags starting with his own. He pulled out a number of smaller bags first each containing different kits. One for medical supplies he set aside this one would need to be updated and another for fishing and fire starting he set aside, these he would just check.

After removing the tent and the space bag holding his dry clothes he began his annual ritual of changing batteries in the flashlights. He exchanged the antibiotics and pain relievers as well as his vitamins. He placed it all back into the pack along with replacements for his freeze dried foods and edibles. Amy's bag was far easier to check, as hers contained only her clothes, freeze dried foods and smaller versions of the kits he kept in his bag.

Feeling satisfied with his day he headed to the kitchen to see what she was cooking up. She was a wonderful cook and it was something she loved to do, he did appreciate the good eats.

Tomorrow he will have to work and was not looking forward to it; he hated his job as an electrician. It made him think of Dez and Matt and how they got to choose their own schedules, he thought 'they sure got it good, what the hell am I doing all this for?' 'I totally should have gone into computers instead of electrical.'

Something wonderful was summoning him from his thoughts; it was a terrific smell coming from the kitchen. He recognized it and knew immediately she had made his favorite.

He practically danced into the kitchen singing, "Yay for me, it is lasagne night."

Amy loved it when he would get excited about what she cooked, and secretly he knew it and would do it often so she knew he appreciated the good grub.

*September 11$^{th}$*

As the morning sun began to shine, John headed outside to take care of making sure Amy had enough wood inside before he headed to work. As soon as he opened the door, he knew it was much warmer today.

He still wanted to bring in the wood and make a fire for her as she was sure to want one. He dreaded going to work today, and it weighed heavy on his mind. Surely they would make this day a day of remembrance like Martin Luther King Day or Presidents Day.

It puzzled him how it could not have gained such a status and sometimes annoyed him that there were observed holidays for stupid things yet not to remember the fallen on this day. 'Maybe it is just that I don't want to go to work that it annoys me.' Laughing to himself, he fixed his lunch and headed out the door.

The morning was the same stuff he had been doing for the past three months.

He spoke hushed to his friend Lefty saying, "Hell man, you would think working on at army depot today we might get to at least see something interesting."

Lefty looked at him, saying, "You know, I was just thinking that. It seems too quiet today, usually we see uniformed guys doing this and that. Today, though, there is nothing, almost eerie."

John nodded and went back to his work thinking, 'it *is* too quiet, and eerie was a good word for this day.' He shrugged to himself and tried to look busy enough to get him through till lunch.

During lunch there was chat about the lack of activity on this date and some speculation, but John just had an uneasy feeling about it all. Looking into his lunch, he could not help but wonder 'What was I thinking this morning?' Inside the cooler was a decent turkey sandwich, but he had also tossed in some random junk food. There was some candy, a Swiss Roll, a baggie full of chips, and a yogurt drink.

Lefty looked at his lunch and asked, "What happened to your lunch? Did a nine year old pack it for you?"

John just shrugged and said, "I was a little distracted this morning. I usually put in some leftovers, not sure what I was thinking."

They both laughed and Lefty stole his yogurt drink, while John headed for the soda machine for something else to drink. The rest of the day was more of the same, John was glad when it was time to go home. He hoped Amy was cooking something good for dinner after the less than appetizing lunch he had. He drove home in his usual mood, with NPR on the radio. However, today he was barely listening to it, his thoughts were elsewhere.

Each day passed much the same and John was finally feeling better about the eerie quiet of the eleventh. Driving to work a few days later he chided himself thinking, 'I always get these feelings of dread, I should not let them get me all nerved up.' Amy phoned bringing him out of his self-reprisals.

Answering the phone he said, "Hi babe, what's up?"

She responded, "Hi yourself, you forgot I had a hair appointment today and needed the truck."

Sighing, he said, "Be ready in five, I'll be right back."

He had forgotten and now this was just one more thing to curse himself over. He would be glad when this week was over.

# Chapter 3

## "Trouble in the wind"

*"Has a remarkable opportunity arisen for President Putin to Bust the U.S. Petro Dollar and collapse the Criminal Banking System behind it?"*
-Preston James, Ph.D.

*September 14th*

John woke before the sun came up; he liked having some quiet time in the mornings. He grabbed himself a cup of coffee and sat down to watch some news, this was unlike him, but lately he had been watching in the mornings. For reasons he himself didn't know, he felt better after the eleventh was passed, but still had this feeling he couldn't shake.

He always said, "The news is full of nothing but fluff and circus acts."

He figured he would watch the circus for a bit before starting the day. He had the day off and planned to make the most of it.

He was half watching the news and half thinking about what he wanted to do for the day. He knew Amy had some plans but couldn't remember what, he also knew he would catch hell for not remembering. As he sipped on his second cup a line scrolled across the bottom that made him take notice. *"Financial markets are experiencing drop today in the wake of the OPEC announcement that the standard for oil sales will no longer be in U.S. currency, all oil will now be transferred in Gold."* He knew what this meant, although most Americans have no clue what the petrodollar is, he knew exactly what this meant.... Hyperinflation was on the horizon.

This changed everything he'd planned to do today, now not only was he feeling like something wasn't right, he was sure something very bad was on the horizon. His mind began to race, going through all the possibilities of how things could go down. He found himself pacing through the house without direction.

Most people would not think anything of this, but he had done a lot of research on the petrodollar and without the oil to back the U.S. dollar, it would crash, becoming nearly worthless. Since going off the gold standard the only thing propping up the dollar had been OPEC and its agreement to trade all oil in U.S. currency.

John knew deep down, that coming soon would be something that was nothing short of disastrous.

He scolded himself as he did often, "I'm not ready for this!"

Checking things off in his mind, he began his mental list of things he wanted to address. "Cache" he thought, he had wanted to get that done this summer and had been putting it off. The thought struck him like a truck when it crossed his mind, 'Matt's parents, I have to go over and see them. I need to see what their situation is.'

John and Matt had been friends since middle school and he was close to his parents. Often just strolling in around lunch time and helping himself to snacks while chatting with them. He decided he would go over this afternoon, coincidentally right around lunch time. He giggled to himself thinking how he would be going to check on them yet helping himself to lunch.

Heading to the barn he got out the fifty-five gallon drums, he had collected earlier in the summer that he planned to use for his cache. Behind the barn was the chicken pen, he planned to bury them in the far corner of it. With the chickens constantly scratching the ground there was no grass anymore, he figured no one would be able to tell something was buried there.

In one of the three drums, he planned to put fuel, he had wanted a diesel truck, but Amy insisted she wanted him to get "normal" gas. She said that she hated the smell of the diesel and said she would not ride in it if he did. Thinking about it, he felt it was a good choice as he would now be able to fuel all the vehicles without the need of different drums. He buried all three of the drums without backfilling until he was done adding the contents. The fuel drum he filled full which took a few trips to different gas stations with his five gas cans that each held 5 gallons.

He then began to decide what he should place in the others. He knew that a time might come when his guns could be confiscated so that was one thing he was going to consider for the non-food drum.

The other was a food cache; he lined the drum with a large Mylar bag and placed 2 cases of freeze dried meals inside with coffee, sugar, powdered milk and chocolate. He also added canned meats of various kinds and fifteen pounds of beans. There was still room in the drum so he added salt and other spices and ten pounds of rice, topping it off with some flour and powdered eggs and a few jars of canned butter and peanut butter. Not wanting to waste any space he poured a large bag of various packets of things he had collected from all his takeout food to fill the voids. He sealed the bag and closed the lid taking care to make certain it was closed properly.

The final drum was non-food items he placed another Mylar bag inside, but only to make sure there would be no damage in case of leakage.

He decided on fishing equipment, a net and some snares. He added zip lock bags full of matches and lighters along with a whole box of heavy duty trash can liners.

He opted for two of his Glock 19's both chambered in 9mm and five hundred rounds for them. He also had a 12ga that he had picked up at the flea market and two hundred-fifty rounds of bird shot and another hundred of double ought buck. Finally, John added his old .22, and five hundred rounds of ammo for it. The gun had been a gift from his grandfather when he was nine years old, and held a special place in his heart.

Standing back looking at it, he knew he could get still more into this one, so he decided on a hatchet and camp saw. Not knowing what else he could add he began to walk about just looking at different things when it hit him, "Water" he said out loud.

Searching through his closet, he found what he was looking for, he had purchased some time back a Katadyn portable water filter, and it even had two replacement filters for it. As he was headed back to the drums, he remembered his other Med kit and decided to add it as well. Feeling fairly content with his caches he added random smaller items. These consisted of some silver coins, five bottles of varied liquor and a few flashlights along with spare batteries.

Once filled and all were sealed he completely covered the drums and spread the rest of the leftover dirt around the chicken pen. He rolled it with a large, heavy roller he used to mash out the mole trails in the yard; I worked well to pack it down. Afterwards he spread some chicken scratch around to get the chickens moving about so it would look like it usually did

Heading to the house to clean up, he asked Amy if she wanted to go over to Mark and Renee's with him.

She said, "Babe, you know I always go out with the girls on Fridays."

John replied, "I know that there sassy pants, I just didn't want you to think you were not invited."

He winked at her as he did his best strut into the house. Watching his strut, she laughed, and shouting out after him, "Oh yeah, shake that sexy ass."

He laughed as he headed for the shower, he loved her playful banter. Driving the five miles over to Mark and Renee's he considered what he might say. They had always thought he was just a little bit "off" where his thoughts on things like this were concerned.

He decided he would just try and play it off light, as though it might cause some disruptions and make sure they go do some food shopping. While there he would look around and quietly assess their situation and get Mark to go out and fill the tanks on the vehicles.

John walking into the house went right over and grabbing a soda from the fridge, sat down in his usual seat. Renee, true to form, started making sandwiches for the guy's lunch. John knew Mark always came home for lunch around eleven o'clock and would time it just right.

Laughing Renee said, "We were expecting you today, being your day off and all."

Mark and John both laughed, while John winked at her and gave her a kiss on the cheek saying, "You know me well, mom."

John talked with them a while about things and felt confident they would take his advice, at least for now. He and Mark went and filled the tanks in both vehicles and picked up a few items from the hardware store. This gave John a chance to talk to Mark about things.

He explained, saying, "Mark, I know you and Renee think I am crazy sometimes, but something isn't right about all of this. I know you know what OPEC is but if the world goes off the Petro-dollar we are in big trouble. It wouldn't hurt anything to do your grocery shopping tonight instead of waiting till Sunday would it?"

Mark agreed to head out to the grocery store this evening just to appease him.

While they were chatting John got a text from Matt that said, "There is going to be an announcement on TV, you need to check it out."

John texted back telling him they would watch. John and Mark headed into the house to put on the afternoon news.

John, waiting to see something other than a circus show said, "You know Mark; the news of OPEC this morning was pretty big. This is all going to cause our money to crash."

Mark just nodded with his usual dismissal of things John would say. John knew he was being dismissed on the subject and left it alone for the moment. Renee had brought them both a cup of coffee while they watched the news.

Mark looked at John and said, "The weather sure has been cold for this early in the season, now they are calling for snow already."

Mark nodded just waiting for whatever Matt had wanted him to see. The news was almost over when the anchor said, *"In financial news, a cyber-attack against the banking industry today has caused some computer glitches in the system. At the close of business today all systems will be offline until Tuesday morning. This bank holiday will allow programmers to correct the problems with the computers over the weekend."*

John hopped up from his seat exclaiming, "I didn't think it would begin this soon. Mark you and Renee need to go to the store now and pull your money out of the bank!"

Mark, waving him to calm down said, "Why would I need to do this, don't worry so much the banks are insured."

John replied, "Listen Mark, if I'm wrong and God help us I hope I am. Then you can just go put it back in on Tuesday right? Please, Mark just this once trust my conspiracy theories. What harm will it do to take it out and put it back in if everything is ok?"

Mark had never seen John so adamant, so he agreed to do as he asked. As they were all getting ready to leave John told them, "Listen, try and get things that won't go bad if we lose power or anything. Plus, if you buy extras it won't take up too much freezer room."

They agreed and each went their own way to take care of what they had planned to do. John admonished them to not talk to people about anything or they might find others looking to dig a little deeper and he did not want anyone questioning anything.

# Chapter 4

## "In the midst"

*"There are only nine meals between mankind and anarchy"*
-Alfred Henry Lewis

John and Amy's checks were direct deposited into their account and he wanted to withdraw all of their money. He did not, however, wish to drain the accounts and cause a red flag to go up. They had a number of accounts so he began with the smallest credit union, they were pretty chummy with the tellers there and he decided to empty all but a hundred dollars in that one.

He went into the bank and filled out the withdrawal slip, taking it to his favorite teller he started making small talk. "Hi Sharon, how ya doing today?"

She replied in her usual cheerful tone, "Sure glad it is Friday."

He nodded and said, "No rest for me this weekend, I'm finally going to be getting that new barn."

She looked at the withdrawal slip and said, "I thought you needed to save up more than this to do that."

He just winked at her and said, "My buddy Matt is going to loan me the rest so I can get it done before winter."

Counting out the cash for him, she wished him luck with it and he waved as he was going out the door.

He was practically dancing at how easily he had fabricated the story for her. Smiling to himself, he thought, 'Well, I'm not really full of shit. I was saving it for the new barn.' While driving to his other bank, he wondered how he might pull most of the money without questions. Many things went through his mind about it; this was a much larger bank and often asked questions about large withdrawals. I was not unusual for him to do so to pay taxes or other things so he hoped he would not have too much to explain. As he approached the line a lady cut right in front of him, with bleach blonde hair and 4 inch heels brandishing her designer purse like it was a trophy. She was demanding everyone wait on her immediately, saying, "I'm in a hurry, so can we please get this place moving?"

John was irritated with her, she had no apologies for her actions just pushing everyone around. He got to the teller and said, "That was probably the most irritating thing I've seen all day, that woman was a piece of work."

The teller agreed while John continued, "I don't know where she thought she was more important than everyone else."

The teller replied, "She's always in a hurry and I'm just thankful it wasn't my line this time. She's always demanding something and being rude to us tellers."

While the teller was taking care of his transaction they continued to discuss the woman, the teller never asked him about his large withdrawal.

On his way home he wanted to buy some extra ammo from a few different stores and pick up a few odds and ends along with some groceries. He knew deep down the banks would not be re-opening, but didn't want to go crazy spending the money just in case. The rest of the way home his mind was racing through all the possibilities. He was sure this was no false flag and that there was something more to it, but what he didn't know was how OPEC and now the banking issues were tied together. He knew this was no coincidence and that he needed to be ready for almost anything.

Over the next few days John was busying himself with various activities and quietly squirreling away things in other places on his farm. He had an old tree stump he had hollowed out a few years back to hide his goody snacks from Amy, he decided to put some extra camping gear into it. Under the stairs, he had made a compartment and kept his.38

special with extra ammo hidden in it. To that he added a bunch of MREs and multiple Lifestraws. John knew all along that his place would not be sustainable long term and had already talked with Matt a few times about what they called bugging out. They had already made maps with directions to his location if the need ever arose. Knowing this, he made sure that what he was stashing were things that were more portable and lightweight.

He visited Mark and Renee a few times over the weekend and was glad to see they had done the shopping and taken the money from the bank like he asked them to. He worried because Renee was not in the best health and that she would struggle on a long journey. He was glad he had asked them in the spring when a late storm had knocked out power for a week to make sure they had extra prescriptions on hand just in case.

Renee had managed to get them into a plan that would give them 3 month prescriptions. John already had found a way for them to have two months in reserve. After the power went he had her tell the doctors that the pipes froze and when the heat came back on the bathroom faucet exploded, ruining their medications. After being scolded by the doctor for leaving the caps off she was given a two month supply. John knew a journey like the one he was sure they were going to have to take would be very difficult for them both. He had promised Matt that if anything happened to make him go, he would make sure Matt's parents came with him.

The one thing he dreaded and was trying to figure out was Matty. Matty was Matt's son and he would be taking him along. Thinking about this made him cringe. Matty's mom was not what one would call an easy to get along with person. When Matt married her, no one could figure out why, no one liked her and she was horrible to Matt and even worse now about things with Matty. He laughed to himself thinking, 'well, if things are bad enough to go to Matt's place, I could just shoot her.'

Shaking his head, he said to himself out loud, "While I might enjoy that and Matt could rest easy, I guess I couldn't do it to Matty. Sure was fun thinking about it though."

He decided he would wait to see what happened with things before contacting her. Thinking of it, he knew his timing on that would have to be just right. She was what he would call a "sheeple", someone who would follow along with whatever the government or others would say, having no real opinion of their own, simply following the crowd like sheep. If something caused a breakdown she would be the first in line waiting for a government handout. He didn't relish the thought of trying to get Matty out of an internment camp or something.

*September 18th*

John sat in front of the stove building a raging fire before Amy would get up. It was cold this morning, he hadn't checked the news yet, but he was sure it was well below freezing. It had been a hard frost during the night, he was sure much of the garden was toast. It was only six, but he still had not been able to check his bank accounts online.

The banks were to reopen this morning and he thought it strange he was unable to even log in. He decided to wait until nine before trying to check at the bank. Turning on the news, he sat watching to see if there was any news on the banking situation. To his chagrin, there was nothing, just more fluff and fiction. The news held little more than the weather forecast and some story about the President and family on vacation again. John was instantly irritated because it seemed like they were always on vacation and usually smack dab in the middle of some crisis.

John headed out to the bank promptly at nine, he arrived to see armed guards outside the bank and a mob of people waiting for it to open. He was going to just leave, but decided to go ask if the guards knew what time the bank would be opening.

As he walked up he overheard people talking in the crowd, an elderly gentleman was speaking to what appeared to be his wife saying,

"If the bank doesn't open soon we should go, there are some very angry people here and I think we would be safer at home."

A very angry man was shouting that it was time for the bank to open and to let them in, along with another man who seemed to be getting the crowd all agitated.

John walked up to the guards to ask when they would be opening, when the guard turned his weapon in a threatening manner, telling him, "Hold it right there buddy!"

John was stunned saying, "Relax man, I just wanted to ask if you knew what time they would be opening?"

The guard looked to ease up a little, but still maintained his stance and said, "We do not have that information, we are here to keep the crowd under control."

John thanked them and turned to leave when the other guard asked him, "Did the news or anyone say anything about this? We have been here all night and no one has come to relieve us or give us any information."

The other guard grumbled at him, saying, "Shut up!"

John just shook his head, "No" and continued to his car. Once in the car he tried to call Matt, but all it kept telling him was, *"We're sorry, all circuits are busy. Please try your call later."*

Leaving the bank he went over to Mark and Renee's to see how things were going. Mark was there when he got there, which was much earlier than his usual time to be home.

When he asked why, Mark just shook his head and said, "The world has gone mad, there is no work for me today. Everyone is in a panic over the banks and wants to hold off on their projects."

John said, "I'm not surprised, you should have seen the mob at the bank. You would think people could go at least a weekend before needing to get things."

Renee was making them brunch and asked John, "Do you think there is anything to this banking issue? I'm glad you made us take the money out on Friday, but when I went to the store this morning gas jumped up another seventy-five cents since yesterday."

John shook his head saying, "And so now it begins."

Renee looked at him quizzically and asked, "What begins?"

John said, "Don't you worry there Mama, you're going to be ok."

Gaining a more serious tone John looked to Mark and said, "I need you guys to be prepared to leave here if you have to. Did you keep the tanks full like I asked you to?" They both nodded and John said, "Good, here is what I need you to do; first I need each of you to pack a bag of clothes. Be sensible, nothing like a vacation, more like what you would take for camping. Don't forget extra socks, gloves, hats and scarves also add your tennis shoes to it. Then I need you to put out an outfit like you might wear for hiking, everything down to the socks and boots. Have this in a spot in your room so you could quickly change if you needed to."

Renee began to get upset, asking him, "Why do we need to do this."

John said, "Don't worry about anything there girlie, it is all just in case."

Once John felt confident they had their bags together, he began helping Mark look at tools and such that might be helpful. Renee was working on what John had instructed her to do with other things inside the house, she had all their important papers inside her purse along with a freezer bag of only the most precious of family pictures.

The goal was to organize things so they could easily and quickly pack up the vehicles and go to John's house. John and Mark made a mini cache for them in a small graveyard down the road, in case all they could take was their bags.

John waved as he pulled out of the driveway saying, "I'll be back tomorrow to check on you. If you hear from Matt tell him I said Sierra Echo Tango. He will know what that means."

John and Matt already had a few phrases that meant different things, this meant all is SET to bug out. Thinking about Matt he knew he had to go check on Matty. This would likely be an unpleasant encounter, but he decided today was a good day to see.

When he got to Rita's apartment, her usual rude attitude was blatantly obvious. She was a heavier girl, but not in a proportionate way, she insisted on wearing tight clothes that would accentuate the worst areas of her body and fail to cover others. She stood at the door, glaring at him, her hair a strange shade of orange and her lips pursed in annoyance.

John said, "Hey Rita, with all the trouble at the banks I just wanted to stop by and see if you and Matty needed anything."

She instantly became accusatory saying, "What? Did Matt want you to come spy on me?"

John replied, "No, he just wanted me to make sure Matty was ok if any trouble happened."

She sneered, "I'm not incompetent you know."

John sighed, "No one said you were, but with the banks failing to reopen I just wanted you to know if you needed anything to stop over, you are BOTH welcome and I can loan you some money if you can't get any from the bank today."

She said, "Fine, but I'm sure we will be ok."

John nodded and said, "One last thing, if any trouble starts because of this, you and Matty come over."

She glared at him sneering saying, "I said we can take care of ourselves."

John sneered back slightly and with a warning in his voice said, "Matty is who matters here and let me give you one word of advice. You will not have to fear bad guys if anything happens to him because of your pride and attitude. Because I will be far worse than any bad guy you can imagine. Matt wanted him taken care of in the event of issues and I will take care of him one way or another."

Rita stepped back a little and stammered, "I'm sorry John, I know you mean well, I'm just trying to keep Matty safe too." She knew better than to make John really angry.

She asked if he could take them to the store for some groceries, telling him she had tried this morning but everyone had gone crazy buying everything in the store.

She began to cry, saying, "They were pushing and shoving and grabbing things out of my hands. One guy pushed Matty into the counter and kicked him."

John was angry now and shouting through the apartment for Matty. Matty came from the back room with a large knot on his forehead, running to Uncle John, as he called him, and whimpering into his belly.

John glared at Rita, "Why didn't you just tell me, why were you being so bitchy?" Rita just stood there with her head low.

John told Matty, "Go pack a backpack for campouts, while I talk to your mom."

He turned to Rita with what he felt was sheer hatred in his eyes and said, "Matty is coming with me."

She began to object when John put his hand up to silence her and saying, "I'm not done, you may come too, but he is not leaving my side until this is all over. Do you understand?"

She nodded and said, "Ok."

He said, "Go, now! Pack a bag, oh... and forget the nail polish."

Rita did as she was told but did not look happy about it, she complained as they were getting into John's truck that he didn't have to be such an asshole. John just glared at her, he was not going to argue with her in front of Matty.

As they started to leave, he remembered Kimmie and Jenny, they were Matt's cousins. They were only eighteen and twenty but had gotten an apartment on the other side of the same community that Rita and Matty lived in. John drove across the parking lot, he felt he needed to check on the girls. He didn't know to what end, but they were not what one would call financially savvy and would not have seen the banking issues and saved some money.

As he pulled into the lot where parking was designated for their building, he saw Kimmie trying to fight off two teenagers who were taking her groceries out of her trunk. John stepped out of the truck Glock in hand and yelled out,

"Hey! You, drop the bags!"

The teen that was closest to him could see the gun in his hand and immediately dropped the bags, but the other one flipped him off as he rounded the corner of the building with his plunder. John smacked the one that stopped in the back of the head and told him to go home.

Kimmie was crying when John approached her and had a long scratch running down her forearm that was bleeding. He motioned for Rita to come help him, but she sat crossing her arms in defiance, she hated Kimmie and would have no part in helping her. He walked up to the truck and told Matty to come with him that he needed him to help. He sneered at Rita telling her to make sure to keep the truck safe.

She looked horrified and said, "You aren't leaving me here alone, are you?"

John replied, "No, you didn't want to come help, you're choosing to stay. We'll be right back."

John and Matty took Kimmie up to her apartment to find Jenny in bed sleeping. He ordered her to get up and start packing a bag for each of them, while he began to bandage Kimmie's arm. Looking over he could see Jenny adding lingerie and dresses and gasped, snapping at her he yelled for Matty to come show her what to pack.

Jenny began to cry, saying, "What's wrong, John why are you yelling at me?"

John stopped what he was doing, he hadn't realized he was so harsh with her. She was sleeping and had no idea what was going on.

John walked over and hugged her saying, "I'm sorry Jenny, and I didn't mean to be so harsh. Things are not going good in the neighborhood and I want you and Kimmie to come with me for now."

She nodded and asked what she was to pack, John told her to have Matty help her that he would know what she should pack for each of them.

The girls grabbed the food Kimmie had just bought along with the feminine products from the bathroom. As he was watching John realized he had not stocked such items for Amy. Hurrying the girls out he said he had to make a stop at a store on the way. All the girls in the truck whined it was too crazy and they were scared. John and Matty looked at each other, Matty rolling his eyes.

Matty would be ten in October, he was small for his age but very quick with the wit. Matty was a good looking boy with dark hair and dark eyes and could win you with a smile.

John remembered hearing Matt say that he had been hoping to get him to grow over the summers and vacations he got to spend with him. It was hard because he was always fighting with Dez, Matt's girlfriend, about not wanting to eat what she cooked.

Matt and John had talked on many occasions about how Matty treated Dez and believed it was Rita's doing. John admired Dez because she put up with Matty's attitude and was always good with him. He silently wondered how he would get through even a day without smacking the daylights out of Rita for all the trouble she had caused them, and the certain problems she will make for him before this was all over.

Making numerous stops along the way, John was able to get a large amount of both tampons and feminine napkins for all the ladies. He also picked up a number of jars of both peanut butter and jelly because that was one of Matty's favorite things to eat. He also got more saltines because they would last better than bread for him.

When they arrived at the house, Amy was standing out front waving to John. He knew this was not like her and worried something was wrong. Hopping out of the truck and practically sprinting to where she was, he looked quickly in all directions before speaking. Panting, he said,

"What's wrong?  Are you OK?"

She said, "Of course I am silly, I just wanted to tell you to park on the other side of my car because Mark and Renee are going to be here in a few minutes."

John sighed, saying, "Oh good, I'm glad they decided to come right away."  Amy looked at him quizzically asking,

"Why honey, what is going on?"

She began to feel alarmed and looking toward the truck she noticed Rita getting out.  With daggers in her eyes, she looked at John and said,

"And what is *that* doing here?"

John told her to relax, that it was a necessary evil for the sake of Matty and he would explain later.

# Chapter 5

## "The End is now the Beginning"

*"War is a way of shattering to pieces... materials which might otherwise be used to make the masses too comfortable and... too intelligent*
-George Orwell

The small group sat around the table after dinner chatting and drinking coffee with various conversations going on, Kimmie was playing cards with Matty while Jenny stared at the TV.

John rose and started speaking, "We need to get the sleeping arrangements worked out."

Before he could finish speaking Rita said she was not comfortable and wanted the room for her and Matty, which John quickly vetoed.

They had a guest bedroom and two sleeper sofas; he assigned Mark and Renee the guest room. Rita would have the full size sofa while Kimmie and Jenny would share the queen. He handed out pillows, comforters and sheets and showed them how to open the sofas.

Matty frowned, saying, "Do I have to sleep on the floor?"

Rita scowled at John, "I guess you're just a kid, you can handle the floor."

She had an uncanny knack for saying exactly the wrong thing. John, giving Rita a disgusted look went to Matty knelt down smiled at him a devious smile saying,

"Bud, you get the best bed in the house."

He looked over glaring at Rita with a look of victory, as he led Matty to an area in the far corner, where he unwound a hammock and attached the loose end to a hook on the opposite wall. Matty giggled with excitement exclaiming,

"This is the best bed ever! Thank you Uncle John."

Hugging John tightly he ran and scrambled into his hammock and immediately got it swinging.

John and Amy wished everyone a good night's sleep and said they would discuss things in the morning. After everyone had settled in Kimmie got up and went over to Rita's bed. She sat on the edge of the bed as Rita rolled away from her. Kimmie had heard her quietly crying and come over; she tried to act like she felt bad for Rita. No one liked her, no one really ever had. She had a miserable disposition and was always saying horrible things about Matt. She hated Dez and tried at every turn to make Matty hate her. Kimmie had been subjected to her harsh words on more than one occasion, so even she did not know why she went to comfort her.

She asked her what was wrong, trying to sound kind. Rita snapped back,

"What do you care?"

Kimmie's tone got sharp when she said, "You know what? I don't, forget it. I just thought you might like to talk about it. Good Night!"

Rita rolled over slightly and said in almost a whisper, "Why do you talk to me? With everything that is going on, why did John even bring me with him?"

Kimmie looked at her quizzically saying, "Because you are Matty's mother, and whether we like it or not he needs his mother and would not have left without you. You really don't matter, but for him it has to be don't you understand anything?"

Rita began to speak when Kimmie cut her off. "You could give people a try and instead of being a perpetual bitch try being kind to another person. I came over to see if you needed to talk and you snapped at me. Rita no one hates you, they hate the way you act."

Rita sniffled and said, "I know… I know I do it too but it just comes out. I was mean to Matt but all of you really have no idea what really happened, you would only listen to him."

Kimmie reached out and touched her arm saying, "Just try not to be so bitchy, and maybe you will make it through this."

Rita felt a horrible fear, but nodded and thanked Kimmie for the chat and saying, "I will try and I know John is just trying to keep us safe. You have been kind and I haven't, I'm sorry Kimmie. I really am." Kimmie smiled a little and headed for her bed. The smile left Rita feeling uneasy, it was a crooked smile with some kind of knowing look in her eyes.

She had hated Kimmie because of a lie she had told Matt about her. Kimmie never liked her and tried to break them up so she told Matt that Rita had cheated on him. The truth eventually came out, but not before Rita had found out many ugly secrets and lies about their whole relationship. She hated anyone associated with Matt and didn't trust any of them. She wanted to keep Matty as far away from them as possible and acted like a bitch to do it.

The next day they everyone was to stay at the small farm except John, who wanted to see if things had calmed and the banks had opened. He exited the long drive, not seeing anything out of the ordinary he headed for town. He drove slowly trying to establish some kind of indication of the state of things, as he entered the town square he found himself staring at something that looked like a scene from a movie. Auburn was a smaller town on the outskirts of Worchester keeping them for the most part away from the city issues. It was a quiet town like one might see on a New England postcard. When he saw that most of the store windows on Main Street lay in shards on the sidewalk, he was in a kind of shock. A car was burning in the square while two others were on their sides. There were a few people walking around trying to gather up things with looks of shock or disbelief as well.

Making a left onto Second Avenue would bring him to the police station and hopefully some answers. He carefully drove along, dodging debris, trying not to damage things that were strewn in the road, when he noticed Ole Ben. Ben was, as near as John could tell, the oldest guy on earth. He was a stout man with a deep laugh and prickly whiskers. John remembered as a kid every time Ben would see them he would give them "whisker burn" as John called it. He pulled over to talk to Ole Ben asking,

"Ben, what happened here?"

Ben looked up at John and waved saying, "Hey there young man, we had a bit of a ruckus around here last night I guess."

John asked, "Do you know who did all this?"

Ben nodded with a look of sadness said, "Young'uns, some of them gang types. There were about fifteen or twenty of them, rolled in here last night. Hollering from their car windows and throwing things like it was one of them crazy parties they like. They broke all the store windows and took all kinds of stuff." John shook his head in disbelief and asked,

"Did the police catch them all?"

Ben shook his head saying, "No, they took shots at the police cars, had them pinned down a while. Then they jumped into their cars and hauled ass outta here."

John waved saying, "I'm going to head on over to the station and see if I can find anything out."

Ben waved back and said, "Careful, I don't know if they are still lurking around or if they headed back to the city."

John made his way to the police station. He noticed as he was pulling into the lot that a number of the police cars had bullet holes in them. All of this seemed surreal; it had only been two days since the banks had not reopened. John entered the police station apprehensively, not sure what he would find.

An officer at the front desk asked him, "Can I help you?"

John replied, "I was hoping to find out what happened here."

The officer shaking his head said, "There was a group of looters that came through here last night, raising hell all over town."

John asked, "Was anyone hurt?"

The officer shook his head "No" and asked, "Are you a resident of Auburn?"

John said, "Yes, I live about 5 miles up Sandy Lane."

The officer asked, "Was there any trouble out that way?"

John said, "No, it was quiet."

The officer nodded and just grunted saying, "Listen, you should make sure to keep your doors locked, I don't think we have seen the last of this bunch."

John didn't want to give away any details about his location or supplies so he thanked the officer and headed home. When he got there Amy was in tears, while Kimmie had been trying to comfort her. John asked,

"What's wrong?"

Kimmie said, "Its ok, she and Rita had some words is all."

John was fuming mad and started for the house, when Renee stopped him saying,

"No, John we all handled it. Amy just needs a bit to calm down is all, she's fine."

John looked back at Amy and she nodded in agreement. Everyone went inside to hear the news about town. Renee made some coffee while John began to explain to them what had happened in town. Everyone sat gasping with horror on their faces and Amy began to cry again. John eased everyone's fears telling them they were safe where they were and not to worry. Deep down though John knew that was not true, they would eventually move out further and further. Looking at his group he knew keeping everyone safe for any time would be impossible. Mark could shoot, but was the only other person who was trained to use a firearm; the ladies had never even touched a gun before. He went to bed that night with heavy thoughts and fears for them all in the future.

# Chapter 6

## "Welcome Friends"

*"Rightful liberty is unobstructed action according to our will within limits drawn around us by the equal rights of others. I do not add 'within the limits of the law' because law is often but the tyrant's will, and always so when it violates the rights of the individual."*
-Thomas Jefferson

*September 20th*

The group sat around the television, having coffee and watching the news. It was shocking that the country had completely gone to chaos in only three short days. It seemed that the bigger cities like Los Angeles and New York were in chaos. Most, if not all larger cities in the country had plunged into riots and looting.

John told everyone that they were to remain inside unless he or Mark was with them. He issued Mark a Glock 9mm for a sidearm and Mark already had his 20 gauge. The girls were all talking when John interrupted them saying,

"Listen up ladies, I know none of you have ever handled a gun but you're going to have to learn to at some point. Right now is not the time because we don't want to go making gun shots for people to find us. It will have to be something you are going to need to get comfortable with."

Rita immediately started complaining her and Matty would do so such thing.

To which John said, "You will when the time comes I guaran-damn-tee it."

Most of the day was spent doing minor chores and milling about the house. John was outside listening to NPR taking care of chickens when something struck him.

The radio mentioned a small snippet about FEMA setting up camps to help house the refugees from the cities. It said they would be going door to door to requisition needed supplies in areas where much of the looting had occurred.

John hurried to the house and without saying a word to anyone he went to his closet and gathered all of his bug out gear and a number of guns. He sent Mark to the storage cabinet and told him to take out all but one box for the .9mm guns and to bring along his 20 gauge. He said nothing to the ladies, but shot Renee a look that he hoped she would understand meant to keep them all there.

The two men went out into the large barn where John slid a large feed trough out of the way revealing a trap door. This had been an old cistern that John had uncovered and kept dry for use as a root cellar. They placed all the firearms, ammunition and emergency bug out gear inside the old root cellar. John gathered up some of the antique tools he had hanging on the walls and placed them inside as well.

Mark never said a word, but looked at him quizzically. John looked at him and put his finger up to say shhhh. They moved the feed trough back and covered the area with hay. When they had come out of the barn Rita was standing next to the truck demanding to know what was going on. John looked at Mark and said to her,

"I was a little concerned about space in the house so to open up some closet space I moved all my hunting stuff out here."

Rita replied, "Well, I don't want Matty getting into any of those guns, are you sure they are locked up?"

John said, "Sure, come take a look."

He went to the side of the house where a mud room was located but no longer accessed the house. He unlocked the door to show her inside saying,

"I like the idea of keeping these locked up."

She snorted in disgust from the odor coming from a few of the hides inside and turned and headed for the house. She stopped and turned, looking from John to Mark asking,

"What was going on in the barn?"

Mark quickly replied, "That dang goat kicked over the water bucket again."

Rita looking satisfied said, "Oh, well, that's all just gross."

John and Mark lingered to lock up the mud room, Mark motioned John to the field for the goats and said,

"Ok John, out with it, what was that all about?"

John replied, "I heard on the radio about FEMA taking stuff for refugee camps and I wanted to get some stuff tucked away."

Mark looked confused and asked, "why would you think they would come take our stuff?'

John shook his head and said, "Because I have a small farm and a while back, I read someplace about the plans in the event of an emergency they would be looking to the farms to supply the camps."

Mark replied, "Do you really think they will?"

John said, "I do."

Mark asked, "Why then did you only hide a few guns and your hiking stuff, and not everything?"

John replied, "Because they know I have guns and other things, if I hid it all they would look further and find the stuff I hid besides this."

Mark asked, "Do you think we have anything to worry about? I know you talk about this stuff all the time, but I never really believed it."

John replied, "I hope not, but it is better to be safe than sorry. Mark, do not speak of this to anyone, I don't know who might say something if they come looking and I believe the less the girls know the better off we are for now."

Mark agreed that was a good idea and told him he would not say anything. They walked back to the house chatting about other things to be done tomorrow when Amy came running out of the house with John's cell phone. Shouting, she came running over, "It is Matt; he says he needs to talk to you right away."

John took the phone saying,

"Hey there guy, what's up?'

Matt wanted to know about his family and Matty; John assured him they were fine. Telling him, he had been checking on them and went over and got Matty along with Kimmie and Jenny when it all started. He told him his parents were fine too.

Mark could overhear parts of the conversation, but not what was said, only that Matt's tone was urgent, and although he couldn't hear what he was saying this made him feel anxious. John just kept making affirmative responses, "uh huh, uh huh."

John said, "Ok theah guy, I will tell the others and we will prepare to head out as soon as possible. Would you like to talk to your dad? He's right here."

A pause marked the response and John said, "Ok, I will try and let you know when we are on our way, here's your dad."

John handed the phone to Mark who said, "Matt, are you ok? How's Dez?" There was a pause while Matt spoke and Mark replied,

"Yes I understand, we will make it son don't worry. We are all in good hands with John, he seems to have things pretty well together." He stood nodding while Matt spoke, "I will, we love you too."

Mark ended the call and handed the phone to John. John asked him,

"Matt tell you what we had to do?'

Mark said, "Yes, and I agree with him. The girls will likely give us a hard time but I know Matty will be thrilled."

John told Mark, "I think we should try and leave as soon as possible. I don't know what we are going to run into out there."

Mark agreed saying, "I also think we should get out some maps and check on some possible routes around the cities. After the news this morning I fear it might not be possible to get near them."

John agreed and told him he had already marked out some routes on the maps and they could go over them and revisit the options, they agreed they would wait before they told the girls what the plan was.

John asked Mark, "Do you think we should tell them we are headed to Matt and Dez's place? Or maybe not till the last second just in case we do get some visitors. We don't need any attention drawn to our leaving."

Mark agreed this was the best idea, especially given all the grief Rita had already caused and that Amy will likely not care for the idea of a road trip.

It was only five o'clock so John decided he would head to town to see if he could find anything left in the stores they might need for the trip. He took Rita and Kimmie with him to keep Rita and Amy apart.

When they got to town there was a roadblock with what looked like the National Guard standing in the road. As they approached, they were signalled to stop. John rolled down his window and asked,

"Is there a problem here?"

The guardsman asked, "Where are you going?"

John replied, "We were going into the grocery store to pick up a few things."

The guardsman said, "The grocery store has been closed do you have any other business in town?"

John said, "I have a friend I was hoping to check up on. Ben, he lives over the pharmacy."

The guardsman responded, "All residents of the affected town have been relocated to the refugee camp in

Devons. If you have no other business here, do you require assistance? I can have a truck follow you to pick up the residents for the refugee camp if you are unable to care for yourselves."

John looked shocked and said, "No sir, we are fine, the ladies here just wanted some chocolate is all. Can I turn around right here?"

The guardsman consulted with another who scurried off to a tent nearby, looking to John and saying,

"I need to see your license, sir."

While fishing it out of his pocket John asked, "Is everything ok? We didn't know this area was cordoned off."

The guardsman looked at his license and made a note on a clipboard saying, "You're fine, we just wanted to know who would still be in the area. Travel is restricted during this period of Martial Law."

John was shocked; he had not heard anything about the declaration of Martial Law. He looked at the guardsman and asked,

"Can we go home now?"

The guardsman was preparing to let them go when the other one came back with a man in a suit. The suit looked like it was big on the man, who was older with a slight limp. He walked determined with his dark eyes piercing the windows of the truck clearly assessing any threats. The man approached the truck and wanted to know what kind of supplies they had at the farm. John told them just the usual farm stuff, explaining he was basically a hobby farm not one of the big farmers.

The man said, "Sir, we will need to come and take an inventory to assess what may be needed for the refugee camp. You're free to go, someone will come by tomorrow."

Before John could object the man turned and walked away. John started to say something to the guardsman who put his hand up to be silent and waved them to leave. John looked at the guardsman who shook his head "no" looking in the direction of the suited man, as if to say that it was not a good idea to object. Tipping his head sideways, and motioning silently, suggesting, for them to leave quickly.

On the way back to the farm John was agitated and was cursing under his breath at how they thought they could just do anything they want, and who do they think they are?

Kimmie interrupted his cursing asking, "John, is something wrong?"

John looked at the girls who both had looks of fear in their expressions. He had not realized that they had no clue what this meant.

He softened his look and tone, saying, "Kimmie, this is not good at all. Do either of you know what this could all mean?"

Both girls shook their heads "No."

John said, "When we get back to the house we are all going to talk about this. I don't want you to worry about it right now, but there are some things we will all have to be aware of and think about."

They drove back to the house in silence, John was deep in his thoughts and both girls were watching the houses go by.

Turning into the driveway John said, "Kimmie, will you get some coffee going and Rita can you please gather everyone to the table? I will explain what some of the things that are bothering me about all this are then, Ok?"

Both girls nodded and upon exiting the truck each went to the task that John had asked of them. John sought out Mark, who was in the large barn tending to some of the animals.

Mark saw him headed for him at a trot and yelled out, "Hey John, what's up?"

John walked up to him, saying, "I think we have some trouble coming, we need to sit down with everyone and have a talk. Let's go inside."

Mark followed John inside where everyone was sitting around chatting with Kimmie and Rita. The girls had already told of their encounter with the strange man in a suit.

Mark and John came in and Amy asked, "What's going on?"

John said, "I see you girls are pretty much up to speed on what happened in town. The guardsman said the area was under martial law and while I don't know what agency the man in the suit was with I have a pretty good idea."

Mark asked, "Do you think it is FEMA?"

John replied, "That's exactly what I am thinking."

Renee asked, "Is it true they want to come out here for stuff?"

John said, "The guy said he wanted to take an inventory of what we had here."

Jenny said, "I don't understand why?"

John said, "They think they can just commandeer whatever supplies they think they need for the refugee camps."

Kimmie asked, "What is a refugee camp? Is it for the bad people who made the mess in town?"

John said, "No, they put all the people from town in the camp."

Mark sighed, saying, "John you've been saying stuff about this for years. Is this what you were talking about when you talked about FEMA camps?"

John nodded his head saying, "This is very bad, think about this, it has only been a couple of days and, other than the banks not reopening everything feels fine, right? If they had a place to house all the residents of the town capable of handling it, when did they build such a thing? Why would they want to house American citizens in it instead of the criminals who messed up town? Why not just bring aid to the town instead of herding everyone off to a camp?"

There was absolute silence as John continued, "I think we have to assume they know something we don't. When they come tomorrow, if they ask, all of you were here for our harvest weekend. If they want to know why you are still here, you tell them when the banks did not reopen we decided to extend it because of the trouble in town. I don't think they will check yet so if they want to know we are all family here."

Rita said, "Won't we be safer in the camps?"

John looked at her and as gently as he could and explained, "It is not a camp that wants to help you. They say they do, but what they really want is to control you. In all likelihood they would put Matty in a kid's tent and make you work all day for the camp.

I have some friends who were able to get some of the information about what was planned for these years ago. The plans they have for the majority of the people are not good Rita. Please for Matty's sake take my word for it. I promise you it will be better and safer with us."

While Rita had a look of doubt, she knew that John would protect Matty with his life.

After dinner a text came through from Matt saying that he would have additions to the group and they would use the code words. He acknowledged the text and organized a watch for the evening, either for them or any threats. Mark would take the first watch and everyone went to bed.

Mark was tired; it was almost midnight when he thought he saw movement in the tree line. Not sure if he was seeing things because of fatigue or if there was something out there, he strained to see the area where the movement had been. There it was! He had seen something! Creeping into the bedroom, he quietly woke John explaining there was movement in the tree line. John quickly got up and fished his night vision scope from under the bed. They quietly made their way over to the window where Mark pointed in the direction where he had seen movement.

John trained the scope in the area and could see two people crouched beside the rock wall. John watched silently as they made their way up the drive, scanning the area looking for the rest of them. He assumed it was the group Matt had texted about, but didn't want to take any chances.

Mark took over watching them while John slipped out the back door. He crept over to a position across the driveway from them and crouched behind a large pine tree. Once in position he called out,

"Stop right there."

A female voice called back, "John, is that you?"

John replied, "What do you want here?"

The female responded, "John, its Morgan and Kevin."

John stepped slightly from behind the tree saying, "Move into the light so I can see you."

The two figures moved up to where the bright outdoor light was shining, and waited for John to approach. As he approached, he recognized them. A little perplexed at why they were there he asked,

"Morgan, why have you come here?" Morgan replied, "The city is bad John, I didn't know where else to go."

John was not exactly comfortable with them just showing up. He knew Morgan but only because she had accompanied Matt over to visit on a few of his trips up to see Matty. He felt it was strange that they had come to his place.

He asked, "Have you heard from Matt?"

She said, "Yes, two days ago."

The guy with her got a strange look on his face that John could not interpret and asked him,

"Is there something wrong?"

He replied, "No, I just didn't know she had spoken to Matt."

John asked, "How do you know Matt?"

Kevin replied, "We've been friends for years, this is my wife, Morgan."

John asked him, "Why did you come here?"

He said, "Morgan told me we had to come here."

John didn't like the way this all felt and had a sinking feeling that something was not as it seemed.  He told them to come inside and they would talk about it.  When they went inside Mark immediately recognized Kevin and hugged him. John felt a little more at ease, but did not know how it could be that he had never met Kevin, yet Morgan had come with Matt on a number of occasions.  Something still felt off to him, but he trusted Mark.

They got Kevin and Morgan a bedroll on the floor and promised to figure out something better in the morning.  John sent Mark to bed and opted to take the next watch.  The rest of the night was quiet, but John was bothered by the appearance of their new guests.

# Chapter 7

## "The Others "

*"How fortunate for governments that the people they administer don't think."*
-Adolph Hitler

Danny said, "Jeremy, I'm so glad we got a hold of you?"

Jeremy could be heard over the speaker phone and almost shouting said, "Danny? Danny is that you?"

Danny replied, "Yeah man, I'm sure glad to hear your voice."

Jeremy with relief said, "Same here guy, how's it been going for you?"

Danny replied "Not good, not good at all. A few days ago after the banks did not reopen riots began almost immediately. The National Guard came in and shot a lot of people and started putting people in a camp at the old Fort Devons. Remember, we had talked about that?"

Jeremy said, "Yea, I knew Devon's would end up a FEMA camp or something."

Danny continued, "Well, we got out of the house, I took Mom, Melinda, Dickie, Jules, Georgia and Nancy up to the old cabin. The one at that pond we used to go fishing at."

Jeremy was just saying, "uh huh."

Danny continued, "I went back to the house to get some clothes and stuff, but the FEMA people had mostly cleaned it out. Man, I gotta tell ya we left just in time. I saw them dragging the neighbors out of their house in cuffs, it is bad here!"

Danny paused a minute taking a deep breath, "We have had lots of fish to eat but not much else. Nancy left last night to go to the camp; she insisted they just wanted to help us. I followed her and watched the camp a while. I gotta say guy, no one wants to end up there! They had the people working like slaves and they were under armed guard. Why would a relief camp have guards watching the people? They looked like prisoners not refugees."

Jeremy said, "Ok Danny this is what I need you to do. Matt's friend John is coming down with some of Matt's family. I need you to get to John's place. He lives out in Auburn; his place is on Sandy Lane."

Danny could hear Matt in the background say, "He needs the code word, when he gets there he needs to say Hannity, John will reply with foxtrot, to be replied with Matt. This will tell John that I sent them."

Jeremy repeated the information to Danny and said, "Danny, it is important you get there tonight!" Danny said he understood and would get them ready to go now and thanked him. I'm going to give the phone back to Toni now, but you need to get there right away."

Danny replied, "Thanks guy we will head out tonight."

Toni said hi to everyone and assured her mom she was ok and that once they got there they would be too. She said her goodbye's and hung up.

Danny hung up the phone and noticed his mom was crying. He walked over to her and hugging her said,

"Don't worry mom, Toni is in good hands Dez would do anything to keep them safe and you know that. We will get there."

Laurie sniffled and said, "I know, I know, Dez has always taken good care of all you kids. You and Jeremy have talked about this before. Let's get things ready to go."

Danny like Jeremy was tall and thin, which was deceiving for many. They were both wiry and excellent shots. They even looked alike with the dark hair and dark eyes. Danny had liked Jeremy since he first started dating his sister Toni. Dez, Jeremy's mom took to the whole Reed family like they were all one big family. Danny knew they would be safe once they got there.

The small group began to gather what little things they had managed to salvage before they had to flee the house. It was around ten miles to John's house and with the girls it would be a long night.

There were only the six of them Danny and Laurie Reed, Toni's brother and mother. Melinda Saunders, Danny's girlfriend and friends of Destiny Dickie and Jules Miller with their thirteen year old daughter Georgia.

Dickie seemed like he was ex-military, He was originally from the UK, He had moved to the states fifteen years ago. Danny was happy they had been sent to check on them before it all started, Dickie had a British DPM Bergan backpack and a fair amount of useful things including a number of firearms and good amount of ammo.

As Danny looked at his small group he pulled Dickie aside, saying, "Listen, I think we should keep the girls between us, we are going to have to walk this. I'm thinking we should go over to the power lines and follow them out of the city, what do you think?"

Dickie nodded in agreement saying, "Danny, I'm worried about Jules."

Danny asked, "Why, is something wrong with her."

Dickie responded, "We didn't get the chance to tell anyone yet."

Danny said, "Tell us what?"

Dickie said, "She's up the duff."

Danny said, "What?"

Dickie said, "She's friggin pregnant mate."

Danny raised his eyebrows and said, "Oh, Well, I guess... Ummm congratulations?"

Dickie looked a little relieved, saying, "I just don't know how she will handle it."

Danny said, "Don't worry about it, we will look after her, but listen when we get to John's don't tell anyone that right now, ok?"

Dickie asked, "Why?"

Danny responded, "I don't know John all that well and I don't want him thinking she will be a burden. We need their help to get to Dez."

Dickie nodded and went over to tell Jules.

They had their stuff all packed up and were ready to go at nightfall. They went around the lake to the power lines and began to walk right up the middle, because there was a trail often used by four wheelers and snowmobiles. After they had been walking along the trail for about thirty minutes they heard some four wheelers coming up the trail.

Danny saw the things in town and hurried them into a thicket off to the side and told them to be absolutely silent and not to move. They could see in the moonlight, three vehicles with multiple riders. They could not see much more than shadows, but the moon glistened off the rifles strapped to the front of each vehicle. They all realized this would be a difficult ten miles.

After the riders had passed, they continued on their journey now staying just inside the tree line that followed the power lines. They would bring them out two miles from John's house.

During the seven hours it took them to walk the eight miles to the point where they would need to leave the power line easement, there were a few more of what Danny and Dickie thought might be some kind of patrols.

The girls were shivering when they reached the point they would exit, so Danny told them that they could take a short break and try to warm up. He wanted to scout out a route that would get them there with the least amount of exposure.

Danny was like Jeremy in that he was quick and stealthy, he and Dickie talked that while Dickie had the military experience, he was not as young as he once was, and carried more than a few extra pounds. He had been injured while training with the military and was no longer as quick on his feet, but he had kept up practice at the range since moving to the states, plus years of playing paintball when he was young taught him how to run and gun. He would stand watch over the girls while Danny scouted the route.

He got them settled under some blankets in a blueberry patch, which provided not only a vast amount of berries that the girls immediately began to collect, but also decent cover.

He crept out of the trees onto the street, looking ahead, he cursed the street lights; they would surely give him away. As he moved from cover to cover he could see that a house was burning around the corner. As he got closer he heard yelling and some gunshots. He moved to where he could see the house clearly and was surprised to find there were no rescue vehicles.

The house was fully engulfed and a second one was starting to burn at the eaves and roof. The yelling was a gang of bystanders laughing and tossing things at the second house.

Danny started to go back the way he came to look for a way around this when he heard a scream. It sent chills down his spine; it was obviously a female scream. He looked back to the scene to see they had dragged the occupants of the house outside. They were holding a young woman by her hair and tearing her clothing off.

He was enraged and it took all he had not to try and intervene. He knew it would only get him killed and he cringed at the thought of the same fate for his family and friends.

After nearly an hour of searching he found an alley and some smaller side streets, he thought they could use to get around the gang. It was already two a.m. and they needed the cover of the darkness.

He returned to where the others were waiting and explained what he had seen.

Jules began to cry, saying, "Danny, I can't go out there."

Danny looked at her and saw the terror in her eyes and said, "I know you are scared, but I've found a way we can get around it. You have to be brave and do everything you are told."

She sniffled and nodded. Dickie walked over to Danny and whispered, "Are you sure it is safe?"

Danny replied, "No, not at all. We have to keep everyone very quiet and they need to only move when told to do so."

Dickie continued, "Maybe we should wait until after daylight."

Danny shook his head no saying, "I think we need the cover of darkness. And Jeremy said that we had to get there ASAP, the other group was preparing to leave."

Dickie nodded in agreement and said, "Just let me know what I need to do mate."

Danny put his hand on his friend's shoulder and said, "Just keep the girls together and pray, pray we can do this quickly and quietly."

They returned to where the girls were packing up their stuff and Danny explained to them what they were to do saying,

"Ok, here is what we are going to do. In some places we are going to need to sneak from one point of cover to another. When it is your turn to move you do it quickly and quietly. You watch me for the signal to come and stay low.

And the most important thing is to stay absolutely quiet, do you girls understand?"

They all nodded and Danny gave them the wave, showing them the hand signal to move ahead. They left the cover of the blueberries and made their way down an alley and over two streets from where the house was burning. Once they reached the point where Danny wanted them to go one at a time they crouched behind a truck.

Danny explained what to do and where they were to move to. He put his index finger to his lips, signaling them to "Shhhhh" and made his way silently through the intersection and crouched beside a dumpster at the entrance to another alley.

Holding his hand up for them to hold in place he scanned the area for anyone who might see them. Once he was ready for the first one to come over he waved his arm signaling come over. Laurie was the first to go; she silently crept to Danny's position and took up look out down the alley. Danny signaled again and Melinda did just as Laurie had and also began scanning the area for threats.

Jules was crying by now and when Danny signaled she did not move. She was immobilized by fear, they could see the gang beating a person in the light from the fire and she was too scared to move. Dickie signaled with his index finger pointing up that they needed a minute. A few minutes passed and Dickie gave a thumbs up they were ready.

Danny gave the signal and both Jules and Dickie began to creep to the position. Jules kicked a soda can on their way over that caused one of the bonfire onlookers to come walking down the street.

They were all hiding behind the dumpster at this point and Danny prepared to pounce on the guy, when Laurie made a loud sound that sounded like a cat preparing to fight. The guy stopped and looked around for the cat for a moment and turned back to the burning house.

They moved quietly through a few yards and up a long driveway to the point where they could enter a corn field. Danny was thankful for the cover of the farm. Once they were deep into the field, he chanced using his light to check the map. They were less than a mile from John's but dawn would be coming soon.

They hurried through the fields and onto a dirt road that would bring them into John's place from the back. By the time they arrived, the sky was beginning to gain light from the impending dawn. They made a quick camp just inside the tree line and decided to wait for daybreak to approach the house.

Danny and Dickie kept watch while the girls tried to get some sleep. As the sun came up Danny saw that someone had come from the house to the barn and decided to approach, leaving Dickie to keep watch over the sleeping girls.

Danny emerged from the tree line with his hands in the air calling out for John. The person he saw go into the barn ran to the house and came out with a large man. He looked like a powerful man with a full beard; Danny prayed he was in the right place.

The man approached the fence line that was at least two hundred yards away and yelled out,

"Who are you?"

Danny remembered what Jeremy had said and responded by saying, "Hannity."

The man replied, "Foxtrot."

To which Danny replied, "Matt."

The man waved him over, and Danny approached the edge of the fence line.  The man put out his hand and said,

"Danny?"

Danny took his hand and said, "Yes, are you John?"

John nodded and asked, "Where are the rest of your people?"

Danny told him of their night and how the girls were sleeping in the woods as he pointed to where they were.  John asked, "Do you have good cover?"

Danny nodded yes and asked, "Why?"

John explained about the FEMA guy and said they would be coming by.  He wanted them to remain under cover and wait until after they had come so he didn't have to explain them.  Danny heartily agreed, saying he had enough of those guys.  John gave him a look with raised eyebrows that meant he wanted to hear about that at some point.

He told him he would send someone out with some breakfast and drinks in a few minutes and admonished that they were to not break cover for any reason.  Danny acknowledged him saying,

"Thank you John."

John shook his hand and said, "We will talk later."

Danny made his way back to where the others were and explained to Dickie what John wanted them to do.  They woke the girls and told them they had arrived, but that they had to wait until later to go to the house, and that John was sending out some food and water for them.

# Chapter 8

## "The Road"

*"It is not power that corrupts but fear. Fear of losing power corrupts those who wield it and fear of the scourge of power corrupts those who are subject to it."*

-Aung San Suu Kyi

*September 22ⁿᵈ*

John went into the house and asked Amy to prepare a large breakfast quickly and package it to go while getting the meal ready for everyone. Mark and Amy were the only ones up so far and he told them to not tell the others. He instructed Mark to quietly make it look like he was taking leftovers or something to the barn for the animals and to bring it to the fence line and call for Danny. John looked at Mark saying,

"Don't linger just tell him we will come for them when the timing is right. Then go straight to the barn and feed the goats make sure there is plenty of hay on the floors."

Mark said, "Ok, gotcha." Nodding his head in understanding that he was to make sure the trap door was well covered.

Amy may not have been the outdoorsy type but she could sure cook. She prepared a large breakfast for everyone with sausages and bacon, scrambled eggs, pancakes, pan fries with corn muffins. She did as John had instructed carefully wrapping up about half of it and placing it into a pail she kept by the sink for the animal scraps. She added some butter, strawberry jam and a loaf of bread that she had baked the day before. She gathered some sugar and a small carafe of milk and put it into a separate pail with a large jug of coffee. She nodded to Mark that the food was ready to go and tossed some scrap lettuce leaves on top of each to cover their contents. With a heavy sigh, she said, "Mark, will you take these out to the animals and compost for me. I can't believe how quickly they fill these days." Mark immediately got up to take them, saying, "Sure, no problem."

As he was going toward the door Matty jumped up and said, "I wanna come Papa." Mark looked at Amy who said, "Not this time young man, I need a strong man here to help get these dishes down from this high cabinet." Matty kicked at the floor and said, "Yes, Ma'am" as he walked over to where the dishes were.

Mark did as John had instructed and reminded them to remain under cover and to rest if they could. Mark then told Danny, "Just stay quiet and someone will come to get you later." Danny thanked him for the food, as he smelled the hot food his eyes beamed with excitement and he hurried back to their hiding place. Mark returned to the barn and was spreading the hay when John came in saying,

"Everything set?"

Mark said, "Yep, but I don't think they have had a hot meal in days. Why are we leaving them out there, it is looking like some kind of weather is coming in?"

John replied, "I don't want any questions about them if that man in the suit comes a calling like he said he would."

Mark said, "Ahhhh, Yes that is smart. Do you think they will really come?"

John told him he wasn't sure, but they would all be leaving by nightfall anyway and didn't want to take any chances. They returned to the house for breakfast with John reminding him that the less people that knew, the less chance of something being inadvertently disclosed. Mark agreed and gave him a pat on the back saying,

"Thank you John, for everything. I fear we would all be in one of those refugee camps already if it were not for your foresight."

John just shrugged it off like it was no big deal. They came in exclaiming how wonderful the food smelled and took their places at the table.

It was not long after breakfast when the man in the suit arrived. There was a loud banging on the door and someone shouting, "Open up we have orders to collect provisions for the refugee camps." John was surprised, he had been told they only wanted to inventory what resources were out here. He opened the door to see the man in the suit standing with a clipboard looking like he owned the place.

John was instantly irritated and asked him what their intentions were. The man in the suit shoved past him, demanding to know the names of all in residence. John tried to object, but was restrained at the door by the guardsman. John looked at him; it was the same one from the roadblock. The guardsman looked at John raising his eyebrows and throwing a quick glance in the direction of the man in the suit.

The man took down the names and asked where they lived and why they were there. They all stuck to the story they had prepared and said they were all family.

The man instructed the guardsmen to take all of the livestock and feed in the barn and to leave them a week's worth of food according to the number in residence. John started to object when the man in the suit quickly turned to him and said,

"This is martial law; you will comply or be taken to the refugee camp as well. We don't need any trouble makers."

John decided to play dumb and asked, "So we can expect that the grocery stores will be open next week?"

The man in the suit replied, "Of course, this is just a temporary measure to assist in the efforts to get things under control. You will be compensated when it is all over."

John knew better and said, "Oh, Ok... I didn't know how we were going to eat after the week. I want to do anything I can to help my townsfolk."

The guardsman who had been restraining him, let him go and gave him an almost imperceptible nod. This man had John wondering what it was that was going on. As the trucks were pulling out with their bounty the guardsman who had restrained him offered his hand to shake. John took it and shook, but quickly realized the man was passing him a note. John thanked them for the information about things and turned and went back in closing the door.

Mark was at the window watching as they pulled away, making sure they did not leave anyone behind to watch them. It seemed they didn't bother to leave a watch so they must have bought the act. But John was sure they would be checking on their story and knew they had to go today.

John looked at the note from the guardsman and in shock, he read it, *"You need to escape, this is not what it seems. If you leave by the Upper Granite Road, I will be on that post tonight and let you through. Stay far away from all cities. There are many of us, but trust no-one."*

John knew already that once the government came for their supplies, it was time to go. He was thankful for the help of the guardsman. It was good to know there were some who would do the right thing.

Mark asked him if he should go get the others, John thought for a moment and told him to hold on for a bit just to make sure also saying,

"I want to be sure we are not being watched. We need to look like we are trying to salvage what is left of the garden and do the chores like bring in the wood and such. I want Amy to watch the tree line for anyone while we all do these things."

Mark agreed it was a good idea and they all began to do the chores assigned. Amy was watching and about an hour and half after they started this watch she saw something. She tapped Rita and sent her to go tell John that lunch was ready and to do it loudly. Rita did as Amy had instructed and everyone began to come inside.

John asked Amy what she saw and she pointed to the place where she had seen someone. John looked and could see him peering at the house from behind a tree. They all took turns watching the man and after about another hour he waved to someone and left.

Once they were sure he was gone Mark went to get the other group, calling out to Danny to bring everyone to the house and to do so quickly. Danny told them to gather everything up in a hurry that it was time. They quickly packed up the small camp and made their way to the house in a trot.

Everyone was gathered inside the house when John returned from what he had hoped would appear to be checking the mail. He had gone to the end of the driveway to make sure the man who had been watching was gone, using the guise of checking for mail.

After a brief introduction of the newcomers John began to speak saying,

"I know everyone has questions, but save it and listen carefully to what I am about to tell you. We don't have much time and we need to move on this quickly."

All eyes were on John as he spoke, "That man that came here today is not offering assistance. They are also not the good guys."

Mark coughed saying, "Well, I think we gathered that the good guys don't come and steal your things."

John nodded and continued, "We need to leave here and we need to do it tonight." He reached into his pocket and produced the note the guardsman had given him. He passed it over to Mark to show everyone as he continued,

"We have some help but this window of opportunity may not last long. We need to gather all we can and load up the vehicles and prepare to leave. Now we have Mark's truck and mine, Amy's car and the old mustang in the garage. The trucks will hold most of the things, but each vehicle needs to have a variety of things in it just in case any vehicle may be lost."

Amy handed him a cup of coffee and he took a long drink and continued, "I need you ladies to gather all the things inside the house that would be useful like you would be going on a campout and place them in the dining room. All medical supplies and food as well, The guys need to come help me gather what is outside, please do so quickly it will be dark in a few hours and we need to leave just after dark."

Everyone started talking at once wondering what was going on. They all saw the note and knew it was bad, but didn't understand what it had all meant. Danny spoke up saying,

"I saw what they are calling the refugee camps or aid stations. It is not what they tell you it is. They have people inside a fence line with guards and not for protection either. They are not watching the perimeter of the camp, but the people inside it. The barbed wire faces inward, not out and the people inside are made to work like slaves."

They all gasped and had questions for Danny who said, "I'm sure we will see more, but John is right we need to move quickly."

Danny, Dickie and Kevin followed John and Mark to the door to help with the supplies outside, while inside the girls did as John had asked and began to gather things into the dining room.

As they were walking to the barn Danny asked John,

"What will we be needing out here? I thought the FEMA guys took everything?"

Mark and John gave each other a knowing look and John said, "Not everything."

Danny seemed unsure of what the look was but nodded at John. While they walked to the chicken pen John grabbed some shovels, which made Danny and Dickie glance at one another. When they got to the corner of the pen John handed out shovels and told them where to dig. It wasn't long before they hit the tops of the barrels. When John began pulling out the cache of items Danny whistled saying,

"This is amazing! You really prepared."

John nodded and said, "I could see what was coming down so I hid a few things here and there."

Danny looked at him a sideways look saying, "Here and there?"

John winked, "Well, ya don't wanna put all yer eggs in one basket you know."

They all laughed and finished loading the contents of the barrels into the truck and moved over to the barn to empty the things from the old cistern, while John went to the stump. Once everything was loaded into the truck they went back to the house and began distributing things between the vehicles, except the mustang. John told them he wanted a lead car with very little supplies in it as a scout car telling them,

"If something happens and we run into something this car can be abandoned and we won't lose any supplies.

Mark asked, "Do you think it could get that bad?"

Danny was nodding his head and said, "I already saw some shit Mark, I think John is right, we should be cautious."

They had equally distributed things into each truck as well as some into Amy's car and the Mustang. The car would carry the kids and stay in the middle of their little convoy. John and Mark wanted to ride in the lead with the mustang but Amy vetoed that saying they wanted at least one guy in each vehicle, and that whoever could shoot the best should be distributed as shotgun to each as well.

John was shocked, thinking about how Amy was only interested in doing her nails and extraneous fluff as he would call it.

He looked at her and said, "Where did that come from?"

She said, "Where did what come from?"

He said, "All that shit hits the fan wisdom?"

She smiled at him, saying, "While you may not have realized it, I heard the things you said. I can fix a car or chop wood... doesn't mean I wanted to, that is what guys are for." She let out a tiny giggle as she turned to walk back to the house. John just stood dumbfounded and shook his head, going back to what he was doing with a boyish grin.

They tried to put things in each vehicle that if a vehicle were lost they would not be without things and could still cook and eat as well as other things they would need to do along the way. Once the task was done, they all sat in the dining room for their vehicle assignments. Amy had already drawn up the assignments and began telling everyone where they were to ride.

She decided, John would ride shotgun in the lead with the Mustang along with Kevin, who would drive, Rita and Morgan would take the back seat. John's truck would be second with Melinda driving, Danny is riding shotgun and Laurie, Kimmie and Jenny in the back seat. The car would carry Amy as the driver along with Jules and Georgia and Matty with Dickie riding shotgun. While Mark follows up the rear and would ride shotgun with Renee, Marks truck had an extended cab, but with only jump seats it was a bit of a squeeze for anyone but kids to ride in.

Rita was not happy about riding separate from Matty, but agreed it was best that Jules needed to ride with them. She was adamant that she not be forced to ride with Morgan but was careful not to seem bitchy about it. She quietly approached Amy and said,

"Can you please place me in another vehicle? I'm not trying to be difficult, but it is Morgan, I can't ride with her."

Amy looked at her angrily saying, "Rita, you don't like anyone. What's the difference?"

Rita began to cry and whimpering she said, "You don't understand what she and Matt put me through and just you wait and see what she will put Dez through."

Amy looked at her in shock saying, "What is that supposed to mean?"

Rita still crying, said, "Morgan won't divorce Kevin but she and Matt have been carrying on for years. How is it you know her and not Kevin? Think about it Amy. He cheated on me with her and he is cheating on Dez with her. She is not what she seems and can't be trusted."

Amy was silent a moment and said, "Let me change you and Laurie but I will need to know more about this later, understand?"

Rita nodded and thanked her, gathering her things she went over to Matty and stood instructing him to be good in the car and not give Amy a hard time. She hugged him and went to put her things in the truck.

Amy went to John and told him what she said; he too was shocked, but conceded it was odd they had never met Kevin before and that she had often been with Matt when he visited without Dez. Amy noted that never when Dez was with him she didn't visit and told him that while she hated the idea of believing Rita, something; even with their arrival was off, that they all thought so when they first arrived. John agreed to the switch and said that he wanted Amy to try and befriend Rita that something about everything was not right. Amy said she would be nice and that she actually felt bad for Rita when she was telling her.

With the changes made to the vehicle assignments and everyone packed and ready, Amy distributed bags of food she had prepared and wrapped for travel earlier in the day. They all got into their vehicles and with a wave of his arm in true John Wayne style taken from an old western movie, he yelled out, "HO!" The convoy was now on their way to Kentucky to meet up with Destiny and Matt, and hopefully safety.

# Chapter 9

## "Out of the Fire"

*"The choice for mankind lies between freedom and happiness and for the great bulk of mankind, happiness is better."*
-George Orwell, 1984

The sky was red as the last of the sunlight passed beyond the horizon, looking back to his home John felt like it was to be like a lost friend he would never see again. A bit of nostalgia gripped him as he swiped a single tear from his eye. He knew the world would never be the same again. He glanced back to the vehicles following and worry gripped his soul. Till now everything seemed surreal, sort of like a bad dream that unfolded before his eyes. He knew his resources and preparations had not taken into account this many people.

He began to run through scenarios in his mind of what they might encounter and it occurred to him that Dickie having some military training and Danny's experiences may just have saved them all. He was glad for their arrival and knew he would have some help with this rag tag group he was leading. He never thought of himself as a leader and wished at this moment this burden had not fallen to him.

He really only knew Matt and while he knew Dez through Matt, he hoped she was the woman he thought she was. The homestead and all the property and assets belonged to her. He worried what would happen if what Rita had said was true, he wondered if she would put out him and all of his kin when she found out about it. So many scenarios were running through his mind that he almost forgot to tell Kevin where to turn.

The daylight was nearly gone as they approached the roadblock the guardsman had told him to go to. John was anxious, worried that if the same guardsman was not there that all their plans and preparation would be for nothing inside of an hour of their exodus. Kevin pulled up to the guardsman and John was relieved to see it was indeed the one who had given him the note. The guardsman looked into the car and said,

"Glad to see you understood my note."

John replied, "I knew already things would go bad quickly, you just confirmed we should not wait."

The guardsman shoved his hand in the window and said, "Ray Saylor, and this big ox is Roger Morris."

John put out his hand, saying, "John Green and this is Kevin Brown, thank you for helping us. But I must say I'm not sure why you do."

Ray responded, "Well, sir, not all of us in the military agree with what is going on and many have no idea how deep this goes. Not all is as it seems."

John said, "I was pretty sure of that already."

Ray asked him, "Do you have a place you are going?"

John replied, "Yes, we do."

Ray nodded, asking, "Got room for two more passengers?"

John looked shocked, saying, "You two?"

Ray looked down, saying, "We cannot in good conscience carry out these illegal orders that require us to round up American citizens. It is all unconstitutional and therefore we cannot comply. If we stay, we either must go against our belief and oath to the constitution or face court martial."

John asked them to hold on a moment while he talked to the group. He got out of the car and walked back to talk to Dickie and Amy. Dickie and Amy both agreed they would be useful and thought that it was not a ruse because most had no idea what was going on yet so they had no reason to try and trick them.

John returned to Ray and asked him, "Why not just go AWOL on your own? Head for your families?"

Ray responded, "I was stationed here, I'm not from here. Roger has some family in Montana but I really have none to speak of. We hoped someone with your kind of file would be a good group to team with."

John looked confused, saying, "My kind of file?"

Ray laughingly said, "You don't think you were randomly selected to visit do you?"

John said, "What does that mean?"

Ray continued, "They had files on everyone, yours was marked survivalist. They kept track of things you did and bought. What they really wanted to know was if you were going to be a threat and to take away your guns and ability to survive outside the camp. They would not have resupplied you."

John said, "Oh… I knew that part would happen." With a sly smile he continued, "We were not willing to give up all, only what they knew we had."

Ray nodded knowingly and said, "Time's a wasting you know. We are due to be relieved at midnight."

John said, "Well grab your gear solider and jump in."

Ray said, "Be right with you."

Ray and Roger walked over behind a stand of trees that shrouded an old barn and drove out from behind in a genuine army issue Jeep. It had not occurred to John that they would take their vehicle, nor what followed. Roger hopped out of the passenger side of the Jeep with some papers and began sticking red stars on the driver side of each windshield. Ray was at the window of the car explaining,

"The red stars and the escort will work for a little while. Meaning you are in transport, with the Jeep in the lead there would be no questions until we are discovered AWOL. We know the guys replacing us and they too are leaving once they head out to their posts. They will not miss us till morning so we better make tracks."

John was impressed that they had so much planned even though they had not been sure the group would even come. He asked him, "How did you know we would come this way or even that we would leave?"

Ray said, "It was in your eyes and answers the day you came into town. I could see you knew what was going down and from your file; I knew you would not stick around to be herded off to the camp."

John replied, "That was a big assumption."

Ray nodded, saying, "I wouldn't say assumption but more like an educated guess."

The group left and knowing they had to get around Worchester and go a more northern route to avoid New York City they made their way to route 9 which would take them north and west. They made good time and had no problems until they reached the Connecticut River. Amherst, where they had planned to cross was in flames. The group could see from a distance the massive fires burning.

They stopped to look at the map; John stretched it out across the hood of the Mustang and consulted with Ray and Danny. They all thought it would be best to continue north on route 116 and cross at Sunderland. It was nearly midnight when they reached the bridge and as they approached the National Guard roadblock John had knots in his stomach. When Ray and Roger began to pull forward Kevin moved the car hesitantly forward, where they were waved past. One by one all their cars were waved through the roadblock. John sighed in relief, hoping their luck would hold.

They continued along route 116 which they would follow taking other smaller roads and routes into New York. By the time they came upon the outskirts of Albany it was nearly four a.m. and Ray waved out the window to them to follow up route 22. They were headed into the Adirondack Mountains and there were not many cities or towns along the route they were on.

After switching direction and going south they stopped at the lower part of Scandaga Lake. Ray came to talk to John saying,

"I think we should make camp here, we can pull the vehicles off the road into these woods and rest up. We need to continue to travel at night. It might also help to know which direction we are headed into besides just getting around New York City."

John nodded, saying, "We will get some food going and sit down and talk. You can meet the rest of the group and we will try and plan out our route more then."

Ray acknowledged him and said, "I'll scout around and find us a place to set up camp. Everyone sit tight for a few." After a few minutes Ray returned and led them to an area of trees where they could hide the vehicles and set up camp. Dickie quickly had a fire going. Amy and Jules were quickly preparing a hot meal for the group.

They sat around the fire after the meal with coffee and discussions about their next move. Dickie had an idea, saying, "We need to get some comm's up between vehicles; if we should get separated we need to be able to communicate."

Rita leaned into Jules saying, "Comm's? What's that?"

Jules giggled a little and whispered to her, "Communications."

Rita nodded a sheepish nod and Jules reached out and touched her shoulder gently saying, "It's ok, I didn't know what that was till a short while ago and I'm married to him."

They both giggled as Dickie shot his wife a stern look. Kevin, who was a quiet man that rarely spoke, said,

"I'm going to do some fishing while we have this fire anyone care to join me. I really don't know much about what is going on but think I can be most helpful catching some fish."

Morgan scoffed at him, saying, "Is fishing all you can think about right now?"

Kevin replied, "It helps me think."

John was curious about him with his gentle manner for an obviously strong man and leaned into Danny saying, "I don't want people out alone can you go with him. I think some fish for breakfast would be a good thing since we don't know how long this is going to take we should try and conserve and gather what we can when we can."

Danny agreed and spoke up saying, "Hey Kevin, I would love to get some fishing in mind if I join you?"

Kevin's look brightened and he said, "Sure, the more the better." Amy curiously watched Morgan as Kevin and Danny left the fire; there was something about this that still bugged her. She got up and went over to where Jules and Rita were talking and quietly asked,

"Rita, there is something I don't understand about what you told me."

Rita looked up saying, "What's that?"

Amy responded, "If she and Matt have been carrying on like you say, then why did she bring Kevin with her?"

Rita said, "I don't know why, but he tolerates her whoring. I think he just loves her although I don't know why. I'm sure she wants something from him because that is what she does, I think most likely it is because he has been friends with Matt for many years and it would look odd for her to be going there without him."

Amy nodded and said, "I'm sorry Rita, I don't know what to make of all this yet, but we only had Matt's word on things until now. I hope you're wrong about all this."

Rita looked at her defensively saying, "You don't have to believe me, but just watch your back. She is a liar and a home wrecker, if she can sleep with any of these guys along the way she will... John included."

On the other side of the fire John saw Amy go over to where Rita was and nodded. He and Dickie were talking with Mark, Ray and Roger about their destination.

He wasn't listening when Dickie nudged him asking, "So what do you think of the comm's mate?"

John looked startled and said, "What? Oh, sorry, what did you say?'

Dickie sighed and said, "CB's? I think we need to find some CB radios for each vehicle. The only problem with CB's is they ain't secure comm's, so we will need to come up with some system of switching channels so we can't be monitored"

John said, "Yeah, that sounds like a good idea."

Re-joining the conversation they were having about the trip, John said, "We are going to need to try and avoid the cities, so we are going to have to think creatively to find them."

Ray said. "We should look where semi-trucks park many of them have CB's, and if we stick to fleets of trucks we could know where we got them so if things go back to normal, we would return them."

They all agreed that it was a good idea, but none believed things were going to go back to what one would call normal any time soon. They sat looking at the map, realizing they had made little progress on their journey. Knowing it would be even harder as they continued because Ray and

Roger were sure to be found AWOL by now and could not get them through roadblocks anymore.

Deciding to head south in the morning, out and around Binghamton down into Pennsylvania. The thought was that if they could get over to route 92, it would take them far west of Scranton, Pennsylvania. Not really knowing much in the way of news they decided to adjust as they needed to along the way.

It was getting quite dark and Kevin and Danny had not returned from fishing. John walked over to the lake to find them. They had already caught twenty-three fish and cleaned them as well. They were already getting the tackle and poles ready to head to camp by the time John found them. The three men walked back to camp chattering about the great fishing.

Everyone was getting settled in for the night while watches were established. Dickie and Danny would take the first watch and moved to an area of cover where they could watch the camp but been unseen. The evening was quiet and

Dickie looked to Danny saying, "This trip usually takes about fifteen hours to drive it and it took longer to just get here. Do you think we can make it in a week?"

Danny shrugged, saying, "I thought we would be there already, I hope it won't take that long."

Dickie replied, "I don't know what to think right now, we saw a lot of shit just trying to get to John's place. How bad do you think it is out there mate?"

Danny shrugged, saying, "Not sure, but I think we are gonna find out."

As Danny continued to talk Dickie looked around and putting his finger up to his mouth indicating he wanted Danny to be quiet while he strained to listen, sure he had heard something. There it was again, they had both heard it this time. It was a rustling in the woods on the opposite side of the camp from where they were.

Dickie indicated to Danny to watch the area that the noise had come from, by signalling with two fingers pointing to his eyes then to the area the sounds had come from. Before Danny could object he turned back to where Dickie had been to find him silently creeping into the woods, in seconds he was gone from sight. Anxiously waiting for something to happen Danny kept scanning the area they had heard the noise, but heard nothing.

After a few minutes Dickie emerged from the woods where the sound had come from and waved Danny over. Danny came over quickly to find Dickie triumphantly holding out two rabbits he said were the source of the noise.

The rest of the evening was uneventful, even quiet. John sat watching the sun rise across the lake and wondered what surprises this trip may offer along the way.

# Chapter 10

## "A changed landscape"

*"There is nothing new except what is forgotten."*
-Marie Antoinette

*September 25th*

The group packed their camp, remembering to place things into the proper vehicles. Taking some time to look at their maps again, they ventured in the direction the road took them to go south into Pennsylvania. They carefully charted the roads along the way to make sure they were avoiding cities like Scranton.

After talking it over the guys formulated a plan to try and obtain some CB radios. They found some information in an abandoned truck, noting a location outside of a larger city on the Pennsylvania state line. It was one they had already noted, seemed like there was no way around. They all agreed it would be best if they found some way to communicate while on the road with the other vehicles, and thought it was worth the risk.

Once on the road, travel seemed slower than it had been the previous day. A few hours into the day they came to a small town that had been burned to the ground, there was nothing left but some brick and mortar shells of what buildings remained. The insides of these were nothing more than ashes, little more than a few memories of the once tiny town.

They slowly made their way through the one stop light town, each car with faces pressed to the windows, staring at the destruction.  No one could believe this entire town had been so utterly and completely erased from the map.

Ray and Roger who were still in the lead at this point pulled over into a secluded rest stop off the roadway.  As each vehicle pulled into the rest stop, Ray signalled that each vehicle was to be backed into a space. This would make supplies for lunch close at hand, but also for ease of escape if necessary.

It was still early in the day, not even noon.  John wondered why they chose to stop so soon and quickly headed for the lead vehicle.  Approaching the vehicle he was nervous about the look on the military men's faces.  There was something very wrong in the way they looked and one thing he was sure of, was that for it to worry Roger and Ray, this was not going to be good.

Approaching them he waved saying, "I'm guessing there is a reason for this early stop?"

Roger nodded waving him over.  Once he was close enough Ray said, "I don't want to panic anyone so lets you and I take a short walk with the map."

This immediately raised the hairs on the back of John's neck.  By this time Dickie had caught up to them and asked the same question. Ray instructed him to follow as well. They walked over to a group of large boulders and spread the map out on one.  Ray began looking it over with an intense and troubled look.

John asked, "Is there something wrong with the route?'

Ray looked at the map saying, "Do you have any idea what happened to that town?"

John said, "No."

Dickie without looking up from the map said, "I have an idea, but I hope I am wrong."

Ray looked at him and asked, "What did you notice?"

Dickie said, "Oh, you mean besides the town being ransacked, and there ain't no fucker around you mean? But what really got me bothered is the partial red X on one of the doors not fully burned, that was what really told me what happened to that town."

John looked at him, "Red X?"

Ray nodded in Dickie's direction, saying, "You're right Dickie, Roger and I saw that too."

John, looking uneasy, began to raise his voice, "What are you two talking about? "

Roger said, "Let's not get worked up, I don't think it is a good time to let everyone else know what we think is going on."

John apologized, saying, "Sorry about that, but how about you guys let me in on this will you?"

Ray nodded and began to speak, "The red X is something FEMA uses to identify houses and its inhabitants in areas of disaster. It indicates a house has been searched and what was found. It gives the date and time of when they were here, who searched it, if anyone was alive or dead and numbers along with what the hazard was. I saw a few as we passed through the outskirts."

John looked concerned, saying, "What does this all mean?"

Ray responded, "Well the best I can figure from the ones I saw is that, they were here the day before yesterday. The reason for the visit and likely the town burned is because of a Biohazard, and there were at least some dead. As for the rest they have likely been sent to a camp."

Dickie and John looked at each other and back to Ray in shock almost in unison saying, "Biohazard?" Ray nodded and replied, "Before we left Roger and I heard some things about what was going on with Ebola. They were not telling the public, but it was spreading in urban areas quickly. Honestly, we think it has something to do with everything that is happening. All of this is just too orchestrated, too much having fallen into place to institute martial law. Look at it, the whole OPEC thing, Ebola and the banking virus at once? It is just too coincidental for us."

John shuffled his feet nervously saying, "I thought so too, but I never thought it was so widespread."

Ray looked concerned and asked, "How far do we have to go?"

John said, "About another eight hundred miles."

Ray shook his head saying, "I think we are in for a tough trip. We are going to need to avoid civilization as much as possible and it has already taken us three days to go less than two hundred miles. I think it is only going to get slower as we go."

Dickie nodded and headed off to where the cars were parked. A few steps away, he slowed and turned back to them saying, "I don't think we should be keeping them in the dark. If it is going to get as bad as you think then we need to start preparing them right now mate, for when the shit hits the fan. I don't think hiding it from them is going to make it any better either, they need a crash course in survival tactics. In fact, I think it will bring us more problems if we don't educate them double quick, they need to be part of the solution not another problem."

Ray and John walked over to him, when they got closer to him John said, "I think you're right."

Looking at Ray, Dickie said, "What do reckon mate?"

Ray nodded and said, "You're probably right, I think maybe it is the military in me telling me to keep the civvies in the dark as usual. We should have a chat with everyone over lunch and maybe think about where our strengths and weaknesses may be."

As they approached the group Ray was already making notes in a little book he kept in his pocket. John asked what he was doing and Ray said, "Just trying to make notes about who might be an asset and who might be a liability."

John said, "How can you know this? You really don't know any of these people."

Ray looked at him and said, "I can't it is just an estimation based on the past few days. Mostly it is just some notes for me to start from. I want to see what we can do about getting some of these people a little more military trained if you know what I mean."

John said, "I agree and there is some good potential in this little group."

Ray said, "I think you and Dickie should do the same, give each person a letter ranking. A for asset, N for neutral and an L for liability and we will get together and compare our thoughts and then see about getting them into better shape and positions within the convoy."

John looked distressed and asked, "Do you really think we are going to have trouble getting there?"

Ray nodded affirmatively saying, "I think it is going to be worse than we even fear. If even some of what we had heard from the FEMA guys is true, we are in for some trouble."

Sighing, John said, "I hope you're wrong on this."

There was a tasty meal being whipped up by Laurie and Jules finishing off the fish from the night before. They had battered and fried it, along with a stir fry made from some of the vegetables that were beginning to wilt. They had made rice and even managed to make some pan fried flat bread.

When John and Ray approached, they looked at each other and smiled.

Ray said, "They are definitely on my asset list."

They both laughed and went over to get a plate of food. When everyone had gotten some food and they were all seated John told them they had some things to discuss.

Mark looked up from his food saying, "About the town we just passed through?"

John said, "Yes, we are worried that we may run into more than just that kind of thing along this trip."

Jenny had a sort of deer in the headlight look and said, "Are we going to die? Were those marks on the houses because of dead people?"

Roger went over to her as she was beginning to cry, sat down and said, "We're not going to let you die."

She looked up at him pleadingly with her exceptionally light blue eyes, and sniffled. She nodded she was ok and said, "I'm sorry; I don't mean to be a baby."

Roger blushed saying, "It's ok, don't worry about it."

John and Ray looked at each other as Ray was shaking his head, he said, "And people wonder why that ox is in the military. Ain't he got the way with the ladies?"

As they talked and ate Rita stated, "I want to learn how to shoot, I might not be able to shoot well, but we all need to know how to load these things and fire them."

John was genuinely surprised when Amy said, "I agree with Rita, you men think all we can do is cook and do dishes, but we can help with keeping watch and fishing and stuff too."

Dickie chimed in, "Sorry guys I'm on their side. Georgia here can catch fish that ain't even biting. And well, about Jules? Well, I wouldn't get between her and Georgia that's all I have to say about that. I personally think it is a good idea that we start getting the girls up to speed on things like this."

Cautiously looking around, he continued, "But ladies I gotta warn ya, if you want me to cook, make sure you ain't got plans for a few days I only know one dish "curry, rice and chips" and my curries will clean you out if you know what I mean. It won't be a good thing I can tell you that."

Jules said, "No one wants to eat his cooking, that I can surely agree with."

Lunch was over and everything had been packed up, they got into the vehicles and hit the road again. They had hoped to make Pennsylvania by nightfall. On a normal road trip they would have made it to Pennsylvania by midday the very day they started out, but this was not a normal road trip. None of them knew what this trip would hold, but they were all beginning to see that it would be anything but normal.

# Chapter 11

## In Darkness... Danger

*"Look at how a single candle can both defy and define the darkness."*

-Anne Frank

Passing abandoned and burned out cars on the side of the road. They watched people as they walked to an unknown destination. The group began to wonder what they themselves looked like to those they passed, sitting on porches observing them as they themselves passed by.

They took minor roads and smaller highways throughout the day avoiding as much civilization as possible. Shortly before nightfall they found themselves in a warehouse district just outside of Binghamton, New York.

Initially apprehension was the first thought, but then Danny said, "We should try and camp inside, being so close to the city it wouldn't be good to be in the open."

Roger admonished, "If we get caught, they could consider us looters. There is still some law... I think."

John considered it and spoke with Ray and Dickie, they all agreed if they were to use an empty, unoccupied unit that there was nothing to steal so they wouldn't be looting. Roger shook his head saying, "Oh sure, rationalizing it is the way to go."

Dickie volunteered to go find the unit and gain entry, grabbing John's arm, he said, "Geeza you just volunteered to go with me."

They then started walking off toward the buildings John turned back and said, "Maybe we should keep everyone in the vehicles, just in case. Wait here for us to come back and keep watch. If you see anything give a signal."

Danny was standing nearby and said, "These girls can make an amazing cat fight. They actually did it when we were trying to get to John's place and it was both realistic sounding and effective."

Dickie nodding said, "Right! It did work well. Danny, make sure to let the girls know to be ready. I really don't want them out of the car either, so use hand signals to let them know it's time for the show."

The rest took positions so they could see each other and someone could at all times see Dickie or John. Once everyone was in place, they slipped into the night. Silently they crept along the side of the building, peering into the office doors, looking for an empty one.

John motioned for Dickie to look into a unit. Dickie nodded and reached into his breast pocket, pulling out a zippered pouch. Opening it John could see they were locksmith tools, Dickie quickly picked the lock and they entered the building.

It was dark inside, but they did not dare to use flashlights. Feeling along the walls they made their way to an inner office where they turned on their flashlights to look around. It was indeed vacant and Dickie was satisfied that this unit would serve their purposes if the warehouse was also empty.

They moved through the office area to a door that led them into the warehouse section, it too was empty. John went to the garage type door to check it for locks and found none. They nodded to each other and moved back to the office area.

Dickie said, "This will work nicely, I will go back for the others. I figure once I leave, you lock the door and watch for us. We will not use headlights, but I don't know about brake lights. When you see us go through and open the garage door, sound ok?"

John nodded in agreement and Dickie slipped out the door. Watching as he made his way back to the others, Johns gaze shifted to a clump of trees. He thought he saw something, but figured after watching a few moments his eyes were playing tricks on him. Still, he could not shake the feeling that they were being watched.

It was only moments before the vehicles began to roll into sight. John hurried to the door and raised it for them just enough for them to get through. He hurried to Dickie and Ray and told them what he thought he saw and how he felt they were being watched.

Roger manned the door as the three of them headed for the office door again. They remained in the shadow of the office as they watched the area John thought he saw movement.

John jabbed Dickie in the ribs pointing to the area said, "There, did you see it?"

Dickie nodded, saying, "Yeah, I saw it mate, but you didn't have to nail me in the ribs like that you wanker."

John stammered, "Guess I was a little over zealous, sorry there guy."

Narrowing his eyes as he strained to see, Ray said, "I think we need to check this out, did anyone notice a back way out?

They both shook their heads, no. Ray instructed John to keep an eye on the place they had seen the movement and to go ahead and appear be looking around inside with the flashlight, but take care not to shine it outside.

Ray explained that he wanted the attention on what John was doing so that he and Dickie could get to them hopefully unnoticed.

John watched as they made their way to the place the movement was observed, he made a big show as he shuffled about the office flashlight flailing wildly about in the darkness. John watched the observers as he continued his distraction. In his clumsiness he stumbled, bumping a light switch. He felt shocked and blinded when the fluorescent lights flickered to life. Frantically he fumbled at the light switch and quickly switched them off. Scolding himself, he said, "Well, I guess that is something that will hold their attention." He grumbled at himself as he continued to shuffle about the office area.

With all the antics and moving around he was doing he failed to notice that there were two other figures in a dumpster directly across from the office door. He slapped his forehead in embarrassment, as if someone were aware of his inattentive moment. To anyone outside he appeared to be occupied with some unknown interest.

Unbeknownst to them, he maintained this appearance of oblivion to keep them watching him, while still he kept his eye on them. He noted one moving from the dumpster to a point of cover near a jersey barrier, shrinking into it until the figure was almost imperceptible; John watched closely and kept a mental note as to the exact shapes in the area.

Flashing his light around, he was sending the beam of light repeatedly out the door. Appearing random, yet it was carefully orchestrated. The movements with his light, he wanted it to look like he was just careless, although he was secretly signalling Dickie and Ray that there was more movement.

John left the doorway and entered an office where he turned off the flashlight, trying to make it appear as though he had gone back inside the warehouse. He crept back to the office doorway to continue in the darkness to keep watch on the figures. The second figure began to dart in and out from behind the office walls, making his way to the spot where the first one had hidden and still remained crouched behind the Jersey barrier.

He could see Dickie and Ray making their way to the place where the first pair sat hiding. Watching the second pair he decided to create a diversion as Dickie and Ray moved on the two hiding nearest them. John slid himself back into the office and headed for the warehouse. Summoning Mark he instructed him to turn on the back office light when he asked him to.

John took a position near the door that still allowed him to see the two behind the Jersey barrier. He watched as Dickie first crept up on his intended target and Ray made his way for the second one. He signalled Mark to turn the lights on. He could see the two lean over the barrier straining to see what might be going on inside the office room.

John signalled Mark to turn the light off by dragging his finger across his throat. Mark understood and killed the lights; this made the two figures strain harder to see and lean further into view. While John continued to keep their attention, Dickie and Ray came up on the others. Before he knew what was going on Dickie and Ray had subdued his audience and were herding all four of them into the warehouse.

Once they could all be seen, it seemed apparent that they were just like them, and simply looking for someplace to hide out for the night. They introduced themselves to the group, a woman spoke first saying,

"I'm Mandy and this is my son Aaron." After which, one of the two teens spoke saying,

"My name is Martin and this is my girlfriend Cindy." Cindy waved in a shy fashion while clinging steadfastly to Martin's arm.

The ladies had already prepared some beans, and canned spam, and they were serving them with a rather odd looking salad concoction that they had gathered on the way. John was sure it was edible because he saw what they had gathered, but not so sure how it would taste. The salad was mostly made of Dandelion greens along with some lettuce and a few tomatoes that they found in a garden behind a vacant house. Most agreed that it was not the best food ever, but they were happy that there was plenty for everyone and that it was filling.

John blurted out, "That salad wasn't as bad as I thought it was going to be." While the men had all been thinking it, the men all looked at John like he had lost his mind and the ladies looked at him like he had just spoken an unmentionable line, one that would surely be considered the crime of the century. At that Danny burst out laughing saying, "Dude, you're in the doghouse for life, even I know better than that." Everyone burst into laughter, even the newcomers were laughing. Amy glared at John like he had done the unthinkable and he shot her his best puppy dog eyes begging forgiveness.

Once dinner was finished and the laughter had subsided Danny said,

"Ok, well, what's your story? Why are the four of you out here?"

Mandy spoke up first saying, "Aaron and I live downtown, that is we did until two nights ago."

Danny asked, "What happened two nights ago?"

Mandy pulled her knees up to her chest and put her head down onto her knees. Her long sandy hair swept down covering her knees as she silently wept.

Aaron, who Danny thought was about twelve years old said, "A bunch of guys, like a gang, came in and took a bunch of stuff. One of them made me carry all of our food out to their truck. Mom kept screaming but they just laughed." He hung his head saying, "I know they hit my mom a bunch of times. Then they burned our house so we don't have any place to live now. Mom said we would look for a new house out in the country near Grandpa's."

Martin and Cindy had similar stories, but something did not sit quite right with them or their story for Danny. He couldn't put his finger on it, but knew there was something gnawing at him about their stories. They felt contrived, a little too similar to Mandy and Aaron.

Rubbing his chin in a thoughtful manner, but not wanting to voice or show his suspicion he got up and went for more coffee. Amy noticed him shaking his head as he walked to the small camp stove and followed him.

Joining him for coffee, she glanced back to the others and said in a hushed voice, "You don't believe Martin and Cindy either, do you?"

Danny shifted his eyes back and forth as if looking for something and said, "They're after something, I just don't know what yet."

Amy nodded in agreement saying, "Food maybe or supplies?"

Danny sighed, saying, "I know this much, we will have our usual watch for trouble on the outside, but I'll be watching the inside, something feels very wrong with this. Maybe I'm just suspicious of people right now, but I feel very uneasy for some reason. Another thing bothers me, we went through all those towns that had Ebola, how do we know they are not infected?"

Mark came walking up and in a loud tone bellowed, "Hey, you guys gonna share some of that joe?"

It startled Amy and Danny, but as he got closer he looked at each of them shifting his eyes with pursed lips.

While moving toward them, he whistled the Folgers best part of waking up tune and then shot his eyes up and to the right, with a barely perceptible head tilt in the same direction as his eyes went. He was indicating they had observers.

Danny, looking at Mark, but past him also noticed Martin with a fixed gaze in their direction, very deliberately focused on the trio. Laughing loudly and seemingly making a show of whatever the joke was, Danny said loudly,

"You know it guy, but we knew if we waited too long you would likely have downed the whole pot before we even got a sniff."

Motioning him over he said, "Care for a cup?"

Mark, moving closer, said, "Don't mind if I do."

Amy was facing where Martin and Cindy were sitting and began chatting in a normal tone about breakfast with the guys, she was seemingly oblivious to the stares from either of the onlookers.

However, Mark and Danny, who faced her had their own conversation going on and talked quietly about their suspicions, they occasionally nodded at her to make it appear they were listening to her. The three felt certain that something was not as it seemed about these two and were determined to keep an eye on them. They began to discuss who should take the first watch, eventually settling on Amy. It was decided that they would lie in their spots and observe the group until it was time for the next watch. The person on watch would have a coughing fit that would continue until the next person responded they were awake with a small cough.

Tonight's watch on the office door would be John with Dickie and Roger to follow.  Mark thought this was good because the three of them were what the group considered to be the most experienced in things like this.

Amy turned, reaching for the fresh pot of coffee, when the lights flickered off briefly before coming back on. She had accidentally touched the hot pot, startling her and causing her to cry out.

Matty and Georgia came running in from the offices telling John that Rita had sent for him.  She was on watch at the office door, they said she had told them to tell him she saw something and wanted him to come and check.

John already wasn't sure how he felt about some of the members of the group keeping watch and this was surely a dog or something roaming through the parking lot.  He let out a heavy sigh and rose to go to the offices.  It was no secret how he felt about Rita and she knew his eyes, she could do nothing right.   As he reached the place where Rita was, the lights flickered again and went out.

John grunted and with exasperation in his tone said, "What's the issue Rita?  Show me what you saw." Rita hushed him by placing her hand on his mouth.  It was dark with the lights out and she could barely make out his form in the moonlight.

They crept up to the doorway and keeping low to the floor, they peered out the door.  John was shocked, she had indeed seen something.  There, standing in the middle of the parking lot, not even trying to keep hidden were five figures, obviously looking for something.

They were silently watching them when John felt a tap on his foot. He looked back in the direction of a whisper, "John a word please?" He could barely see that it was Mark waving him to retreat into the next office.

Looking at Rita he pointed to his eyes and then to the outside hoping she would understand that he wanted her to keep watching. She nodded that she understood and responded by pointing to the small flap on the door that mail could be dropped into and tapping her ear questioningly. John was impressed that she not only understood, but had the idea to try and listen to what they were saying outside.

He signalled her no, but put up his finger meaning 'in a minute' pointing in Mark's direction and covering his ears. He figured she would figure out he didn't want to take the chance of them hearing him and Mark talking in the next office. She nodded in agreement and understanding as John slid himself backwards into the next office.

Mark whispered to John, "What's up?"

John said, "There are about five people outside in the parking lot sniffing around."

Mark said, "I needed to let you know Amy, Danny and I were observing our new guests and we don't trust that couple. Something isn't kosher there."

John nodded as he replied, "Dickie and I were just discussing the same thing a little bit before we ate. We were planning on keeping an eye on them."

Mark replied, "So what's up at the door? Do you think there is a threat out there?"

John said, "I don't know, but I don't want to give away that we are here either, so go get everyone into the very last office and have them stay quiet."

Mark nodded and turned to leave when John added, "And keep a close eye on those two, I'm curious if they are somehow tied to this group outside."

Mark nodded and headed off in the direction of the warehouse, while John crawled back to the doorway, tapping Rita's foot as he crept alongside her to let her know he was there. Rita looked at him with wide eyes that instantly sent chills down his spine. Rita was tipping her head toward the door indicating for him to look outside. He leaned in her direction and saw what had her scared, one of the guys was sitting outside on the step in front of the door smoking a cigarette. It wasn't the person that had her nervous so much, as it was the shotgun carelessly slung across his back, as he sat smoking.

John motioned for her to retreat into the office doorway and followed her. Once in the office, he whispered to her, "Go get Dickie and Ray, but be quiet about it. Just tell either one of them that I said 'it is go time and I have no fire'."

She whispered, "They will know what that means?"

He replied, "They should get the hint, but mostly I don't want to give anything away about the situation. I have a bad feeling about that couple and in case they are involved with these guys we don't want them to try to send a warning."

She nodded in understanding, but stood wringing her hands as if overcome with anxiety.

John could see how unsure of things she was and continued, "After that I need you to go to Roger and quietly tell him what is going on, he will tell Mark. Then go get Matty and sit near Amy, make sure to keep the kids quiet. Let the girls know what's going on too, but do it quietly." She nodded; a tiny tear glistened on her cheek in the moonlight.

As Rita turned to retreat into the darkness of the inner offices, John whispered, "Oh, and Rita? Good job spotting these guys."

She smiled and returned the thumbs up before disappearing into the darkness.

Rita went into the warehouse and quietly made her way over to Dickie and Ray, telling them what John had instructed her to. Hoping they understood, she looked at each of them with raised eyebrows seeking acknowledgement, both nodded to her and silently made their way to the office door; hoping to not raise suspicions that there was anything out of the ordinary.

Moving to gather the children to Amy and share what was going on she failed to notice the strangers were keenly aware of her every move.

Mandy spoke, "Excuse me, miss?"

Startled, Rita turned, looking at her like she had seen a ghost.

Mandy came close and in a whisper said to her, "I'm sorry I can't remember your name and I don't know what is going on. I can tell there is something so I think someone needs to know… so can they."

Tossing her head in the direction of Martin and Cindy she continued, "I don't know if it is anything but, they are watching every move you people make and whispering."

Rita squinted her eyes to see in the dim light of the candles and it took only a moment to see what Mandy had been talking about, Martin and Cindy were definitely keeping tabs on everyone. Tilting her head quizzically at Mandy she gave her a slight nod and motioned for her to follow.

The ladies made their way to where Amy was sitting; with her were Jules, Matty and Georgia. When Rita approached, she looked relieved and let out an audible sigh of relief to see Matty. After Rita conveyed John's message to Amy and the others, she sat with Mandy and Aaron, and motioned for Matty to join them.

Everyone sat quietly, looking about the room waiting to hear from the guys at the door. Kimmie let out a faint scream when a bright flash lit up the room, immediately followed by thunder sounding like an explosion. Mark quickly cupped his hand over her mouth. Between the lightning and the scream it had inadvertently triggered Martin to act.

# Chapter 12

## "The Storm"

*"I have noticed even people who claim everything is predestined, and that we can do nothing to change it, look before they cross the road."*
-Stephen Hawking

The lightning flashed, illuminating the silhouettes of at least six people, John could see that they were each armed with some kind of long guns, although in the darkness he couldn't make out what kinds. He felt a tap on the back, turning he could see Dickie. He handed him his M9 and gave a slight nod with his chin, silently asking what was going on and with a toothy grin he whispered,

"Someone order up a rifle?"

Grateful they had understood what Rita told them he quickly made hand signals for silence followed by pointing to his eyes, then out the door, the sign for watching.

John glanced over to Ray, who was looking back into the offices with a troubled look. He tapped his ear pointing into the offices and whispered,

"I heard something."

John tilted his head as though he were straining to hear and shrugged his shoulders, nodding a 'No.'

With a slight head shake Ray disappeared into the darkness, back the way he had come to investigate. John and Dickie look at one another, wondering if they should follow or continue to keep watch at the door.

John whispers to Dickie, "I think we need to keep an eye on these guys. If Ray needs help he will let us know.

Dickie nodded in agreement and whispered back, "So what's is going on here? Have you been able to figure it out?"

John crouched low and waved Dickie over to where he could see the door. He pointed to the guy still sitting on the steps saying, "This guy has been sitting here the entire time smoking or just making hand motions to the others over near the dumpster."

Dickie asked, "The leader?

John replied, "Maybe, but I'm not sure. Something doesn't look right about him. I'm thinking maybe just scout or decoy."

Dickie raised his eyebrows as if to express wonder and said, "How many?"

John put up 6 fingers pointing to the guy on the steps. They both slid backwards into the shadow. The guy who was sitting was now climbing the steps towards the very door they were just observing from. He put his hands on the glass to cup his face so he could peer into the office. Pulling on the door, he shouted behind himself,

"It's locked, try the other one."

Dickie quietly pulled the slide back to check he had a round chambered, taking up a crouched position on the opposite side of the doorway from John. He had done the same, maintaining his position lying flat on the floor, his eyes straining in the darkness to see.

Ray entered the room where the others were sitting, it was as if everything was happening in slow motion. He could only watch in horror as the pale light of the candle glistened off the knife, Martin lunged at Danny seemingly without provocation. Danny hadn't expected it and wasn't quick enough to avoid Martin's attack. The knife met his flesh with ease sinking into his thigh, creating a long gash as Martin drew the knife back toward himself.

Like a nightmare, out of nowhere Cindy fired a pistol at Mark missing him but hitting Jules in the back between her shoulder blade and spine, covering Ray in her blood as she fell limp to the floor in front of him. Danny cried out in pain, writhing with Martin, who was inching the knife toward his neck. Danny's eyes filled with fear when it became clear Martin was a lot stronger and would eventually win this struggle for his life.

No one noticed Amy grab the mop, swinging it with all her strength she hit Cindy in the face. Cindy stumbled backwards, dropping the gun reaching for her face. The metal clip holding on the mop head tore into Cindy's face just below her right eye.

Seeing his moment Ray fired at Martin, killing him instantly with a single head shot. Barely noticing the blood that splattered him, Danny scrambled out from under the lifeless body of his attacker.

Amy was already at Jules's side checking her while Laurie was in a trot headed for Danny. Rita ran to the truck and grabbed the first aid kit and was feverishly pulling gauze from its packaging for Amy. Leaving a number of packets there she made her way to Laurie and began opening gauze for Danny's leg. His leg had a gash in it about 5 inches long and was very deep. Laurie began to cry, saying,

"There is so much blood."

Rita took the gauze from her saying, "It's not all Danny's blood. We just need to get this a little closed up so we can get it covered."

Laurie looked at her with a spark of realization, saying, "I'm sorry, I am generally good with this sort of thing, but when it's your son?"

Rita nodded eyebrows raised, "I know I would lose it if anything happened to Matty. Let me take care of Danny, how about if you go help with Jules, ok?"

Laurie nodded, and reaching out she brushed a wisp of hair from Danny's face. Danny shrugged and said, "C'mon mom don't get all weird. I'm ok."

Ray reacted instantly and was standing over Cindy, who by now was whimpering and cursing at them. Shouting profanities, bellowing in some form of guttural howl and at times screaming that they had killed Martin. Ray kicked her in the side scolding her to shut up. She continued her tirade until Ray hit her harder, knocking her out.

Mark came over and started tying her up, looking at Ray he said, "Something is not right here Ray, we have been keeping an eye on these two. You need to go check the front with John and Dickie, I have a bad feeling about all this. I can handle this one, I'll come check in when I'm done."

Don't say anything to Dickie yet about Jules. I'm sure she will be ok, it is not that bad, the bullet passed right through missing anything important I think."

Ray agreed and was headed for the front office when they heard multiple gunshots. He dropped to the floor motioning everyone else to do the same and began to crawl toward John and Dickie's position.

Roger, who was on watch at the rear of the warehouse came running to the group, panting, he said, "There are two guys at the back door trying to force it open. I jammed a pry bar in it to help secure it, but I don't know if it will hold."

Amy heard him, looking up, she said to Renee, "Can you get the kids into the vehicles and have Kimmie and Jenny help you get things packed into the vehicles for what I think may have to be a quick exit?"

Barking out instructions Amy had everyone doing something. She and Rita were tending to Jules and Danny, while Mark and Kevin were attempting to question Cindy. Renee had the rest of them breaking down the camp getting ready to move out.

They had no idea that there were at least six more at the front door, but Mark was sure Martin and Cindy were connected to them.

They could hear gunfire from the front offices and a lot of it. Roger and Mark returned to watch the back entrance while Kevin was to continue to question Cindy.

Kevin was a quiet man who could not get any information out of her. His wife Morgan came over to help him, she was a brash and loud woman, Amy didn't like her, but Morgan was quite chummy with Renee and Kimmie, which made Amy not very fond of them either.

Something felt wrong to Amy about Morgan but she was pretty sure it was just because she was so loud and uncouth that she grated on her nerves. Renee and Kimmie were much the same and likely why they were close with her. What Rita had said before they left was a constant source of wonder whenever she observed her. Amy found herself constantly wondering even what could have made John and Matt such unlikely friends.

Shaking her head, she considered herself and John, many would think they were an unlikely match. She was already sick of this nomadic adventure and feared it would last forever.

Getting Jules to her feet, she helped her into the vehicle and instructed her not to move around too much, telling her, "You need stitches, but I can't do them now, we need to keep you still so you don't start bleeding again."

Jules said, "Thank you Amy, is there nothing I can do to help?"

Amy chided her, "Yes, stay put unless you want me to tie you down. I need to help Rita with Danny and get us all together."

Jules reluctantly agreed and slumped into the seat with a sigh.

Approaching Rita, Amy asked, "How's it look?"

Rita shook her head saying, "It needs stitches, but for now I have it closed up with some medical tape and the bleeding has almost completely stopped."

Amy asked her, "Can we get him moved into the truck?"

Rita said, "I think that is a good idea." Then looked at Danny saying, "I know you think we're just girls but no pressure on that leg."

Looking at Amy, she said, "Let's get him up."

Her and Amy each grabbed an arm, Amy put her foot in front of the foot on his good leg and said, "On three, and don't use the other leg."

Danny did as he was instructed and hopped over to the truck and was settled into the passenger seat.

He said, "Rita, can you give me my gun?"

Rita went over and picked it up, wiping the blood off it as she handed it to him.

He said, "At least I can be on watch."

Rita nodded and returned to Amy's side waiting for instruction for what to do next. She was scared and wished for the gunshots to stop. Amy saw the fear in her eyes and said,

"I know, I'm scared too. Last week my biggest fear was that the colorist at the salon would make my hair too brassy."

Rita laughed with tears in her eyes as Amy continued, "We have to try and keep it together, I mean look around you. The only other woman amongst us with any kind of backbone just got shot."

She handed Rita a Glock 9 mm and asked, "Can you shoot this?"

Rita shook her head and Amy said, "Well, we ain't got time to teach you right now. So this is the crash course."

She handed her two extra Mags and showed her how to eject the old one and saying, "Other than that just point and pull the trigger."

Rita said, "I don't think I can do it."

Amy looked at her sternly and said, "If someone were trying to hurt Matty you would surely find the courage in an instant, don't you worry about that."

Glancing over to the offices she noticed Kevin gathering the sleeping bags and wondered who was watching Cindy. Snapping her head in the direction Cindy was tied up, she saw Morgan hovering over her.

Morgan had her back to them, but she could see Cindy's face, there was something about the mannerisms in their conversation and the look in her eye that made Amy feel like she needed to look closer at the situation.

Going over to them she thought she heard Cindy say, "Company."

Morgan stood abruptly and shouted at Cindy, "You better start talking." Half-heartedly kicking her in the leg.

Cindy cried out, "You didn't have to kill him." As she glared at Amy with hatred in her eyes.

Amy instructed Morgan to go help Kevin and she would watch Cindy.

Morgan glared at her saying, "We are all adults, and we don't need you to babysit us or tell us what to do."

Amy defiantly looked at her and said, "No one said you did. I need to sit for a few minutes and thought I would take over watching her till the guys came back."

The gunfire was slowing down, but still steady so Amy said, "Never mind, I'll go see what else might need doing."

Morgan yelled out to Kevin, "Hurry up with that before Miss Bossy Pants here starts ordering you around too."

Rita watched the exchange and saw Amy look back in her direction. She nodded at Amy and gave her a thumbs up. Rita knew Morgan all too well and hated her. Morgan had been part of the reason she and Matt divorced. Although there was no proof of anything going on between them, Morgan was always right in the middle of every issue they ever had.

Amy crawled into the office and to her horror saw that John had blood running into his eye.

She turned and screamed back through the doorway, "Rita, I need the first aid kit now."

Rita grabbed it and sprinted for the office, she saw why Amy was so shaken and quickly started wiping the blood from his face.

John shooed her away and continued to fire into the darkness when Rita said, "You can't even see what you're shooting at with blood in your eyes."

Amy took up a position beside him and began to fire blindly at the unseen foe just to make John let Rita look at his head. The bullet had grazed his head, leaving a two inch gash from his forehead back. Rita quickly planted a gauze pad on it and wrapped it with a bandage.

Dickie shouted to the girls, "Get everyone ready to move out." they both nodded and made their way for the door.

Amy was crying by now saying, "I can't do this. I tried to be strong, but I can't handle it."

Rita shook her and said, "Look around you. Remember what you told me? You were right, we have to step up. Let's do this."

Amy sniffled and nodded and began grabbing the things that were strewn around the office saying, "I don't think it matters where we put everything let's just get it all stowed."

Entering the warehouse, she shouted, "Everyone into your vehicles. Kids in the back seat on the floor."

Ray came running from the offices asking where Roger and Mark were, Amy pointed by the bay door. He ran over to them, told them the plan and ran back, hopping into the driver's seat of the jeep.

Everyone else was getting into the vehicles, Ray beeped the horn when he saw all were loaded. Out of the offices came Dickie and John, hopping into the vehicles they headed for the bay door. Mark and Roger flung open the door and began firing through it.

As the vehicles passed by Mark and Roger jumped into the back of the pickup and continued to fire at the attackers until they were out of range.

# Chapter 13

## "Treachery"

*"It's hard to tell who has your back, from who has it long
enough just to stab you in it"*
-Nicole Richie

Speeding south they drove a few hours until it felt safe to make camp. They found themselves along the bank of a river, certain they were not on the course originally intended they pulled into a place amongst some pine trees close to the river bank to make camp.

Remaining in the vehicles seemed the best idea for the night so each vehicle had one person stand watch at a time while the others slept.

Once the sun rose they would be able to see to assess their situation, injuries and location. John was worried and couldn't sleep. For the hours they travelled they saw no lights, he wondered if the lights were out everywhere. He wished he could talk to Matt or anyone who could tell him what may lay in store for them on this journey.

The sun rose in a few hours and the weary travellers began to emerge from their vehicles. Looking at the vehicles they could see the many bullet holes and realized just how lucky they were.

Rita collected sticks for a fire and asked Matty if he would help her saying, "Let's be helpful and build the fire."

Matty happily skipped alongside Rita gathering small sticks and playing chase in the woods with her. John watched this looking at them when Amy walked up to him.

She looked at him asking, "Whatcha looking at?"

John said, "Do Matty and Rita look to you like she is mean to him?"

Amy said, "No, as a matter of fact she looks quite good with him. Why?"

John said, "I don't know, Matt is always telling me how mean she is to him and how she only got custody because he couldn't afford a lawyer."

Amy shrugged and said, "Well I just thought she was some psycho we got stuck with because of Matty but she was the only one to step up and help out back at the warehouse."

"See." John said, "That's what I mean."

"Well, who knows really, it is always he said, she said in these things. For now all I see is a mom taking care of her kid and participating in the needs of this, this… whatever we call this trek we are on." Amy replied.

John nodded and Amy asked, "Morgan is my question what is up with that piece of work?"

John said, "I don't really know her, I know Matt does and Kimmie and Renee but other than that? I honestly tried not to, she is just about as low rent as they come."

"You can say that again." Amy scoffed.

Right then Melinda came walking up asking Amy to look at Danny's leg.

She said, "It's starting to bleed through the bandages."

Amy said she would be right there and asked her to go get Laurie and also to get the med kit out of the truck.

Amy kissed John and said, "I'm glad you're ok, I don't think I could do all this without you."

John hugged her close and said, "I am always amazed at not only your beauty but also the way you handle things. We both know that camping and such is not your forte' yet you come through in every instance without skipping a beat."

Amy laughed, saying, "Only cause I've been hanging around a caveman like you." Winking at him she headed to tend the wounded.

Cindy was causing a scene yelling how her face hurt and how they could leave Martin just lying there a crumpled heap on the floor of the warehouse.

Amy walked past giving her an uncomfortable look and wondering why Morgan brought her with them. She thought she best not say anything and leave it up to the guys to question her. It seemed like Morgan had found a new playmate of sorts and this was profoundly disturbing to Amy.

Kevin came walking up and said to Amy, "The stream is clear and fast flowing. Looks like some good water, would you like me to get some boiling for you to clean these wounds with?"

Amy hadn't heard Kevin say two words since she met him, it shocked her that he offered to help. She agreed and went to cleaning up and preparing for stitches with Laurie.

Laurie had an interest in herbal medicines and was always trying to learn new things. But all of this was way out of her league she said. Amy told her not to worry that she could do the stitching, but that she needed her help just to assist her with it.

While each were doing their own set of things, the not so insignificant task of interrogating Cindy was John's priority on this day. One thing he was sure of was that he would not allow her to continue with them and needed as much information about who they were dealing with back there.

Grabbing her by the arm, he said, "You, come with me."

Morgan began to protest, but John gave her a look and she knew he would not be reasoned with on this. He dragged her to the water's edge and told her she would drown today if she didn't start talking.

She cried out for Morgan to help her saying, "You said no one had balls enough to really hurt me."

John sneered right in her face, "She lied!"

Cindy immediately began to talk, he didn't even have to do anything, just the fear of torture was enough.

She said, "Martin and I were supposed to go in and find out what supplies you had and sneak out in the middle of the night and let the others know."

John pressed her, "How did they know we were there?"

Cindy crying now said, "They watched you from the water tower. Simon has binoculars and told us to get inside and see if you had many weapons. They could see the military jeep and the clothes on those two."

John asked, "Who's Simon and why was he watching us?"

Cindy was begging to not be left there by now and told him he had to take her with them or Simon would kill her. John told her if what she told him was acceptable he would think about it.

Cindy explained, "Right after the banks didn't open Simon opened up shop, he had a bunch of biker guys that would enforce for him. He had lots of supplies and everyone had to give up what they had for protection from what they thought were the bikers."

Sobbing, she continued, "He said he would take care of us with all of his supplies and even shot one of the biker guys. Martin found out later that he was a guy they made drive through town like that just so that they could shoot him."

John asked her, "How far away do we need to go to get away from them?"

She said, "We should be far enough now, they stay pretty close to the city and wait for people to come into town."

John thought her story a little too organized and feared they may still be in danger, none the less he allowed her to stay with them just in case she was telling the truth and needed to get away.

He told everyone what she said and that he figured it was probably safe to set up camp. But there would be no fires, they were to cook over the camp stove and keep everything put together just to be safe.

Morgan went to Cindy and told her she was sorry, "There was nothing I could do, believe me."

Cindy sat staunch not really speaking to anyone and scowling at John.

Laurie was staring at Morgan and Cindy saying, "What the hell? Her and her boyfriend just tried to kill Danny and she's all BFF with her. Can we even trust her?"

Amy overheard her and said to her, "I am wondering that myself."

John, Ray and Dickie sat looking at the map trying to figure out where they were. They knew they went south because the direction showing the mirror inside the truck. They tried to find the river on the map, but there were at least five possibilities. They wanted to get back to their original route, but also needed to get Mandy and Aaron to their family.

Dickie said, "I'll go ask her what town her family is in, so we can see if it is even possible for us to take them."

Ray said, "Why wouldn't we?"

Dickie replied, "There is no way I want to go east at all or go into another city."

John interjected, "I agree with Dickie to a point. I'll not bring them to a city, but slightly east as long as it is south I could live with."

Dickie was growing agitated and said, "I don't want Jules to have to travel any longer than necessary."

John sighed, saying, "Somehow, I think this is going to be a long and perilous journey. I thought we could get there in a few days since it was merely a fifteen hour drive a few bumps might slow us down. Now I can see we are in for I think a little more than we bargained for."

Ray looked down and said, "You don't know the half of things. Roger and I saw the FEMA relief camps and there is nothing to do with relief in them. By now Ebola will be rampant in them as well as the cities. We need to limit our contact with people, all people. We have no way of knowing who is friend or foe."

Ray and John agreed with Dickie that the injured needed a day to rest and recover a bit. Ray and Roger would do a bit of scouting to see if they could determine their exact location. They tried the map program on their phones but there was no signal. John cursed himself for not thinking of grabbing Amy's GPS.

The pine grove they were in offered shade and cover, but they found that where they stopped they could be easily seen from the road. Moving further off the road they felt they could conceal the vehicles better and set up a more comfortable camp.

There would still be no fires until they could determine where they were. Roger and Ray would set out in the Jeep and head down the road to check out the area and determine where they were. First, they wanted to take all the supplies out of the vehicle and leave them with the group. Ray said there were a few reasons why, but mostly for fear of losing them if anything went wrong.

The afternoon was cool, but agreeable, they commenced with setting up their camp. With all the pine needles they made beds under each of the tents that would help with comfort while sleeping.

Mark and Jenny set up a tent for the family and offered to let Rita and Matty share it with them, but Amy said she already had a place for them in their tent. Kimmie and Renee just sat and talked to Morgan all afternoon while Laurie tended to the injured.

Laurie approached Cindy with some salve for her cheek, and Cindy backed away saying, "What are you trying to put on me?"

Laurie said, "It's nothing really just a little bit of salve to help heal your face."

Cindy looked disgusted, saying, "Why did you spit the green stuff in it?"

Laurie smiled, saying, "Its plantain."

As she reached over and plucked a leaf from a weed explaining, "You have to chew it up to get it ready, it has amazing healing abilities and I want to get that cut cleaned and covered before you get an infection."

Cindy reluctantly allowed her to clean and dress the wound and thanked her for her kindness.

Laurie looked at her sternly, "Don't thank me, you can thank Amy. You and Martin tried to kill my son. Amy insisted I help you."

The camp was set up including some firewood that Jenny and Melinda had gathered and said it was for just in case. When they started gathering it, Mark also started gathering rocks to make a fire pit and said it was also for just in case.

John began to get concerned when Ray and Roger did not return for a number of hours. He sat on a rock near the water's edge, staring into the river.

Kevin approached saying, "I want to help but I don't know what I should help with."

John didn't know what to make of Kevin, Morgan constantly yelled at him calling him stupid and worthless. John wanted to ask him why he stayed with her but didn't.

Instead, he asked, "Has anyone determined a watch schedule yet?"

Kevin replied, "I don't know, I'm not usually involved in that kind of stuff."

John considered what he said and told him, "Well, you are now. If for some reason Ray and Roger don't return we need enough people to stand watch in twos throughout the night."

Kevin said, "Should I ask for volunteers?"

John thought a moment and replied, "No, only schedule those with shooting experience. That would include, myself, Dickie, Mark, Amy and Danny. Can you shoot?"

Kevin replied, "Not well."

John said, "That's fine schedule yourself with me or Dickie. On second thought, let's make shorter shifts and add Rita and Laurie to the list."

Kevin said he would do so and report back to John when he had the schedule and a lookout point. John thanked him and asked that he also keep an eye out for Roger and Ray while he did. Kevin agreed and said it would be good to get some time to himself anyway.

With that taken care of and the camp set up there was little to do but rest, so John stretched out on the rock and settled in for a nice quiet moment.

The sun sank lower in the sky and Kevin had not given John the watch assignments. John went over to the camp and asked Mark if he had seen Kevin.

Mark said, "As a matter of fact, I haven't seen him since he was talking to you earlier. He went up over that way." Pointing in the direction they drove into the grove.

John said, "Take a walk?"

Mark Said, "Sure."

John waved over Dickie and said, "We need to go check something out, keep an eye on things and stay alert?"

Dickie said, "Sure mate, anything I know?"

John said, "It's probably nothing but we haven't seen Kevin in a while."

Dickie looked off like he was thinking and said, "I ain't seen him either."

John said they would be right back as he and Mark walked up the embankment they drove in the night before. About half way up, Mark grabbed his arm and put a finger up to his lips. Listening, he jerked his head to the left, something was rustling in the bushes. They both crept up to the bush and parted them startling a trembling Matty hiding.

Mark scooped him up and seeing tears streaming down his face asked him, "What's wrong little man?"

Matty didn't speak, he cried harder and buried his face in his grandfather's shoulder. John told Mark to take Matty back to camp and to send Dickie up to meet him.

John waited for Dickie and the two of them crept through the brush instead of walking up the path between the pines. As they reached the roadway they could see nothing wrong, but also saw no sign of Kevin. They walked just inside the brush alongside the road looking for him and could find no sign of him.

Mark was walking back up the path through the pines looking for John when something caught his eye on a large rock. It looked like blood. He called out to John and Dickie who came running.

Mark looked closer and said, "This is blood and it is fresh, it has hardly dried."

John and Dickie both drew their handguns and watched in both directions as Mark investigated closer.

They heard Mark as he gasped, "Oh no, no this is bad."

Scuffling around behind the rock he shook Kevin saying, "Kevin, Kevin…"

He shouted to John, "I need some help, Kevin is hurt…bad!"

John put his firearm away and helped Mark get Kevin out from behind the rock. Dickie said he would keep a watch from the brush alongside the path while they brought him back to camp where Amy and Laurie tried to revive him.

Amy could see someone hit him in the head, she looked at John terrified, saying, "Whoever did this meant to kill him."

John said, "How do you know that?"

Amy with tears in her eyes said, "He's been hit with something hard like a rock at least five times. There are five or more distinct impact points on his skull, and look at his side. He was kicked or beaten besides the blows to the head."

John asked, "Is he going to be ok?"

Amy shook her head saying, "I don't know, he is barely alive. I would say, chances are not good, even in a hospital, and we don't have much more than a Band-Aid to work with."

John sent Mark to get Morgan and bring her to her husband's side. Thinking she may need moral support he grabbed Renee to be there for her at this time. John and Danny each set up watch posts around the encampment feeling like a threat was still nearby.

When Mark approached with Morgan, Amy was shocked to see a lack of emotion from Morgan.

She looked at him like she was surprised he was alive and said, "What happened to him?"

Amy said, "We don't know, we found him in the bushes like this."

Morgan shrugged, saying, "Well, who tried to kill him?"

Amy was shocked as she replied, "No one said anyone tried to kill him."

Morgan laughed nervously saying, "I was joking, he's not very graceful if you know my meaning. Did he fall down?"

Amy looked at her coolly saying, "I don't think he is going to live Morgan."

Morgan never once reached out for her husband, nor did she shed a tear. She simply shrugged, turned and walked away. Amy asked Laurie to keep him comfortable and let her know if anything changed while she went and talked to John.

Amy told John about how Morgan acted and said, "Someone did try to kill him, and I think it was her."

John scolded her saying, "I think you are over reacting, some people handle grief differently."

Amy said, "Mark my words, this is not the last bit of treachery, we will see from her."

John thought about it a moment and remembered Matty crying in the bushes. Horrified, he ran to Rita, who was putting him down for a nap in the tent. He asked her to come out of the tent a moment.

John said, "Did he say anything yet?"

Rita said, "No, he hasn't said a single word, he just cries."

John said, "I think he knows what happened to Kevin, don't you leave him for one second. If you need to walk away get me or Amy to watch him. No one else do you understand?"

Rita became fearful saying, "Do you think he is in danger?"

John said, "I don't know, but don't say anything to anyone about it. If anyone asks, say he has a temp, ok?"

Rita agreed and said, "Thank you John, for everything."

John nodded to her as he turned and went to find Mark and Dickie. Something happened to Kevin and Matty knew what. He was scared, not just scared, but terrified which to John meant the threat still existed somewhere.

He set the watches to be all day as well as all night, he didn't know where Roger and Ray went either and was feeling like everything was falling apart right before his eyes.

Melinda and Jenny made dinner and for being just peanut butter and jelly it sure hit the spot. There were sandwiches made with the biscuits left over from the previous night along with some mixed fruit they cut up after finding some blackberries along the path.

There was also other snacking type foods like crackers and that cheese spread stuff that squirted from a can. They also had out some teriyaki beef jerky, chips and cupcakes.

When everyone saw what was for dinner they all looked astonished that a smorgasbord of snacks could be called a meal.

Jenny with a look of indignation said, "Well, smells are smells, no matter if it is firewood or baked beans cooking would have given us away."

John smiling, said, "Good thinking ladies and this looks wonderful. I for one love PBJs."

# Chapter 14

## "Trouble Doubles"

*"Strength does not come from winning. Your struggles develop your strengths. When you go through hardships and decided not to surrender, that is strength."*
-Arnold Schwarzenegger

Through the evening the watches were quiet, uneventful even eerie. The majority seemed to sleep well, except John, he couldn't sleep at all. The events of the day were plaguing him, Kevin had died mere hours after his discovery and still Morgan seemed to have no feelings about it. Except maybe relief was all John could think as what she showed.

This made John replay the day in his head over and over again. Who could have done this to him? And for that matter, why? Kevin was a quiet man, one might not even know he was around were it not for Morgan's incessant nagging of him.

Morgan almost seemed gleeful at the evening meal, John felt sure she had something to do with it, but also felt it was wrong of him to think that about a woman who just lost her husband.

Matty cried out in his sleep many times that night. He had indeed seen who had killed Kevin. The attack was brutal and bloody, there was blood all over the rocks surrounding the area, he was found and John felt sure it was more than one person because of the scuffling of the leaves in the area. Finally drifting off to sleep the morning's fears would materialize all too soon.

John woke long after the sun rose and even until he could smell bacon and a wood fire. He thought he was dreaming until he fully awakened and realized someone had started a fire and was cooking bacon.

He emerged from the tent to see Roger and Ray sitting around the fire with the others waiting for the Bacon and eggs to be done.

He called out, "The fire, someone is going to see it."

Roger looked over his shoulder at him, saying, "Not likely there sleepy head, we've managed to park ourselves at nearly the end of some poe dunk little access road to the cell tower.

John rubbed his eyes and scratched his head, yawning as he said, "Well, it's about time you two got round to showing up."

Ray laughed and said, "We have a good idea of where we are and after breakfast we will pull out the map and go over some of what we found."

John couldn't help but smile at the breakfast he was looking at, eggs, bacon, biscuits, beans and hash browned potatoes. He thought he'd died and gone to heaven.

Looking at it all he shook his head and glanced up saying, "Now if only there were coff…."

Cutting him off as she shoved a steaming hot cup of coffee under his nose, Amy laughed. She knew he loved his coffee and just how to make it for him. Sometimes he thought she was practically perfect. Thinking to himself, 'especially when she brings me coffee.' He sat smiling at his feast, forgetting for just that moment the events of yesterday.

After breakfast John and Dickie went to show Roger and Ray the spot they had found Kevin while Mark was finding an appropriate spot to bury him.

John said to them, "Something stinks here, you would think if it was an invader or something they would have continued until they got what they wanted. Do you think he happened upon someone and they ran off?"

Roger was busy looking at the prints and the scuffle, commenting, "See these marks here? He was clearly bigger than whoever hit him and they must have tried to quiet him or something by the dragging over here." He said pointing to an area John never noticed yesterday.

Ray said, "Over here, I think this may have been used as a weapon." Pointing to a large rock with blood stains on it.

Roger frowned, saying, "I'm sorry John but there are no tracks leading away from this scene that are not for you. Looking at the struggle and the drag marks along with the prints over where he was we are looking for a much smaller foot. Maybe a woman?"

John looked angry, saying, "I don't want to believe it, but Morgan could care less that her husband was injured yesterday as a matter of fact Amy said she looked surprised when she told her he was alive."

Ray said, "Cold brother, real cold… Do you really think she could have?"

"Maybe not alone, but her and that Cindy girl have been real chummy." Shaking his head, John continued, "I don't know, it just seems weird she didn't care he was dead."

Dickie came up with a theory saying, "I think we all know if she didn't do it, but I'm pretty sure she is somehow involved."

Nodding in agreement John said, "You guys didn't see her yesterday, I'd bet money on it."

"Well." Ray said, "Can we prove it?"

They all stood shaking their heads, John becoming angry said, "How can we prove it, other than the tracks and a good guess we got nothing."

Ray said, "We'll just watch her, she will give herself away if she is guilty. There had to be a reason she did it, all we have to do is find out what that is."

After looking over the scene they walked back to camp to figure out the best course to take. Roger pointed out that they were not really that far off course.

Ray said, "I think it is actually a better direction than we had originally planned."

They pulled out the map and Roger showed John and Dickie where they estimated their location to be. Pointing to a small lake they indicated where they were.

Roger saying, "We are here. This is Quaker Lake, it is just over the Pennsylvania line. We actually made some good progress last night."

Dickie asked, "Where is Fallen Timber, from here?'

Ray said, "What? Is that a place?"

Dickie replied, "Yes, it is, that is where Mandy and Aaron need to go. We might be able to get them close to her parent's house. It is where they were headed and we should try to help them if we can. As Long as we don't put ourselves in unnecessary danger."

The rest agreed they should and said they would try and determine a route that could at least get them close. After figuring out where it actually was they found it was not only likely, but could be even beneficial to them to pass in that direction.

John glanced toward camp and noticed Morgan and Cindy in an argument with Rita. He motioned to the others to him as he sprinted toward them. It was quickly apparent that he was too late. He was shocked at the violence when Cindy came at her from behind and hit her in the head with a large rock. After she fell Morgan was kicking her repeatedly, finally pushing her into the river.

John ran right past them to the river frantically looking for Rita could see no sign, but the bloodied rock in Cindy's hand.

Lashing out he screamed, "First Kevin and now Rita? What is wrong with you two?"

Morgan just glared at him as Cindy spoke, "She was accusing us of something to do with Matty. I thought she was going to do something to her so I hit her."

There was no denial of what happened to Kevin from either of them, only protests about Rita's accusations. John frantically searched for Rita in the water, it was a fast moving river and though they ran down the bank of it, she had already drifted downstream. Dickie arrived and joined the search for her, but she was nowhere to be found.

Roger and Ray grabbed hold of the girl's arms and brought them to the rock where Kevin was assaulted. Not wanting to have a spectacle in front of everyone they secured them there and joined in the search for Rita.

John walked more than a mile downstream and saw no sign of her. Everyone feared the worst and took care to make sure Matty didn't hear anything about it quite yet. This was going to be hard on him and John wanted to make sure he and Amy both could be there for him. He knew he had family alongside them, but Matty was withdrawn and sullen since Kevin died, and would only talk to Amy.

Later in the evening they all talked about what to do with Cindy and Morgan. The guys were sure they were the ones that killed Kevin and that Rita was no accident either.

Amy argued, "We can't do anything, we are not the law."

Dickie heatedly responded, "There ain't no law, Sweetheart."

Amy was furious yelling, "Don't call me Sweetheart."

Dickie conceded, saying, "I know, I know this is not a reason for us to argue. I do have to say that they are not riding with me and Jules and I'm pretty sure you don't want them in your car with Matty either."

Amy nodded, saying, "This is true, but there is no law saying we can't just leave them here."

John chimed in, "That's true. We don't have to take them with us."

Mark nodded and said, "I can agree with that."

Roger stepped up and said, "Then it is settled, we leave them here."

Renee thought they should be left some food, but that was vetoed by the majority of the group. It was decided that they could have their backpacks and that was it.

Ray said, "In my opinion, it's better than they deserve. John saw them hit Rita on the head and the brutal beating they gave her before tossing her in the river."

They kept a guard on them during the night and everyone went to sleep. They would be moving out in the morning headed southeast towards Fallen Timber and closer to their friends in Kentucky.

# Chapter 15

---

## "Grief and Guilt"

*"Negative emotions like loneliness, envy, and guilt have an important role to play in a happy life; they're big, flashing signs that something needs to change."*
-Gretchen Rubin

The sun rose slowly in the eastern sky, seemingly taking forever to give its light. By Dawn they had the camp completely dismantled and packed up. Breakfast was cooking and they would be ready to go within the hour. No one knew what might be ahead, but Roger and Ray had scouted a route and thought they could make good time this day.

Cindy and Morgan were handed their backpacks and told to leave. The one thing that really bothered John letting them go was that Morgan knew where they were going. She and Matt were friends, although for the life of him; John couldn't figure out why.

She was not an attractive woman and would be considered as coming from what was once called 'the wrong side of the tracks.' With stringy shoulder length brown hair, it always had a look like it needed washing. She was a brash and vulgar woman that most in the area considered trashy.

She constantly cheated on Kevin which made John wonder even more why Matt would have anything to do with her. John never liked her and was frankly glad to be rid of her; although he did feel bad for Rita. A few eye opening moments had shown him, maybe she was not entirely to blame in the mess between herself and Matt.

He thought of Dez and how much he thought Matt had jumped above his station in life. She was older than Matt but quite well off, owning her home and the one hundred fifty acres. She was quite beautiful and John asked him more than once how he managed to gain her favor. He would simply shrug and with a sly look say, "I guess when you got it, you got it."

Preparing to leave, they loaded the vehicles and prepared to pull out of the pine grove, but before they could Matty began to scream and call out for his mother. John and Amy told him what happened that night, but the feeling of leaving her there was overwhelming him.

They paused so that he could go to the river and look for her one last time. Roger assured him they would be following the river for a ways and would make regular stops to look for her when they could. The river flowed into Quaker Lake and they planned to stop and look in the areas where the river slowed and opened into it.

Most of the day they drove and stopped, looking for some sign of her, but they found nothing, not a shoe, a footprint, nothing that would even indicate if she were alive or dead. Finally, they had to move on, Matty cried the whole day.

Matty cursed Morgan saying, "I will do to her what she did to Kevin and for hurting my mom."

Shocked Amy asked, "Matty, did you see what happened to Kevin?"

Matty nodded his head and said, "Yes, I told my mom what happened and Morgan killed her too."

Becoming more and more angry, he said, "She told me she would kill anyone I told. It is all my fault, what happened to my mom. I shouldn't have told her, they did it just like she said her and my dad are going to do to...."

He stopped talking and looked out the window and asked, "Do you think it is my fault my mom is gone?"

Amy hugged him saying, "Oh no Matty it isn't your fault at all. Why would you think that?"

Crying, he looked at her, "Because I told."

She said, "No, it's not because of that."

Amy wasn't sure what he almost said earlier that his dad and Morgan were going to do, but she didn't want to press him. He would tell her in his own time, but she didn't want him telling anyone else what he told her for his own safety. She didn't trust everyone, especially not Kimmie and Renee. They both were spending a lot of time talking with Morgan and Cindy and she was worried they might know something.

The trip to Fallen Timber that should have taken an afternoon, seemed like it was going to take a whole lot longer, after the time they spent searching the river and the lake. It was getting dark already and they had only gone forty-five miles in total.

Staying on the lake a final night seemed like the best idea. They had water and could do some fishing, there was really no one around it felt safe and could offer one more night of rest for their injured friends.

Again, they found a pine grove to set up in, the pine needles many said helped make the sleeping nicer. Laurie started the fire and prepared to make some supper.

Announcing, "It will be biscuits, with corn chowder… and of course… Spam."

John groaned loudly saying, "Spam again, can't we have something else already."

Laurie laughed and said, "Sure, we can have Spam and beans."

Everyone laughed as John grabbed his fishing pole and stomped off to the lake saying, "I think we need to make this a fish chowder instead."

Roger and Dickie grabbed some poles and followed him while Mark helped Ray set up tents and try to get the perimeter secured.

While he was setting up one of the tents he said to Ray, "I don't know how Matt could have anything to do with that Morgan and worse yet Renee and Kimmie complained the whole time about how we left them."

Shrugging, he continued, "Am I missing something with these women?"

Ray shrugged and said, "I didn't like leaving them either."

Mark looked shocked and said, "You didn't?"

Ray said, "No, we knew she killed Rita and we're pretty sure she killed Kevin, her own husband. Who's next? I would have taken the law into my own hands if Amy hadn't argued for them."

Mark looked at him, "Really?"

"Yep, I said we should string them up." He replied.

Mark asked, "Do you think we will hear from them again?"

Ray said, "If we do, I'm not waiting for a committee. I'll shoot both them bitches on sight."

Mark replied, "Well, I for one hope we don't."

The evening was quiet and there were no fish for dinner, but a great big pot of Spam and corn chowder with tons of biscuits. Watches were in twos, each pair taking a four hour shift.

In the morning they broke camp and made for Mandy's Parents. Both she and Aaron were quiet, no one even at times aware of their presence. Amy asked her if everything was ok, she just said they didn't want to be a burden. Amy reassured her that they were not a burden, and said it was their pleasure.

Patting her hand, she said, "We don't mind, we're going that way anyway."

Mandy thanked her and said, "Once we get there my parents have a lot of stuff stored. I'll make sure you are supplied for your journey. "

Winking she continued, "And I'll see if we can find something other than Spam."

They both laughed as they got into the vehicles and prepared to leave their camping area. Matty was already in the back silently staring out the window at the water.

Amy felt bad, "A boy so young should not carry the thoughts of guilt he has." She whispered to Mandy.

Mandy replied, "Maybe when he gets to his father it will be better."

Matty spoke just a single word saying, "Dez"

Amy was shocked and asked, "What did you say buddy?"

Matty replied, "Dez, I wanna see Dez."

Amy looked at him, he had tears in his eyes as he stared blankly out the window at nothing but trees as they whizzed past.

Reaching into the back seat she brushed a lock of hair from his eye and said, "I know buddy, we are going there. Pretty soon you will see them both."

Sitting forward, she turned and looked at John, then shaking her head she choked back tears. John reached over and took her hand, giving it a gentle squeeze he nodded in understanding.

Mandy leaned forward and whispered, "Who is Dez? Is that someone in his family?"

Amy turned and said, "No, that is his father's girlfriend Destiny. That is where we are going, to her place in Kentucky."

Mandy nodding in understanding said, "Oh, okay. I have heard the name a few times but didn't know who it was. He seems very fond of her."

John looked back saying, "She really is good to him."

Matty tears full flowing turned and looked at everyone with angry eyes and said, "I need to get there to keep her safe!"

Amy reached back for him and asked, "Safe from what buddy?"

He looked down and said, "Bad people."

Amy reassured him they would get there as soon as they could and that she would be safe until he got there to protect her. Not satisfied with the response he insisted she was in danger and they needed to hurry. John told him they would do their very best to get him there soon.

Travel that day was quiet, sticking to only smaller roads they avoided many of the towns and cities along their path.

Stopping in a parking lot of an abandoned office they paused for lunch. John sat by himself absent minded he munched on his sandwich as he watched the bright red maple leaves fall from the trees.

Mesmerized, he watched as the breeze shook them from their perch high in the air. Considering the journey that lay ahead of them and what was behind. He wondered as they fell into blood red piles on the ground, if it were an omen speaking towards what they would face. Like tiny embers from a fire rising, the blazing colors of fall illuminated by the sunlight reminded him of the world that was quickly fading into the ashes of what was once considered a civilized country.

Packed and ready to move on the group pushed for Mandy's family. Hoping they would be safe for the night and given something other than Spam for food as Mandy promised, looking forward to some rest and a change in diet before continuing their trek southward kept spirits a little brighter.

All of them except Matty, who retreated further away from even Amy, as the miles faded into memory; he seemed to fade with them. She worried he would retreat so far into his own misguided guilt they would never be able to bring him back.

The smells of burning debris and smoke filled the air each time they drew near a town. Left… right… left… right… they would turn as though they were mice in a maze, trying to get to the end of the road while avoiding hazards along the way.

Dickie and Ray were in the lead with the Jeep with Jules and Georgia to help with the mapping. Since the shooting at the warehouse, Dickie refused to let Jules and Georgia out of his sight.

Approaching an intersection Dickie's arm could be seen held upward closed fist out the window. Everyone stopped, then frantically, his arm began to wave for them to pull off the road. The road was narrow with trees on either side, the shoulder was level and grassy with only a slight cement ditch that was easily crossed.

The Jeep and the two trucks could easily pass into the woods with the four wheel drive on but the cars could not. Quickly they emptied what they could from the cars and ran into the woods to hide with the trucks.

It was only minutes until they saw why the cover. A large group of motorcycles pulled up to where the cars were parked and began to scavenge what they could use from them. Holes were drilled in the gas tanks for the fuel and the food left in the trunk along with two sleeping bags and some other items.

The speed at which they picked over the carcass of the vehicles was astounding. Each person going here and there like a choreographed routine, John whispered to Danny,

"They must be doing this up and down the roadways."

Danny nodded and motioned off to the left, where a guy was standing and leaning into a tree.

One of the other members of the gang shouted at him, "Jim, c'mon man let's go."

He shouted back, "Hold on, can't you see I'm trying to take a piss?"

Zipping up his zipper he looked in their direction, the expression was quizzical, like he wondered if he'd seen something, but shrugged it off and returned to the gang.

John didn't realize he was holding his breath and let out a long sigh when they began to leave. Leaning over to Ray he asked,

"Do you think we should camp or keep moving?"

Ray said, "I'm not sure, but either way we are too close to the road right here."

John waved for Dickie to join them, they came over with Jules spreading the map out for everyone to look at.

Pointing at two intersecting roads that didn't even have names on the map she said, "We are here. Those guys came from the north and left to the east. We are only about thirty miles from Mandy's family."

John looked at Ray and said, "I think we shouldn't risk it, if we go over that hill we can cold camp for the night."

Roger volunteered to scout the area for an acceptable camp while everyone else repositioned the supplies they salvaged from the cars before abandoning them. Afterwards, they sat behind the trucks and waited for Roger's return.

After about fifteen minutes Roger returned with good news. He said there was a gully between two hills about five hundred yards to the west of where they were.

Ray asked, "Terrain acceptable for vehicular travel?"

Roger replied, "Roger that."

Ray shouted, "Ok everyone, let's move out and make camp."

Moving the vehicles around behind some low bushes and covering them on the road side worked out well hiding them even further from view. Lined up at the top of the gully they also made good cover from the road. Below the vehicles tents were set up in the flat area with a makeshift latrine across the gully. Smoke was already in the air so a small fire was started to cook on and Mandy and Melinda began to make the evening meal.

John came walking to the cooking area and practically pleading he asked, "Coffee?"

Melinda turned with coffee pot in hand and smiling said, "Quick as I can get this pot on."

John smiled, thanking her and turned to chat with Dickie about the last thirty miles to Fallen Timber. They checked the map and determined they were in the Black Moshannon State Park and why they had seen so few people. Getting to Fallen Timber meant they would have to pass very close to Osceola Mills and while it wasn't a city it was not like the small towns they had been passing.

Roger said, "I think we should try for Fallen Timber in the morning but stop short of Osceola Mills so we can scout it before trying to pass."

John said, "I agree, it may be that it is like most of the smaller towns we've passed and be deserted, but this one is big enough to worry me."

Ray said, "Agreed."

Mark and Dickie nodded in agreement and they adjourned to go see what was for dinner. John smelled something wonderful and hurried over to ask what they were cooking. He was sure it wasn't spam again, it smelled too good.

Approaching, he inhaled deeply, trying to decipher what that delicious odor was. Looking to the ladies practically pleading with his eyes for it not to be spam, hesitantly he asked,

"What's cooking?"

Melinda grinned at Laurie, who said, "Stew."

John said, "It smells divine, for once not spam."

Melinda giggled a little as Laurie shook her head saying, "Why are you always hating on the spam? You're the one who stored it all?"

John replied, "I didn't think I would be eating it for every meal."

Laurie shaking her head said, "Well, I guess the old hindsight adage is appropriate here. "

Turning to walk away, she added, "It's not easy on those of us trying to keep *spam* interesting you know."

John nodded and said, "I know and you do a wonderful job, I'm sorry to complain."

Brightening up his look he said, "But hey, it's not spam at least."

Laurie looked at him laughing out loud saying, "Who said it isn't spam? I said it wasn't easy keeping it interesting. I feel like I have succeeded in that task as even you did not know it had spam in it from the smell. I guess the taste test will be the judge, you might as well start things off and give us your unbiased opinion,"

Melinda snorted, "Ha, Unbiased."

Laurie handed John a bowl of the stew and he went off to sulk with his spam stew while she continued to dish it up. Sitting on the hillside he dipped his spoon into the stew and drew up a nice bite with both a potato and carrot. He paused to blow on it to cool it off and took a bite. He was amazed at how tasteful it was, although he could still tell it was spam; he thought it was very good.

He held up his spoon calling out, "Well done ladies."

Waving the spoon like sceptre, while the ladies all bowed. Mandy was the one who used some of the spices and bouillon cubes to give it a more beef stew like taste. Everyone was very grateful for the effort they put into making it feel like beef stew. As he looked at this raggedy bunch he felt a warm sense of gratitude he had their company.

# Chapter 16

## "The Camp"

*"In the concentration camps, we discovered this whole universe where everyone had his place. The killer came to kill, and the victims came to die."*
-Elie Wiesel

The morning was warm with a slight breeze, fall was the only way John could describe the smell in the air. It was both a pleasurable scent and yet disturbing because it meant winter was closing in on them.

It took them almost two weeks to go the roughly four hundred miles to where they were now. John thought it was about half way and if it took them another two weeks it would be the first week of November before they would arrive in Kentucky.

November in Kentucky wasn't what it was in Massachusetts, but it was still getting quite cold especially in the evenings. He hoped Mandy's parents would have some warm clothes or blankets they could spare. Mostly for the women and kids. Matty and Georgia were generally dressed pretty warmly, but he also knew Rita did not grab any winter wear for him.

"John.... Earth to John." Amy shouted

John looked up, "Hua?"

Amy said, "You with us?"

John replied, "Yea, sorry was just thinking about our travel time and trying to figure out how long it will be till we get there."

Amy stood, hands on her hips and said, "Mhmm, well can you take a break from your calculations to help us with the fire?" Winking she cooed, "I promise there is coffee in it for you."

John nodded and got up, walking toward the fire pit, looking at it, he could see the fire going nicely. Confused, he looked at Amy, and suddenly everyone jumped out shouting,

"Happy Birthday!"

He'd forgotten it was his birthday. After shooting Amy a death look, he told everyone, "Thank you."

Matty came running up to him, saying, "But we have pancakes with frosting on them."

He said, "Oh well that is different, I guess we better eat them."

Matty seemed a little brighter for the first time in days, although he didn't smile he did hop up on a rock and jumped off, then went and sat near Georgia and Aaron. They were close to own age and he seemed to be more at ease around them.

John approached Amy and said with raised eyebrows, "Pancakes and frosting?"

"Yeah." She said, "Get it? PanCAKE?"

He replied, "That's just wrong."

Amy said, "Chill out grumpy pants, I have syrup for you. They are even blueberry pancakes, Matty found some blueberries over the other hill and picked them for your birthday pancakes."

This choked John up, that after all he had been through to be so thoughtful, he went over to Matty and thanked him for the blueberries saying,

"Those blueberries made it the most extra special birthday pancakes I ever had."

Matty smiled a real smile and hugged John saying, "Happy Birthday Uncle John."

John enjoyed the pancakes, maybe more than any he had ever eaten before. He sat eating his pancakes, thinking about the journey that lay ahead and found himself again worried about the time it took them thus far.

After breakfast John grabbed a second cup of coffee and sat down with Roger and Dickie to discuss moving forward. They planned to try and make the thirty miles before noon by moving quickly down the main road until they reached Osceola Mills. Being a slightly larger town they thought it best to go around it.

With the plan all set and the camp packed up they packed into the three vehicles. The loss of the cars made the seating space cramped. Danny's leg was healing, but it was still difficult for him to use it. He sat in the Jeep with Roger with Melinda and Laurie in the back seat. John's truck had a full back seat so he and Amy had Mandy and Aaron come with them, Matty liked having Aaron to hang out with and it kept his mind off things. Ray rode in the back of John's truck as lookout and since Dickie would be in the back of Mark's truck Jules and Georgia also rode with them.

This left Mark's truck, which had space in the back for seating, but not full seats. He and Renee sat up front while Kimmie and Jenny sat on the jump seats facing each other.

Driving for a little over an hour and so far the day was uneventful and even peaceful. The air was crisp with the sights and smells of fall. It was hard to think of all that was wrong with the world when leaves of red, orange and yellow were lazily falling in the breeze.

Roger turned down a dirt road that was not on the route they previously mapped out. John wished for the communications they were looking for that night they went into the warehouse area. The vehicles followed down the long dirt road to a cell tower site. Parking they all got out and clamored for information about why they stopped.

Roger said, "We need to take a break and I need Amy to come up here and take a look at Danny's leg."

John waved Amy over and said, "Can you go have a look at Danny's leg?"

Amy said, "Sure, what's up?"

Roger said, "I'm not sure, but I think there is something wrong and he isn't saying."

Amy let out a heavy sigh, saying, "Men, needing to be all tough and shit. More like stupid."

Amy knew as soon as she approached him that something was very wrong. Danny was sweating and looked to have a greyish or ashen colour about him. Amy knew instantly that he was in critical shape.

Wearing sweat pants to fit over his bandages she quickly stripped them off of him. She wasn't expecting the sight she saw. The leg around the bandage was bright red and as she touched it he winced in pain. It was swollen and hot to the touch. Already knowing what she would find she gently cut the bandages off. She lifted the bandaging and turning her head to the side as the odor of the infection assaulted her.

Looking at Laurie she said, "Laurie why didn't you tell us?"

Laurie was crying as she said, "He didn't want to slow us down."

Amy scolded her, "Well, it is definitely going to do so now."

Calling out for John and barking out orders for boiling water and some clean bandages she had everyone hopping and jumping double time.

She had them set up an area where he could be stretched out and under a cover. Jules came over to help her as Dickie and Roger got a fire going. John approached her with apprehension knowing she would be demanding something bigger from him.

Amy looked at him with pleading eyes, saying, "Let's talk a minute over there." She pointed to an area away from the others.

She began, "John we need antibiotics and a good amount of them."

John said, "I have a few with us, but I'm not sure if it is enough for something like this."

Amy shook her head saying we need something strong and preferably something I can inject. I'm no doctor and my limited medical training in the nursing homes doesn't even come close to medical training, but I have seen what infections like this can turn into in a hurry."

John nodded in agreement saying, "It wouldn't hurt Jules to get a round of them as well."

Do you think a couple of you guys can scout around for a hospital or a veterinary clinic for some? I doubt at this point anything would be left in the pharmacies, after what most of the towns we passed looked like."

John agreed and said, "I'll get Dickie and Ray and we will go right away. It will be good to get an idea of what our location is anyway."

Amy looked at him and said, "John, hurry please. I am going to open the wound and try and drain it, but he is already starting to show signs of sepsis. We need a broad spectrum antibiotic because I don't know what kind of bug caused the infection."

John's eyes widened, "What does broad spectrum mean?"

Amy said, "Just that it kills a bunch of stuff."

John asked her, "Do you know what we should look for?"

Amy sighed, "Not a full list, but, most cillins, as in penicillin. A really good one might be Cipro or Tetracycline but get anything you can get would help."

Laurie and Melinda made Danny comfortable while Amy prepared to lance the wound. She put a sharp knife in the boiling pot along with some strips of cloth to be used as hot compresses. Gathering all the sterile gauze she could find she organized herself and checked on Danny a number of times.

Roger opted to just set up camp and had the others doing chores like gathering wood and setting up tents. Nearly dragging Laurie and Melinda away, he put them to work as well he left Jules to attend to Danny till it was time to do the draining.

Matty and Aaron decided they would be lookouts by climbing the cell tower. A shrill screech alerted Roger and Mark that something was wrong and they ran to the cell tower. Mandy was shouting at the boys to climb down that instant.

They had gone too high and were now afraid to climb down. Growling as he began to climb Roger quickly reached the height that the boys were waiting. As he climbed he noticed something that didn't look right about the city in the distance. It was Osceola Mills but just outside of the city was a huge complex with what looked like tents or barracks.

After hurrying the boys down the tower, he went for the binoculars and headed back up. Only going high enough to be able to see the camp, he began to scan it from his perch. Looking down, he could see Matty still standing at the base of it.

He called down to him, "Matty do you think you can go grab the small satchel from the jeep and bring it to me?"

Matty yelled back, "What's a satchel?"

Roger shouted back, "It looks like a purse for an army man. It has the same pattern as my shirt."

Matty turned and sprinted into the woods in the area of the camp. In only a few minutes he returned with it and began climbing the tower again. He handed it to Roger and turned to leave when Roger said,

"How about a helping hand?'

Matty nodded agreement and sat waiting for instructions.

Roger handed him back the satchel and said, "I have one pad there is another in there, can you write about it some things for me?"

Matty said, "Yes sir." Sitting up straighter and saluting him.

Roger said, "I'm going to make a map of the camp and I need you to write down things I tell you, Ok?"

Matty nodded and got his own pad and pencil ready.

Roger busily created his map, looking at the camp with the binoculars then drawing things.

He looked at Matty and said, "Armed guards."

Matty quickly wrote it on his pad. Roger and Matty mapped out this camp and gathered intel on it for the next forty five minutes before taking a break to go to eat.

Once back in the camp, Roger wanted to discuss with Mark the layout and the information they already gathered on the camp.

Mandy came walking up to them and said, "I know Osceola Mills well, maybe I should come and have a look when you go back up."

Mark said, "Little lady we can handle this."

Mandy was furious, saying, "Don't start that I'm just a girl bull shit. I can climb a tower as well as you."

Mark laughed, saying, "And put an old man in his place too."

During lunch, they sat and went over the map that Roger drew and the list that Matty made. Looking it over closely, they saw that it had guard towers and barbed wire on the top of the fence. Roger explained that there were big tents set up with smaller ones intermingled.

Mark said, "I wish John were here, he had some stuff about these things he was looking up all the time."

Roger said, "I have seen a few and these are not refugee aid stations, they are more like internment camps."

Roger paused and looked up at the sky saying, "Where the hell are those guys anyway? I bet they don't even know what is out there. Damn, once again we could have used some kind of coms to warn them."

Mark looked at him and said, "Do you think they are gonna run into any trouble?"

Roger knowing he was nervous about it shook his head saying, "Nahhh, they ain't that dumb. It'll be ok."

Jules came over and asked if Roger would help with Danny because she was feeling faint and needed to lay down and Amy didn't want Laurie or Melinda to help with this. Roger agreed it was best and got up to go help her. Matty jumped up to help too.

Roger said, "Not for this mister, sit tight for now."

Matty sat back down looking dejected and folded his arms. Mark seeing this began to tell him how he was too young and needed to go play.

Matty was angered and said, "I'm helping with the soldier work."

Mark began to object when Roger stepped up and touched him on the shoulder saying, "Yes, he is, and a very big help he has been."

Looking at Matty he said, "Soldier, its chow time. Go get your grub and report back in thirty."

Matty cocked his head to the side and looked at him confused. Roger whispered to him, "Time to eat, go get some food and meet me back here in half an hour."

He jumped up running over to where Renee and Jenny were passing out the food. Grabbing a plate as he darted by to go sit with Georgia and Aaron and tell about the soldier work.

# Chapter 17

## "In Darkness we move"

*"True courage is being afraid, and going ahead and doing your job anyhow, that's what courage is."*
-Norman Schwarzkopf

John pulled in behind the veterinary clinic just north of town. As they made their way along they noted that the entire town was completely deserted. Osceola Mills was not a large city, but was big enough to have a Walmart and its own high school.

Dickie asked, "Where is everyone?"

Ray responded, "This is not good, there is a camp here somewhere. We need to get what we need and get out quick."

John looked at Ray and asked, "A camp?"

Ray responded, "Yea, they call them refugee camps but they are really like prison camps. We need to be quick here."

The rear door was locked so Ray grabbed a crow bar from the jeep and pried it open. Once inside they could see that it had been ransacked. Fortunately, it seemed it was most likely junkies or someone not knowing what they were looking for.

They began to collect the bottles of medicine when Dickie called out to John, "What are we looking for?"

Ray said, "Grab everything you can, we will sort it out later now let's double time this and evacuate the area pronto."

John found a whole cabinet full of dressings, tools and gauze, grabbing a trash bag he emptied the whole thing of its contents. The meds were strewn all over the floor and Dickie was tossing them haphazardly into a tote he found.

John remembered Amy had requested injectable antibiotics and began looking for needles or any bottles and vials. Coming across a locked cabinet that was as yet untouched, he motioned for Ray to pry it open.

Once open they could see they hit pay dirt. Inside was all the meds and equipment they could need for this. John carefully put it all into a box he emptied of dog treats and they quickly exited the building and made their way out of town.

At a crossroad headed toward the area of town where many of the stores were located, John looked at Ray and asked, "Should we check out the Walmart?"

Ray said, "It is highly unlikely that there is anything left and anything that is wouldn't be worth the risk. I think we need to get these meds back to Amy."

Dickie agreed and said, "We need to look over the maps and find a way around this place anyway."

John agreed and continued back to where the others were camped. They had to take many little side roads and at one point became lost. Cursing Dickie hung his head out the window and looked around.

Pointing to a street going left, he said, "It's that way."

John scowled at him, "How would you know?"

Dickie smirked, saying, "Cause the cell tower is right there."

Shaking his head, John turned up the road that would eventually bring them to the dirt access road leading them to the tower.

Pulling into the campsite Mark hurried over asking, "Did you find anything?"

Ray responded, "Better than we expected."

"Well, come on over and help us with Danny then." Mark said.

As they approached the tented area they noticed Amy was trying to sharpen a knife. John smiled, handing her the bag of tools and dressings, somewhere in there would be the things she needed all sterile in packages.

Amy looked into the bag and immediately began unpacking the items, seeing gauze, tape and latex gloves she was thrilled, but when she found a scalpel she hugged John and began to get organized.

They showed her the box with the vials in it and she quickly looked over the options saying, "Some of this we will need to get information on but I do know that lidocaine will dull the pain. Let's get him numbed up and get started."

Amy applied the hot compresses to the infected area and washed the area around the wound. She carefully took the scalpel and opened his wound, allowing the infection to ooze from it. They began to clean and scrub the wound while she probed the inside of it for any pockets of abscess.

Once they felt the puss had been mostly removed, she left it unstitched and packed the wound with sterile gauze to help the drainage. Giving him a shot of Penicillin and some Motrin to lower the fever, she instructed Laurie to keep an eye on him and come get her if his fever went up or there were any issues.

She approached the guys; who were discussing the camp and said, "Can we hold off on leaving at least for a day or two? He's in pretty bad shape."

Ray replied, "Whatever we need to do will be fine, I'd like to do some recon on that camp anyway."

Ray went with Roger to the cell tower to have a look at the camp. It was starting to get dark and they thought it would be good to observe what goes on in the evenings. After some time on the tower Ray told Roger to keep watch and he would send relief soon.

When he reached the bottom of the tower Matty stood pencil and paper in hand and said, "Reporting for duty sir."

Ray looked at him with warm eyes and asked, "What has been your duty today soldier?"

Matty replied, "Writing sir, I write down what Roger tells me, sir." He then stood tall and straight.

Ray looked up at Roger and said to Matty, "Carry on soldier."

Back at camp Ray talked with John and Dickie and asked that they set up a watch schedule for the camp. He wanted to know what was going on in there.

Pulling Dickie aside, he said, "We need to do some up close recon."

Dickie nodded and said, "I'll get my stuff."

Ray told John that they would be out doing recon on the camp and asked that he set up a watch schedule for the tower. They all thought it was a good idea to have camp only partially together in case of the need to move fast.

John asked Mark to see to it that all unnecessary items were kept put away and that it be a cold camp this evening. No fires were to be lit and everyone would have to sleep either in a vehicle or in the one large tent that was set up.

Dickie said to John, "If the watch should see a blaze kick up out of nowhere, know it is time to pack up." He reached into his pack and pulled out a jar of liquid John assumed was gas or something else flammable.

The two left and John allowed Mandy to take the next watch, telling her what Dickie had said they should do if she saw fire. Mark was next up on the tower followed by John, who hoped that Ray and Dickie would return before then. He didn't like hanging around so close to one of those camps.

The night was cool without any fires, but there was no frost so the brisk morning was somewhat bearable. After the lookouts watched the camp all night, John said they could start a fire, but to keep the smoke to a minimum. They could see and smell small fires in the woods surrounding them all night long; apparently not all the residents of Osceola Mills were interned in the camp.

Shortly after the coffee was done Mandy brought a cup with her to relieve Roger at the tower and told him John wanted to talk to him. Matty followed her and began to turn and follow Roger once he came down.

Roger returned to him and said, "Soldier I need you to record what Miss Mandy sees today. Can you handle this mission?"

Mandy looked at him like he was crazy, but Matty stood stiff and tall in salute. Roger sent him to get his pad and pencil instructing he was to bring a snack with him.

When he left Mandy asked, "What was that all about?"

Roger said, "He seems to be acting out, I think it is because he felt so weak watching what happened to Kevin and then after telling his mom about it that he couldn't protect her. I don't think there is any harm in it, just a way of coping for him."

Mandy nodded, saying, "I figured it was something like that."

Matty returned with his pad and pencil along with a satchel full of snacks and some water for them and started climbing the rungs on the tower. Mandy climbed up behind him and got settled in for the shift.

In camp Danny was already noticeably better and taking in fluids, Laurie was fastidiously watching over him and making sure he got the oral antibiotics Amy said he should take.

Renee and Kimmie were yelling at Jenny about something to do with, her inability to understand something they refused to discuss when Roger approached to see what was going on.

Jenny looked up at him from the rock she was sitting on, tears in her eyes. This infuriated Roger, he liked Jenny's quiet manner and felt all along the brash and crudeness of Kimmie and Renee did not seem to fit with this family, but more into the kind attitudes that he'd seen Morgan exhibit. Scowling at them, he lifted Jenny by her arm and asked her to come help him clean up the breakfast area.

Jenny liked Roger and enjoyed chatting with him about almost anything. Kimmie flirted with him shamelessly even pretending to need his help to undo her bra one day. Roger unceremoniously brushed her off telling her, "Get your mom to help you."

As they walked to the area the food had been prepared in Kimmie glared at her calling out, "She's not worth the effort soldier boy."

Roger now angry retorted, "Correction, it takes no effort to enjoy the company of one so lovely. Yet is agony to even tolerate the presence of someone like you."

Kimmie snorted and huffed back into the tent where she angrily tossed all Jenny's things out the door grumbling about how she is useless and worthless. Jenny started back for the tent to gather her things when roger stopped her.

"Hold on girl, that is just what they want you to do."

He turned to Laurie and asked, "Laurie will you be so kind as to go and gather up this young lady's items and bring them over here?"

Laurie brushed her hand down Jenny's long blonde hair in a motherly fashion saying, "It would be my pleasure."

Roger said, "There will be new riding assignments, effective immediately."

Looking at John he nodded and John nodded back saying, "Will you take care of setting them up?"

Roger nodded and taking Jenny's arm headed to clean up the breakfast mess. Reassuring her things would be ok, he asked, "What is wrong with them to treat you like that?"

Obvious that she knew something, but, she hung her head and said, "It's best I just leave it alone, I wouldn't want anything to happen to anyone else."

Roger glared in the direction of Renee and Kimmie saying to no one particular, "If I find out...." Trailing off, he didn't finish the sentence but continued to glare at them as he thought about it.

Ray and Dickie returned to camp and asked that Mandy be relieved on the tower. John asked Mark to relieve her and he would brief him afterwards. He thought it strange that nothing seemed out of the ordinary at the camp. Walking over to Ray and Dickie he remarked to Roger,

"Maybe it is just a refugee camp or aide station."

Ray overheard him and said, "It is by no means ordinary." Then he looked to Mandy and asked,

"Are you familiar with the warehouse section of town right next to the camp?"

Mandy shook her head yes and said, "I know it well, what do you need to know?"

Ray said, "The train tracks next to it? Do you know if they are ever used?"

Mandy said, "I have never seen a train on them. I know they were not exempt from when I drove the school bus, we tried to get them declared exempt because we had to stop at them and they are not in use. The town refused to because they said they had some purpose to the government."

Ray said, "Well, they are in use now. We saw refrigerated cars parked on them. They never moved, but the refer units were running. They are heavily guarded and we saw nothing going on with them."

Mandy said, "I saw someone putting packages on them last night, maybe fifteen or more."

Dickie looked at her saying, "Can you describe those packages?"

She replied, "Well, it was sort of hard to see, but they were black and were brought out on carts. It took two men to lift them into the rail cars."

Roger and Ray both looked at one another and giving a nod, Ray said, "Great job Mandy, did you see anything else? As a matter of fact did anyone see anything else?"

John told them about the small fires all around them during the night. While Roger produced the map he drew the day before. Dickie and Ray began to add things to the map that they discovered on their recon trip.

There were guard towers that Roger already had shown, but added to it, guard shacks on the ground. Also noted that the fence was a double row of fencing with barbed wire on both inner and outer runs of fence line.

While they watched the camp, they had the chance to peer inside some of the tents. A few had people walking around inside while others had multiple lines of cots inside. That one appeared to be a kind of infirmary with the workers suited up in Biohazard suits.

One was clearly a latrine, another a mess hall and one tent housed only children. The thing that they found curious was that there were armed guards all around; and the inhabitants appeared to be in a sort of prison, even being escorted to the latrine.

After watching the camp for the past twenty-four hours they all agreed it would be best to get around the city at night. Ray and Dickie would recon the area for the best way around later this night and they would leave the next.

After grabbing a bite to eat they both grabbed some shut eye while everyone did other things to occupy their time. John took over on the tower and sat with Matty for a time just calling out things for him to write down. Just before the four hours were up for a change in lookout, something was happening at the camp.

While not taking his eyes from the binoculars he said, "Convoy coming in, seven trucks with a jeep on either end."

Matty feverishly wrote all Matt was saying and when he finished with the first part he said, "Got it."

John continued, "Non-military persons in the front jeep giving orders. Civilians exiting trucks and being segregated into three groups, can't see reasons for each group yet."

Looking down at Matty writing asked, "Are you getting this?"

Matty looked up saying, "Yes sir."

John went back to watching while Matty waited for him to say more. John watched as they led the first group to the tent they had determined was the infirmary. The next group was let to a tent on the far side of the camp that looked like it was all alone in an area. The third and largest group was lined up at the fence line while the military officers spoke animatedly with the non-military leaders from the first jeep.

Suddenly John gasped, and Matty asked, "What do I write Uncle John?"

John replied, "Nothing buddy, that was all there is. We need to go see the other guys and report. You ready to get off of here and go report what you have written down?"

Matty nodded and put his pad away as he prepared to climb down.

Once back in camp, they waited for Ray and Dickie to join them for the reporting of the refugees coming into the camp. Matty gave the report about the trucks and the groups of people and was praised for his excellent work. They sent him to get cleaned up and eat so they could discuss it.

Once Matty left John said, "That's not all I saw."

Ray responded, "What else?"

John said, "I didn't want to tell it to Matty or in front of him but the last group? They were executed at the fence."

Ray jumped up almost yelling, "What?"

John continued to tell them what he saw, "They lined them at the fence like Matty said, but after the others were carted off to their respective areas there was an argument. The non-military guys from the front jeep, and what looked some officers from the guard argued in a very animated way for a moment. After that two men got out of the jeep in front and just mowed them down. I didn't hear any shots, but there was no mistake that they shot them all."

Roger looked at Ray saying, "Silencers I bet."

Ray nodded and shook his head in disbelief. He asked what fence line they were on when shot and John pointed out the place on the map. Ray showed Dickie and told him they would check out that side of the fence during tonight's recon.

All those who heard the news were quiet and considering their own thoughts about the goings on at this camp. John was particularly disturbed thinking at how close they were to ending up in one if they decided to not just take his supplies and taken them to a camp like this one.

It was difficult to think about how close they really were, when Roger seeming to read his thoughts said,

"We gave you that note when we came because they were planning to round you all up at the end of the week for the camp at Devons."

John looked up at him, saying, "I was just considering how close to that we really had been."

As the sun sank low on the horizon Dickie and Ray prepared to leave. They mapped out some smaller roads that would get them within a mile of the camp without being seen. From there they would go on foot to get a closer look at that fence line.

They told the others that it was likely fine to keep the fire going, but advised they should build up rocks around it and keep it low so the light didn't attract any unwelcome company. With the fire lights the evening before they knew there were others in theses woods; not knowing if they were friend or foe. A watch was set for camp as well as the tower that evening and again all were packed for a quick exit if it became necessary.

# Chapter 18

## "Wolf in sheep's clothing"

*"The world will not be destroyed by those who do evil, but by those who watch them without doing anything."*
-Albert Einstein

Ray and Dickie drove out of camp turning the jeep left with another left not far up the road, the road would take them along the river that flowed right past the camp. It was dark already and Ray drove with the headlights turned off. It was still a mostly wooded area, but he didn't want to draw any unnecessary attention to themselves.

They followed that road for nearly eight miles before Ray turned down a road that would cross the river and went into a large warehouse complex. There were hundreds of trucks it seemed.

Ray and Dickie looked at each other before Dickie said, "It feels kind of strange to see all these trucks just sitting here, I wonder if they have anything to do with the camp?"

Ray turned and looked out the window saying, "I hope not or we might find ourselves stranded."

Dickie replied, "Yeah, there was a road about a quarter mile back on the left that went into the woods, maybe we should high tail it over there and hump in."

Ray nodded in agreement and turned the jeep around, once they found the road it didn't take them long to get the jeep parked in a pile of bushes and covered.

As they started to walk out of the cover a voice whispered, "I would wait a few more minutes if I were you."

Both of them immediately crouched lower and put their hands to their side arm, as they began scanning the area Ray said, "Who are you?"

The voice whispered, "Keep it down and look to the road. Now take cover and wait."

Both men crouched behind a stand of trees and watched the road. The trucks that were parked not even thirty minutes prior were pulling onto the roadway.

Ray whispered to Dickie, "That could have been bad."

Dickie nodded and said, "I want to know who our guardian angel is though, makes me a little nervous he knows where we are but we can't see him."

Ray glanced over his shoulder at him and nodded as he scanned the trees looking for him. They sat quietly as they watched the convoy of trucks exiting the warehouses occasionally shifting their eyes to look for their guardian angel. The traffic slowed and eventually stopped for what seemed a sufficient amount of time. They began to rise from their positions when again the voice instructed them to lay low. They didn't know why, but they trusted it and crouched just before one last smaller convoy of pickups and varied cars exited and sped off away from their position.

They remained crouched and were startled when from the very tree they were crouched under dropped a spry older man. He was dressed in all camo and slung across his back was a long bow. His beard was grey as was his hair, but under the netting of his hat it did not show.

He stood and held his hand out to shake saying, "Emmett Rabin, at your service."

Dickie extended his hand replying, "Dickie Miller here and this is Ray Saylor."

Emmett shaking his hand said, "What brings you into these parts?"

Ray said, "We are travelling and had to make a stopover for a few days."

Emmett nodded his head and asked, "I saw you hightail it out of the warehouses. What were you doing in there?"

Ray responded, "We were trying to get a look at the camp to see what is going on in there. Do you know anything about it?"

Emmett nodded, saying, "I've been watching for a bit now and it seems that anyone goes in… well they don't come out. Least wise not alive anyway."

Dickie's eyes widened as he spoke, "Are they executing them all?"

Emmett said, "Not exactly, you see they got that Ebola in there and even the healthy ones are crammed into the tents all the same. There are some that go into the smaller tents and they seem ok. But anyone that makes trouble or seems like trouble, well, they are just taken to the fence."

Dickie asked, "The fence?"

Emmett replied, "Yea, some they line up at the fence and just shoot em as soon as they arrive."

Ray said, "We're trying to get to Osceola Mills and need to know the routines of the camp to pass."

Emmett looked nervous saying, "What business you got there?"

Without saying any names, Dickie explained how they had come to bring Mandy and Aaron along.  He told him about the gang ransacking their home and that they were trying to help her get to her parent's house.  They did not know much about Emmett and did not want to jeopardize Mandy and Aaron's safety.

Emmett shook his head saying, "There ain't no one left in Osceola Mills, that's where they keep all the black suits."

Confused, Ray said, "Black suits?"

Emmett replied with a chuckle, "That's what I call the guys that are running the show.  I don't know who they are but they all wear the same damn black suit.  They look like there was a going out of business sale at J. C. Penny on black suits and everyone got in on it."

Ray and Dickie shared a look and knew it was the same as the things they saw back in Auburn.  They thanked Emmett and turned to leave. They both knew this was not going to go well for them if they were caught.  At this point they were deserters and figured it was best to move along and avoid the camp and Osceola Mills entirely.

Emmett said, "Hold up there.  We got some folks from Osceola Mills right here in these woods, maybe someone knows your friend's parents."

Dickie said, "It is worth a try, how can we find out?"

Emmett said, "Well, we can check in with Frank and Ruth, they know just about everyone who's out here."

Ray looked at Dickie and said, "We don't know her parents' names."

"Well, let's go see Ruth and see what she knows anyway." Emmett said.

They both nodded and followed Emmett down a trail that led back into the woods. It wasn't long before there were a number of ragged looking people looking at them as they passed. All had hollow eyes and quietly stared as the strangers walked past. These people had a grey look about them almost as if death had already come, but they didn't know it and lingered in this world.

Coming into what looked like the center of the group they found an older man sitting on an old stump smoking something that looked like rolled up leaves. He didn't look as ragged as the others they saw. With his large round belly and stubby fat fingers, he looked well fed.

Emmett asked him, "Where's Ruthie gone to?"

The man looked up and said, "She's just over the hill, she'll be right back. Whatcha got with ya Emmett?"

Emmett said, "These two are looking for the parents of a few people in their *group*."

Ray looked at Dickie, neither one of them liked the way he said *group*. Something was not right here, although neither of them could put their finger on what was wrong, they passed knowing looks that told one another OPSEC was important.

Dickie said, "Yes, they lived in Osceola Mills."

Stepping out from behind a stand of trees a surprisingly lovely woman stood before them. She did not look worn or grey like the others. Her shoulder length blonde hair hung in her eyes a bit. She was older, but seemed fit, even formidable.

Extending her hand, she said, "Hi, I'm Ruth, how many are in your group?" It was almost as if she didn't hear what Dickie said, but only cared about their numbers.

Dickie picked up on this and said, "Well, Ray and I have been helping others get to their homes. Seems like most of them are just families and couldn't defend themselves. We have been trying to help them get home. Not really sure of how many there are, it changes along the way, but we're just a small group maybe fifteen or so."

Nodding to Ray he said, "Sound about right Ray?"

Ray looked at each of them, pursing his lips like he was thinking and said, "Yea, I'd guess that is pretty close."

Ruth asked, "You say they are defenceless?"

Ray nodded, saying, "Mostly, you see... we scout ahead and then go back and bring them up. Because there is only Dickie and I to keep them protected, we need to take things slow."

Ruth looked almost excited saying, "Well, just bring them on over here. We can look after them while you two do your scouting."

Dickie trying to look impressed with the suggestion said, "Wow! That would be great. You sure you wouldn't mind the extra burden?"

Ruth responded, "Not at all, shall I have some of our guys come help escort them?"

Ray shrugged, "Do you think it will be necessary? It seemed pretty quiet."

Emmett looking them over said, "It'll be alright if you just wait until after dark."

Ruth agreed and sent them to get a cup of coffee and rest up before dark. Dickie and Ray took the opportunity to look around at the group. The people were ragged and hungry looking. Dickie noted an almost savage look about them and that some were shaking. He couldn't put his finger on what it was, but knew there was something very wrong here.

As night fell and the two prepared to head back to their camp planning to fill the others in on their explorations. They were startled by someone while they were uncovering the jeep, a weary woman and a small girl in hushed tones signalled them from the woods. Hidden in the trees near their vehicle the two begged that they take them away from there. Dickie looked at Ray, turning to them silently he nodded directing them to get into the vehicle. They crawled to the far side of the jeep and Ray acted like he was checking something allowing them to slip into the back unnoticed by the ever watchful eyes of Emmett.

They had been driving for only a few miles when the woman asked, "Is it safe yet?"

Ray asked, "Safe from what?"

The woman began to cry, begging, "Please don't hurt us."

Ray was confused and turned to her asking, "Why would we hurt you?"

She responded, "I don't know, I didn't think about whether or not you were bad guys. We just needed to get away from there or we were going to be dinner."

Ray gasped, "You mean…"

She nodded, saying, "When we were found by Emmett, there were six of us. They actually only unchained us because you were there, we were told that if we said anything to you that they would make us suffer when it was our turn."

Ray asked, "Why didn't they just take us captive?"

The woman responded, "They wanted to follow you to find out where the rest of your group is. I overheard Emmett talking to Ruth and that's why we snuck out to try and go with you."

Ray looked over to the young girl and back to the woman and said, "Where are you from?"

The woman replied, "Altoona, but the black suits have been bringing people to the camp from all over. When they came to start taking people away in our area, we left and hid in the woods. We were pretty hungry when Emmett found us and brought us to their camp. At first they were very nice and gave us food and water, a place to sleep and clean up."

Pausing, she looked out the window and continued, "Then on the second day they burst into the tent taking us all prisoner."

Tears streamed down her cheeks as she said, "Ron, my husband, fought hard and was killed in the scuffle. They were like animals, cutting him up and carrying off the pieces."

Ray sat with a look of horror as she continued, "At first I didn't know why, but once we were taken from the tent I understood what was happening. I watched the man who killed him as he brought his head to Frank and Ruth like it was a trophy."

Sobbing the woman could hardly continue to speak, yet she went on describing the horrors of the small encampment, "Every few days they would come for one of us. Missy was the last one taken, she had been at the college in Altoona when we met up with her. The women were given to the men of the camp the evening before they were to be eaten for what they called pleasuring. We could hear her screaming long into the night. I think Ruth wanted to save Mary here for Sunday dinner. She said the young ones were the most tender."

Pulling the child closer to her, she sobbed great heaving sobs, speaking between sniffles and broken words she tried to tell them more, but Ray reached out for her hand saying, "Later, it can wait."

Dickie said, "I don't know whether to be pissed off or terrified, we need to get everyone packed up and leave this area RFN."

Ray said to the woman, "There is no time for introductions or formalities. You are welcome to sit tight and come along or you are free to go when we get to camp. We don't have a spare vehicle, but might be able to offer you some supplies."

The woman replied, "I don't care where we are going, any place is better than here. I have some family in Ohio and could try and get to them."

Ray replied, "We are going south and can take you south until you would have to head west to Ohio."

The woman nodded, thanking him, saying, "My name is Julie and this is my daughter Mary. Thank you both for your help, I promise that we won't be a bother."

Ray turned to Dickie and said, "No time for explanations, we just need to get everyone into the vehicles and get gone. Hopefully we can get out without a scuffle. I think we need to have John and Roger watch the perimeter with us while everyone else gets loaded up."

Dickie said, "Gotcha,"

The Jeep sped up the dirt road to the camp, lights shining across the camp's occupants. John immediately knew something was wrong and ran to the Jeep.

Ray poked his head out the window as he ran alongside saying, "We're leaving... Right NOW!"

John ran ahead to the tent and told everyone to pack up and get ready to pull out in minutes.

Roger was on the tower and came running asking, "What's going on?"

Ray said, "Packing up, need to DiDi and do it RFN. Explain later but make sure we have everyone there will be no going back because there will be nothing to go back for."

In less than five minutes all of the gear was stowed and everyone was in a vehicle as they sped out of the encampment and made their way to route 53, the route they mapped out earlier.

# Chapter 19

## "Luck can change"

*"Shallow men believe in luck or in circumstance. Strong men believe in cause and effect."*
-Ralph Waldo Emerson

They were well on their way and headed south on route 53 by morning, the horror of what they learned spread through the vehicles horrifying some but most just felt anger. Mandy cried and was almost inconsolable at the thought of such a fate for her parents. Julie tried to convince her that her parents were probably just off with family somewhere, but Mandy was sure they would have happily accepted the FEMA offers for help.

John figured she, of all people, knew her parents and was likely right about their fate, but also that they were lucky in the sense that it was a better fate than that of being lunch. Shaking his head, he shrugged off the mixed feelings of anger and disgust. Fear lurked in the back of his mind of the distance they still had to go. It had only been little more than a month and already people had resorted to cannibalism. It suddenly occurred to him that it had been over a month and they had made it little more than half way.

Much of the day was spent in slow progression south, avoiding roadblocks, vehicles and other things in their path. John, who was in the lead vehicle, pulled over at the on ramp as leading onto interstate 22.

Jumping out he said, "Hang tight, I'm going back to talk to the others about the highway."

He reasoned that taking the highway might be just the same as the back roads, but would get them to their next route quicker. Everyone agreed they might give it a chance. Cautiously, they proceeded up the on ramp to the interstate. There was apprehension because they knew if there were trouble on a highway there were few places they could escape it.

The road was clear all the way to route 219, where they began to move south. It too was a highway, but was eerily void of any vehicles. On route 22 there were a number of broken down vehicles on the roadway, but none on route 219 at all. They saw nothing along the route, no sign of people anywhere, just the roadway. No one said anything, but all were feeling uneasy about the ease of travel and the lack of abandoned cars.

Finally, Amy said, "It is funny that only a few months ago we would be angered by traffic and obstacles in our path and now we feel uneasy about how clear the road is."

They all laughed a little and eased the tension as they came upon the interchange for I-70.

Pulling over, John said, "I think we should take a lunch stop and see about looking at the map again. It will be good to get our bearings and plan the next leg of the trip."

He hopped out of the Jeep and headed back to talk to the others about it.

When he returned, he said, "We talked and think it would be best if we move forward through the town, then stop in an area where we can have more cover."

Climbing in, he smiled over his shoulder, for the first time in a long time feeling hopeful. A few miles beyond the interstate they found a small dirt road leading to a dried creek bed, beyond it was a small pine clearing. After checking the area surrounding the little nook for any threats, they were all permitted to get out of the vehicles. Everyone began to murmur about the quick exit the night before.

Most of them got the quick version during the trip, but everyone wanted to hear about Julie and Mary. Renee and Kimmie were clamoring for the attention of the newcomers being overly friendly, when Roger came over to the group.

Looking disgusted at the pair then back to the newcomers, he said, "Excuse me Julie, John would like to talk to you if you feel up to it."

Julie appearing to welcome the relief from the questions said, "Sure, who is John?"

Roger said, "Follow me, I'll show you."

Glaring as Julie and Roger walked away Renee scowled. She made her way back to the vehicle mumbling how much she hated him, Kimmie was hot on her heels agreeing with her making animated gestures in his direction.

Julie watched them as she followed Roger and asked, "What is wrong with them?"

Roger shook his head saying, "They're just dead weight, don't pay any attention to them."

John held out his hand to greet Julie saying, "Hi Julie, I'm John and this is Amy." Motioning to Amy as he introduced them.

Julie reached out and shook both of their hands, thanking them for all the help the group had given them in escaping Ruth and the others.

John said, "Dickie has already filled us in on what happened so there is no need for you to go over it again. I'm very sorry to hear about your husband."

Julie nodded, saying, "Thank you."

John asked, "Where is it you are hoping to get to?"

Julie responded, "My uncle lives just west of Zanesville, My dad's side of the family are all there."

John nodded and said, "Ok, let me talk with the others to see what we can do about helping you get there."

Julie nodded to him and turned, walking back the way she came.

The sun was getting low on the horizon, the clearing they were in afforded them some cover from the road and the stress of their escape was just setting in. Settling in for the evening would give them some time to assess the area and look over the map.

Small pockets of conversation could be heard as Roger walked through the encampment. He was looking for Jenny to see if she wanted to eat with him. Standing near the end of the truck he leaned on the tailgate. Glancing around, he lit up a swisher sweet that he had been saving since the last scout. Inhaling deeply and blowing out a huge smoke ring, he watched as Jenny excused herself and walked in his direction.

In the brush behind him, he heard a rustling and immediately turned to investigate. The sun was setting and the twilight made it hard to make out what it was, he squinted to see. Watching a moment he realized that the figure moving through the brush was only Kimmie. It was clear that everyone was feeling uneasy, the events of the previous night had them all slightly edgy.

Smiling at Roger as she approached, Jenny said, "Are you hungry?"

Roger turned to look at her saying, "Starved, how about you?"

Jenny nodded in agreement and poked her hand through his arm, practically escorting him to the meal. Amy and Laurie had cooked a large stew with some cast iron corn bread. Almost everyone was seated around the fire talking about the past few day's events and what might be ahead for them. John and Dickie were talking with Ray about their next direction and how far was left for them to go.

Mark asked Ray, "Do you think it is safe to continue on the main roads and highways?"

Ray said, "Honestly Mark, I'm not sure any roads are going to be safe at this point. People are getting desperate, I think things are worse than we really know. We haven't had any real news for quite some time, I think we need to get some Intel soon."

Laurie came over to the group saying, "Danny said maybe we should look for an antenna."

Ray looked up, with an almost shocked look. He got up and headed over to where Danny was lying. Danny's fever was lower and he was awake. The antibiotics and lancing of the wound seemed to have had a positive effect, he was already looking better.

Approaching Danny he saw Jules as well and asked her how she was feeling.

Jules said, "Not too bad for a girl who just got shot and has morning sickness."

Ray laughed, saying, "You're quite the trooper."

Jules hopped up off the chair and saluted saying, "Yes sir."

Ray shook his head and said, "Knock it off. Can you ask your husband to come and chat with Danny and me?"

"Yes, sir." She quipped as she marched off to find Dickie.

Roger stood nearby watching the brush where Kimmie had gone, he thought it was moving on a few occasions but could see nothing.

Turning to Jenny he asked, "Care to go for a stroll? I'd like to make a check on the perimeter before everyone settles in for the night."

Jenny said, "Yes, I would like that. I would like to know more about what you guys are always looking for. Then I could help too."

Roger acted uneasy, something was bothering him, although he said that he couldn't put his finger on just what yet. They checked the perimeter and all seemed clear.

Arriving at Jenny's tent he said, "Don't wander far from your tent ok?"

Jenny nodded and went into her tent. Roger headed back up to where Ray was still talking to Danny.

Mark walked up to Roger saying, "All clear?'

Roger nodded, saying, "Yea, I guess. I haven't seen anything as yet. Who's on first watch?"

Mark replied, "You're looking at him." Smiling and pointing his thumb at himself.

Roger looked around anxiously, turning abruptly to Mark he said, "Something doesn't feel right, I'm going over to speak to the others but be on guard."

Mark nodded his head saying, "I've been feeling it too."

Roger made his way back to where Danny and the others were, looking nervously around the camp as he walked.

# Chapter 20

## "Light at the end of the tunnel"

*"The thing about a hero, is even when it doesn't look like there's a light at the end of the tunnel, he's going to keep digging, he's going to keep trying to do right and make up for what's gone before, just because that's who he is"*
-Joss Whedon

*November 2ⁿᵈ*

Amy and Laurie were already preparing the morning meal when John came walking up with Roger and Dickie. Roger grabbed a cup of coffee, Dickie his Tea, and continued to move throughout the camp, making sure everyone was packing up the gear and preparing to head out.

Roger was telling them of his uneasy feeling the night before, when Mark walked up saying, "I had the same feeling, almost like someone was watching us."

Roger said, "Yes! That is exactly what it was. I felt like I was being watched."

Dickie looked around them and said, "I'm not sure if it is just residual fear that had set in from the run in with Frank and Ruth's group, but I too feel like we should getta move on pretty soon."

A chill shot down John's spine and he shivered, trying to shake it off.  Just thinking about that group made him cringe.  Telling them to get everyone packed and rounded up for breakfast, he turned and walked to the vehicles.

In less than thirty minutes everyone was packed up and sitting around the campfire eating the morning meal.

Renee remarked, "What is John in such a snit about this morning?"

Mark glared at her saying, "It is not a SNIT, and John is concerned for your safety and wanting to get back on the road as soon as possible."

Melinda gasped, "Is everything ok?"

Mark replied, looking around to everyone, "Yes, everything is fine. We just want to pick up the pace is all. There is still a long way to go."

Mark got up and went over to where Dickie was talking to Ray and Roger asking, "When do you want me to start getting them to load up?"

Dickie said, "Let's say about ten minutes."

Looking at the others who were nodding in agreement. They all refilled their cups with the fresh pot of coffee Amy brought over and stood with the map stretched across the hood of the Jeep.

John said, "It looks like if we just take the highway straight west we will hit West Virginia within a few hours.  I think we should go for it."

Dickie nodding said, "We need to make some better time and I too think it is a good idea to just high tail it down the highway."

"Ok then." Ray said, "Let's get loaded up and head back to the on ramp and get moving."

Dickie said, "Question for everyone."

John replied, "Shoot, what is it?"

He responded, "Do any of the vehicles have issues with doing a higher speed? We are going to be on the highway and it is mostly clear. I think we should put the slowest vehicle in front and just go!"

John was rubbing his beard looking at each of the vehicles when he responded, "You're right! Let's put Mark's truck in front with the Jeep in the middle and my truck bringing up the rear."

Amy was standing nearby and said, "We should make sure those in the back of the trucks are comfortable with the speed and just in case it should also be able to shoot well."

John nodded in agreement and said, "Look here at the map." Pointing to where they were camped.

He continued, "If we head back up this road and take the highway, there are no real cities till almost Pittsburgh."

Ray standing over the hood of the Jeep pointed to a southern route, saying, "After looking at this I'm wondering if the southern track might be a better choice. Pittsburgh is too big a city to get that close to, even if we skirt around it there will be more people in the outlying areas."

John asked about Julie and how they could still help her get closer to her family. They talked for a few minutes studying the map and thought that once they got to the Morgantown, West Virginia area they could head south and over route fifty towards Parkersburg. She would have a much better chance even though it was south of where she was going. It would get her past most of the cities she would encounter.

Roger said, "We also have another issue."

"What is that?" asked Ray

"Mark's truck only has a quarter tank of fuel and the other two are under a half. All of the gas cans are empty now and we haven't seen another tanker."

John said, "Remember that pile up of cars at the off ramp? Most vehicles we see abandoned are because of fuel but these might still have fuel in them."

Nodding his head Ray said, "You're right Roger, let's check it out."

Ray and Roger took Mark's truck and all the gas cans back the two miles to the crash scene.

John and Dickie began to get seating arrangements figured out. Both trucks would hold shooters in the back and the Jeep the children in the center.

The Jeep would be driven by Amy with Jules riding shotgun. In the back was Matty, Georgia, Aaron and Mary. They knew Julie would object to Mary in a different vehicle, but it would be safest.

Front vehicle would be Mark's truck it was the slowest vehicle and also the one that regularly needed fuel first. This vehicle would seat Mark driving with Mandy riding shotgun. Kimmie and Renee would ride in the jump seats with Dickie and Ray in the back

Leaving everyone else in John's truck, he would drive with Jenny shotgun. Laurie, Melinda and Julie in the rear seat Roger and Danny would ride in the back. John tried to seat

Danny in the front, but he objected, saying he needed to help. His leg would not interfere with him sitting in the back.

By the time Roger and Ray returned everyone was ready. The vehicles all had fuel, they were able to fill Mark's truck and gather an additional thirty five gallons of fuel. Filling up the Jeep and the other truck and still left a full five gallon can and another half full.

Setting out, they followed the route they planned and for the first two hours they saw nothing, no one anywhere. It wasn't until they reached the outskirts of Morgantown when they began to see evidence of people. Some of what they saw made them anxious.

One whole section of the city was completely burned and further up the highway, they heard shots being fired in the distance. They needed to get to route fifty, and right now John was wishing they stayed on the original route two-nineteen that would eventually meet up with route fifty. They had covered a greater distance than they had in weeks but now he was wondering if it was worth it.

They reached route fifty and it too was a highway, they stayed on the highway and kept up their speed right around Morgantown, down route seventy-nine and were about an hour's worth of travel along route fifty. They would reach Parkersburg within the hour. With the exception of a new bullet hole in the side of John's truck they made it without any confrontations.

Traveling along route fifty, John almost forgot that the end of the world as they knew it had really happened. Watching the trees whizzing by like they were off on vacation, his thoughts were elsewhere. The sun was high in the sky meaning it was barely even past noontime, John began to listen to his stomach and started thinking about lunch. Passing a sign for McDonalds he thought, wow, would a Big Mac taste really good right now. His thoughts on almost anything but the travels and the reason for them.

Suddenly, WHAM! Something hit them from behind. Roger and Danny were firing their rifles in rapid succession, poking through the open rear window Melinda was also firing at the big black pickup. The tailgate of John's truck was caved in more and more with each hit. The truck behind them had a beefy brush guard that was delivering devastating damage with every hit.

John began sounding the horn loudly for the others in front to go full speed. Jenny was hanging out the side window waving at the Jeep in front of them to go faster who in turn had Jules doing the same to Mark's truck. Speeding along at over ninety-five miles per hour the truck following dropped back.

John sped ahead and indicated for them to follow him, something told him this was not over yet. Taking a quick left onto Dutch Ridge road they found themselves in a mostly residential area. Following it around to Mill Run road brought them into a wooded area, on the left they found a smaller unnamed road the turned onto it. Following it to the end they found they were in a quiet wooded area and could stop and assess their situation.

They didn't realize that they too had been shot at, John's truck was leaking badly. They checked it to find it was a hole in the radiator.

Looking at the other vehicles John said, "These shots were fired from the sides and in front of us."

Ray nodded, saying, "I think that was supposed to be an ambush."

The others said they agreed and thought they should hold up for a few. Check to see if they could fix John's truck and have a bite to eat.

John and Dickie ventured out on foot, to see if they could find some parts while the others rested and prepared some food.

They followed the road back to Mill Run road and went in the opposite direction from where they came in. Sticking to the heavy brush along the road they made their way along until they found themselves in another residential area. They didn't see any sign of people living in the homes, but stayed out of sight just to be safe. They found it difficult to see any vehicles creeping through back yards and moved out into the open on the street, ducking behind any cover they could find.

Just as John was about to run for the cover of a hedge Dickie grabbed his arm, put his finger up to his lips and pointing to the house diagonal from them. It looked unkempt and abandoned, but it had one of the huge antenna's Danny was talking about.

Dickie said, "I just saw the curtains move in the house with the antenna."

John looked at the house, saying, "Do you think someone is in there?"

Dickie said, "Hopefully, maybe we can make contact with the group and make sure there is even anyone there."

John nodded and stood straight up, Dickie gasped saying, "What the bloody hell are you doing?"

John responded, "If there is someone there, then we don't want to go creeping up on them, might as well just stand up and flag em down."

Dickie said, "Yea? Well... what if they start shooting?"

John responded, "Then we'll know they aren't real friendly then won't we?"

John began to wave his hand like he was saying hello to a long time neighbor. Dickie watched and saw the curtain move aside in the same window, he saw movement before.

John continued to wave and eventually the figure came into full view. John put his hand to his ear like he was talking on a phone and pointed to the ham radio tower. The man waved them to come closer where they could talk.

John and Dickie walked up to a spot right behind a car and John said, "Is that a ham radio tower? I would like to know if we can find out about some friends in Kentucky."

The man was guarded, but said, "What do you want me to do?"

John said, "We would like to know if they are still at the location and let them know we are ok."

The man motioned them inside, which shocked Dickie. He was apprehensive about going inside but knew it was better than shouting in the street. Once inside they could see why the man was not afraid to let them in, there were fifteen odd guns trained on them.

The man held out his hand, saying, "I'm Gerald and you are?"

John shook his hand, saying, "I'm John and this is Dickie."

"Who do you wish to contact and where are they?"

John replied, "His name is Matt and they are south of Richmond near Berea, Kentucky."

Gerald told him to hold on while he pulled out a book and began looking something up.

John asked, "Can you help us?"

Gerald barely glancing up from his book and looking over his glasses said, "Likely."

Gerald was older with gray hair and coveralls on. Not at all what you might think of living in this area. It was upper scale houses, new construction all looking nearly identical. It felt like forever until Gerald told them to come into the radio room. "I have a few fellow hams listed in this area, I will try and find one that knows of your friend. Are there other names they might recognize?"

John said, "Dez, I mean Destiny but she goes by Dez."

Gerald began turning dials and listening, asking his hams to find someone who knew these two. After a few minutes Gerald was amazed that one did know about them. He told John that he had found someone who knew ole' Arthur, they were pretty sure he knew them.

John was ecstatic asking multiple questions all at once, "Are they ok? Still at the same location? Can I talk to them?"

Gerald said, "Hang on, hang on, we still need to raise Arthur. This could take a little bit."

Looking over his shoulder into the room they were just in he called out, "Rosie can you fetch us the scotch? I think these gentlemen need a little snort."

Gerald continued to listen to his headset waiting for a response. He turned to them pushing one of the earpieces behind his ear and said, "Are you the group that left out of Massachusetts?"

John tilted his head to the side and asked, "How did you know that?"

Gerald said, "We heard about you a while back, it just didn't register it was you until I started looking for the contact there. Your friends are well known there as a good group of people, we'll get your information to them."

John was moved saying, "Thank you so much, it is good to meet some nice folks."

Gerald responded, "I have heard stories over the radio about how it is out there, how are you getting along?"

John said, "I has had its rough patches, but overall it has just been long. We ended up here because we ran into an ambush and the vehicles got shot up; we were actually looking for a radiator for my truck and that's how we found you."

Gerald admonished them, "Keep off the roads there are some bad gangs here bouts. Where are the rest of your people?"

John and Dickie were somewhat guarded after what could have been a disastrous meeting with Ruth and Frank's group. John hesitated to say anything, and looked to Dickie who said,

"If it is all the same mate, we would rather not say."

Gerald clicked his tongue and said, "Already seen some action have ya? A little gun shy I bet.?

Dickie looked at him with a downward nod, saying, "The worst kind."

George turned from the radio and said, "I have heard of some crazy things already, but do you mean it's worse than the gangs committing all manner of violence?"

John and Dickie both nodded as Dickie said, "The last group we ran into lured weary and frightened people, by inviting them to dinner without telling them they would be the main course."

Gerald looking horrified said, "Cannibalism, already? It hasn't been but few months surely there is still food around."

Dickie said, "I don't know if it was just a decadence or because the government boys had the whole town taken over. We saw the camp up close and they shoot anyone with any objections. There were trucks and train cars hauling off bodies."

John said, "We have been lucky, a few scuffles. We have injuries and lost a few, but we got a lady and her daughter away from them and they have seen even more horror."

Gerald said, "Most of these houses are empty, there isn't any water or electricity, but it is shelter and it is getting cold. We have a house we have rigged up with hot water for showers and maps of gang activity from the other hams. If you have guns keep them and stand guard. Helping others is what the network of us hams have been doing."

John asked, "Let us go and talk with the others, Ok?"

Gerald said, "The white house at the end of the block with the green shutters has a good line of sight for you to feel safe and it has four bedrooms. If you want to settle in there and we will see about getting you to your friends."

John said, "Thank you, we will let you know."

Gerald replied, "It will be dark in a few hours. Do you have a message for your friends? It is not likely we will talk to them, but I can get them a message."

John thought for a moment, saying, "Tell them you spoke to John and Danny. Everyone is ok and Matty is doing great. Tell them travel is slow and getting slower."

Gerald said, "We should let them know that you may be walking soon."

"Walking?" John said

Gerald nodded and in a more serious tone said, "The cities are rough, real rough. Even the smaller towns are rough and travelling on the roads makes you a target."

John said, "Thank you for everything, we should get back to the others and talk to them."

Gerald said, "I'll send someone over to open up the house in case you and your group want to use it."

"Thank you." John said

They returned to the group to discuss what Gerald had offered and talk about the road ahead.

# Chapter 21

## "Unexpected friends"

*"The best way to find out if you can trust somebody is to trust them."*
-Ernest Hemingway

The first reaction of all of those in the group was fear. There was chatter amongst them about the cannibals and the shots that were fired at them earlier. It began turning into an argument when Dickie stood and said,

"Listen, there is a chance that they could be trouble, but after looking around at everything, I don't think so."

Ray spoke, saying, "What gives you that impression Dickie?"

Dickie said, "Mostly a gut feeling, but it was the stance of those with the guns. They were not at all comfortable with them. I think they genuinely want to help."

John stepped forward saying, "I think we can trust them. We will post guard shifts just in case, but it is what we would have to do anyway. One thing that helps is we will have better cover there in the house than we have here in the woods."

Once they gathered everything up and got into the vehicles it only took a couple of minutes to get to the house. A gray haired man, with tattered coveralls, was standing on the lawn when they arrived. He waved them across the lawn to the back yard, putting John's truck in the garage to be worked on.

Approaching John he said, "Gerald sent me to find out what parts you needed."

John showed him the radiator, he made some notes in a miniature composition book, then turning he left without even telling them his name. Watching him leave John noticed standing in the driveway was two of the ladies. Each held a casserole dish in their hands. The younger one, walked toward them with an obvious limp. Her hair was a long silky brown which she carefully kept hanging across one side of her face. It was also obvious that she was hiding it.

The older woman confidently strode up chattering away at the younger one about being rude. John noted that it was not in a chastising way. He noticed how she gently brushed the younger girl's hair over her shoulder, holding her hand to her back with a gentle pat to encourage her to speak to them.

The group seemed to be a collection of fragmented families from some of the surrounding areas. The ladies dropped off the casseroles for the group and said that everyone in their community had given up one of their shower privileges so that each of them could have a hot shower. She told them that Gerald would be by after dinner to show them around.

John looked at Dickie and said, "Hot shower?"

They both grinned and almost skipped into the house to tell the others.  They sat eating the casserole and talking about the hospitality.  A few were worried it would come at a high price.

A short time later there was a knock at the door, it startled them and everyone jumped up as if ready to bolt. Roger opened the door slightly to a smiling older gentleman who said,

"I bet you all want to know about them showers."

Roger opened the door the rest of the way for Gerald to enter.

Gerald looked around saying, "Are you settling in ok?"

John approached him with his hand out and said, "Everyone, this is Gerald."

Mark hurriedly came over and asked him, "Did you talk to Matt?"

Gerald said, "Unfortunately, no I didn't.  I did talk to Arthur and he says they are all fine."

Mark looked relieved and asked, "Did he say anything about how things are there?"

Gerald replied, "Arthur said that he and Dez had a small group that were doing well.  Jeremy and Matt had a good handle on things in the area and that the militia in the area were active and helping to keep things from getting too crazy."

Mark looked at John and they both knew he had actually spoken to someone who knew them because he talked about Jeremy.

Laurie jumped up asking, "Toni, what about Toni?"

Gerald said, "I don't know, but I got the feeling that everyone was fine."

Laurie nodded and went over to where Danny was sitting.

Seeing her disappointment at not hearing about her directly he said, "Don't worry mom, I'm sure she's good, there is no way Jeremy would let anything happen to her, and you know how Dez is fierce over them. She's fine too, I guarantee it."

Everyone was excited about hearing some news and the prospect of a hot shower. They began to outline the order of the showers. Giving the ladies and children the first showers with the men to follow in the order. Jules was to be first, given a towel and some toiletries she stood to go, becoming dizzy she sat quickly. Roger looked at Dickie as he hovered over her.

He went to them asking, "Is everything ok?"

Dickie looked up with worry on his face and nodded that she was fine, but Roger knew something was wrong. Dickie asked that someone else go first. As Jules sat regaining her sense of balance, Dickie brought her a root beer that she sipped.

Renee approached Roger as he watched the exchange saying, "I've been watching for some time, I think it is gestational diabetes."

Roger asked, "How do you know?"

Renee said, "I have type two diabetes and I know the symptoms.

Since no one has said anything I assume it is due to the pregnancy or they would have had us look for insulin. "Roger nodded to her and walked over to speak with Dickie.

Midway across the room Laurie stopped him, pulling him aside said, "I need to talk to you."

Roger, had become close friends with Dickie and was concerned for his friend's wife. Laurie was insistent that he come speak with her telling him it would only take a few minutes. Roger nodded and followed her to the far side of the room.

Laurie spoke softly saying, "Roger, I know what you are going to say, but I need you to listen to me."

Roger looked at her confused and said, "What do you mean?"

Laurie said, "I saw you talking to Renee and she is right in a way, but not entirely."

Roger asked, "How did you know?"

Laurie told him that she overheard them and wanted to talk to him about it before he talked to Dickie. Roger asked her why and she explained that they already knew what was wrong with Jules.

Roger asked, "What's wrong, is it gestational diabetes?"

Laurie said, "No, it is type one diabetes. They have known since she got pregnant that the pregnancy could be dangerous to Jules, even with the best care the outlook wasn't good. They were talking with a specialist before everything happened, who told them the pregnancy might be too much for her."

Roger looked horrified, getting agitated he said, "What do we need to do, can we find her some insulin?"

Laurie said, "They have insulin, we have been keeping it cool with cold packs but it is losing its effectiveness."

Roger asked, "Why have they not told anyone?"

Laurie said, "Because there is really nothing to be done. We thought maybe she would miscarry, but she is nearly six months along now so we are hopeful. Unless something changes this is a death sentence for her, they are mainly just trying to save the baby."

Roger looked away angrily glancing over to where Dickie was anxiously fussing over Jules. Looking back, he said, "What about the camps? Maybe she can get help there."

Laurie looked at him with sadness saying, "You of all people know the truth about that."

Looking down, he mumbled, "I know."

Laurie said, "In the days ahead Dickie will need a friend like you. Amy is already studying up on C-sections. Let's let them have this time without everyone causing more anxiety for them."

Roger looked at her and nodded, turned and left. Laurie went to Dickie and Jules to see if she was ok. Knowing it was likely time for a shot she grabbed the pouch with the test strips and insulin in it. Dickie saw her coming with the pouch and nodded to her as he stood to leave.

Laurie reached out saying, "You need to go to go talk to Roger… he knows."

Dickie put a hand on her shoulder and thanked her before leaving to go find Roger.

The shower rotation was a huge success, Jules finally got hers and everyone felt clean and rejuvenated. A home cooked meal a roof over their heads and a shower made it seem almost like everything was normal. Until the topic of what to do about the vehicles and direction of travel came up.

Gerald came back once the showers were finished and asked how everyone felt. He was greeted with overwhelming gratitude and questions about how they maintained things there. He explained that they kept low key and had an agreement with a local gang. He explained that they were safe there and said they could relax.

Motioning John and Ray to follow, he said, "I need to talk to you about some things."

They followed him outside where he told them of some dangers he had heard over the airwaves. He admonished them to steer clear of the cities, and that they would need to stay off the roads as much as possible.

John anxiously asked, "How are we supposed to travel if we can't drive on the road?"

Gerald said, "I am part of a network that will help you get there, but it will be difficult."

Gerald continued to explain that the gang that watched over them were also not accepting of visitors. He said they needed to be ready to go in two days. The plan was to get them out of the area over the power line easements. They had a relay of four wheelers that could carry them as far as the West Virginia, Kentucky line. After that they would have to walk.

John said, "I think we would rather take our chances in the vehicles."

Ray reached out and touched his shoulder saying, "I wanna hear the rest of what he has to say."

He continued, "I spoke with Arthur and he believes that overland is the way to go as well. The breakdown in the cities is beyond any hope of control and FEMA is still trying to round people up."

Ray asked, "What about Mandy, Julie and the kids?"

Gerald said, "At the border of this territory there will be two groups, one to continue with those going to Kentucky, the other to take them to the territory of Ohio."

Ray looked confused, asking, "Territories?"

Gerald looked troubled, saying, "Much of the area has been split into territories, much like turf that gangs fight over. I told you they don't take kindly to visitors, especially ones that haven't paid tribute."

Again, Ray asked, "Tribute?"

Gerald was frustrated, saying, "Tribute, yes… they will take whatever they think they deserve. Do you remember Lana, the young lady who brought casserole? She was the tribute and that is what they did to her. We need to get your women out of here. If they catch you inside their territory they will not look kindly on it and exact a high price."

Ray nodded and said they were grateful for all his help asking, "When do we leave?"

Gerald said, "Morning after next, I need time to set up the relay and supply caches."

The group enjoyed a few days of rest before the final leg of their journey would begin. They talked about the plan and expressed excitement over their impending arrival.

Mandy and Julie were told of the plan to get them to Ohio and were sent to get the information to Gerald.

The next day was spent repacking what could be taken and relaxing, again, they were brought dinner and took showers in preparation for their journey.

As the sun set everyone settled in for a good night's sleep only Roger remained awake watching out the front window. Just about the end of his watch he saw a figure darting across the yard. Jumping up his hand on his sidearm he made his way to the side door. It was the young lady whom had brought food that first day.

Roger let her in where she hurriedly gave him her message. "Gerald said, be ready to go in five minutes, also to tell you, time is up and to hurry."

As quietly as she came, she left back out the side door and along the row of houses.

Roger woke Dickie saying, "It's go time, get everyone ready. Five minutes is all we have been given so let's get everyone ready."

They were all ready and packed in five minutes waiting for the word to move.

# Chapter 22

## "The Relay"

*"All Tyranny needs to gain a foothold is for people of good conscience to remain silent."*
-Thomas Jefferson

The knock came right on time, when they opened the door Gerald stood in the doorway a look of horror on his face.

"Quickly." He said.

They followed silently into the night, not even sure of where they were going. As promised they were lead to a group of four wheelers waiting to take them out of the territory. John turned and shook Gerald's hand, thanking him for all their help.

The coordination needed to pull off such an effort was staggering John at one point had explained to Amy. The first day brought them to the edge of the territory at the southernmost point. What they witnessed was what Dickie called amazing.

There were cache points all along the trail. They stopped for breakfast and fuel where they were given coffee, eggs, bacon, grits and hash browned potatoes. Snacks and drinks were handed out and drivers were changed four wheelers fueled. Again at lunch the same thing, hot soup and sandwiches with lemonade.

By the evening meal they were all exhausted but still could not stop. They were fed a hearty stew with fresh biscuits and more coffee. They were each given a small sack with snacks and supplies for the evening. At the edge of the territory they were told to camp until the next territory's relay was to begin.

They camped two days before they could safely travel through the territory. During the two days of camping again, they were provided with meals and essentials. They were instructed to have no fires or flashlights and to remain in camp and as quiet as possible.

During the second evening a patrol was spotted walking the power lines and the group then understood the caution of their benefactors. At one point Amy asked one of the men guarding the camp his name.

He kindly refused and said, "I'm sorry ma'am but we don't want to know your names and you can't know ours. We don't even know where you are going except our specific leg of your route. Don't be offended if we don't talk to you much this is for your safety and ours. If anyone is questioned none of us can give any information.

Amy went to John saying, "I'm not sure if I should be grateful or terrified."

John reassured her saying, "I know babe, but I believe they are truly working this to best help us while insulating themselves."

Dickie overhearing them told her that he agreed with John. They were instructed to have all gear packed at all times in case they had to leave quickly. This was also part of the reason food was provided, they could not cook and gear remained intact except when in their tents.

They had all been saying goodbyes to Mandy and Julie, Aaron and Mary for two days, but this morning the time came, they were first to head out.

Jules was struggling more each day as her insulin became almost useless. Laurie seeing her condition brought her behind a tree to administer a triple dose of insulin in hopes it would keep her going.

One of the drivers saw this and asked about her supply. He was told it was almost worthless at this point. He nodded and returned to his position without another word.

Laurie insisted on having Jules sit in the cart with Matty and the gear, afraid she was too weak to hold on. Periodically during the morning ride, Laurie noticed the driver who had asked about the insulin, looking at Jules. When they stopped for lunch, she told Amy what happened at camp. Amy reassured her that his ride was over.

Four wheelers fueled and the group fed it was on to the next leg of their journey. But as they were preparing to leave Laurie saw the man pointing to her and talking to another driver that would be carrying them to the dinner location.

Laurie approached the driver and said, "I know that last driver is concerned for Jules but please do not tell the others about her."

The driver said, "Don't worry ma'am, I won't say anything."

The road was rough in this section and a few times they had to go through some of the wooded areas off the main access road, making the trip very bumpy. The travelers were weary by the time they arrived at the dinner rendezvous.

When they arrived the driver Laurie had previously spoken with immediately went to the lady handing out the food. They both then searched inside a cooler, when he returned, he asked Laurie to come and check on something for him. Once away from the crowd, he handed her two insulin pens. Apologizing for it only being two he told her they were good and that she only needed the normal dosage.

Laurie began to cry thanking him. She quickly led Jules to a private area where they could test her blood sugar and administer the fresh insulin. Jules was crying because the muscle cramps were so bad she could hardly walk. This was one of the signs her kidneys were failing and both she and Jules knew it. Laurie went to Dickie and told him that he and Georgia needed to spend time with her.

Again their meal was filling and they each were given a small satchel of things for the evening. After the meal they returned to the vehicles with the fresh drivers and set off for the territory border. It would only be one more day of travel and they would reach the Kentucky border.

Much as the previous nights had been they were to have no fire or lights of any kind. They were once again instructed to remain quiet and alert. Everyone settled into tents except those on watch. John and Dickie were on first watch and each sat motionless, watching in the darkness.

John whispered to Dickie near midnight, "You've been quiet these past few days is everything alright?"

Dickie nodded up and down silently, his eyes never leaving an outcropping of bushes to his left. He signaled John to be silent and move around to the side of the bushes. John immediately took the cue and began moving laterally from where they were to a position near the bushes, while Dickie approached them head on.

The bushes rustled and something moved startling John into action. John leapt at the place he saw the silhouette, while Dickie moved in closer. John surprised the figure who made a low growl in anticipation of his attack. Dickie, stopping his advance, frantically waved to John but it was too late. John was already into the bushes with the intruder. The bear howled loudly as its massive paw struck John, knocking him to the ground. The claws leaving behind a set of bloody gashes across his chest.

Dickie could see John laying lifeless in front of the bear. Trying to think he began waving his arms, he ran right at it, just hoping he could look big enough to frighten it off. The bear pawed at John a few more times before retreating into the forest. Dickie rushed over to John and checking him could see he was still alive.

By now everyone was up and wondering about the noise. Dickie grabbed Amy and ran back to John, Mark followed with Ray right behind. They carried him to the tents and got him comfortable in their tent.

Amy with tears, said to Dickie, "I can't see anything to check on him."

Dickie looked thoughtful a moment, then said, "I gotta idea."

He went outside the tent and asked everyone for their blankets, coats and anything that would block the light. In moments they returned, arms full of the requested items.

Looking at Ray he said, "In World War two, they would block out the light because of air raids. Let's just black out the tent."

Ray immediately understood what he wanted to do and they began to drape the tent with blankets. Once they were finished Amy was told to turn on the lantern. A few small cracks of light could be seen which were quickly covered. She could now assess the wounds and check him out. The entire time she scolded him for his carelessness.

Amy began to look at the gashes and check him for other injuries. She requested her first aid bag and some water, which Roger and Jenny had already gone for and handed it to her through a small opening in the tent. By now John was awake and except for needing stitches was doing fine. Amy stitched him up and gave him some pain killers to help him sleep.

Roger and Ray took the watch lasting until daylight and talked of what they would do once they reached Kentucky. The ride through the power lines would end when they reached the Kentucky border and there was no telling what would be their options from there.

The morning of their last day on the four wheelers they were served a large breakfast and told that Arthur was updated on their location and situation.

An older lady approached Laurie handing her a small pouch while grasping her hand said, "I hope this helps." Laurie opened the pouch to find five more insulin pens, in tears she thanked the lady and hurried over to show Amy.

John was up and moving when the guys came over to talk with him. Setting up a map of Kentucky that had been given them, they showed him red dots on it. There had been caches set up and the locations marked on the map.

Ray looked up from the map saying, "I figure it is about one hundred forty miles left to go."

John did some quick math in his head and said, "If we can go ten miles per day we could get there in about two weeks."

Roger looked around their group and said, "I wonder if we could maintain that pace."

Dickie looked at Roger, who nodded to him and began to speak, "I don't know if Jules could keep up, you may need to leave us behind."

They all looked at him and simultaneously began to object. John waved his arms for them to quiet and spoke, saying, "We are not leaving anyone."

Roger nodding said, "We will find a wagon or something, it will help with gear as well."

John patted Dickie on the shoulder and said, "We are all family now and there will be no further discussion about leaving anyone. We will figure it out if we have to build a litter and take turns carrying her."

Roger looked at Dickie who was already humbled by the gesture and said, "Tell them."

Ray looked at Roger and said, "Tell us what?"

Dickie had tears in his eyes as he spoke, "Jules is going to die."

John gasped asking, "What do you mean, she is going to die?"

Dickie continued, "Her kidneys are failing, the pregnancy is too much on her. She is diabetic and they warned us that even with the best of care there was a chance her kidneys would fail. We were planning to have a backup plan for her sister to donate one if they did. Jules really wanted this baby and now her only wish was that the baby be ok. The kidneys are struggling and Amy isn't sure the baby is far enough along if something goes wrong."

The men all stood silent processing what Dickie had just said.

Dickie continued saying, "We didn't want to be a burden on the group."

Ray angrily said, "You could have told us, we could have been looking for insulin or other things she might need."

Dickie said, "We have insulin, Amy and Laurie have been closely monitoring her blood sugar. We knew when she fainted before the shower that something was wrong and have been just trying to keep her going."

John stormed off grumbling something that had multiple expletives inserted. Talking to one of the riders he asked if there was any way that they could find a wagon or garden cart along the way, that they would need it for Jules.

The rider told him he would see what could be done and walked over to one of the relieved riders and began talking to him. He returned to John explaining that it seemed that the people who had been transporting them knew she was in bad shape and had been getting them insulin and other things. He told John that there were things for her care at the final drop and said they should get moving.

The day's travels were much like the others before, except there was a more somber attitude among the travelers. When they reached the final stop at the Kentucky border, there was a very nice garden cart for Jules that had cushions in it for her comfort, and a second cart for gear.  There was food and solar showers set up for everyone to get cleaned up.  They would sleep in beds this night at an old hotel that seemed like it had not seen guests in many years.

The following day would launch them into the final miles in their journey. With almost seven hundred fifty miles behind them the last one forty seemed like a cake walk.  Some of them worried about what lay ahead while others just reveled in their showers and grand meal that was set before them.

John could not help but feel grateful for the assistance Gerald had mustered for them and wished that someday he could repay the service.

John and Dickie were outside watching the sun set as two of their drivers approached.

One who had been the driver for Kimmie and Renee said, "Be careful of the ladies they are not your ally."

John looked over to where Kimmie and Renee were animatedly talking, saying, "This we know, they cannot be cut loose, yet cannot be trusted either."

The other man handed John a paper saying, "Do not let anyone see this outside of you two."

John looked to the paper and began to ask, but was swiftly cut short by the man who said, "For now just put it away, look at it when there is more privacy.  Another thing to keep in mind, this is Appalachia, people don't take kindly to strangers.  Be very careful who you talk to and who you trust, stick to the map you were given."

John nodded and thanked them, as they walked away Dickie looked at John quizzically and they both shrugged and went inside to eat.

Mark was visibly unsettled and John asked him what was wrong. Mark replied, "I am not sure, something is somehow off about things."

John said, "I agree, we will keep a good eye out and start off early."

# Chapter 23

## "Overland"

*"The flaw in being civilized is that it permit's the uncivilized among us to perpetrate horrific crimes against us in the name of freedom and equality."*
-M. J. Croan

*November 9th*

The morning came too soon for John, he felt as though he'd been beaten and tortured, his wounds aching and bruised from the impact of the bear claws the night before. John, Mark, Dickie, Ray, Danny and Roger sat at a table scrutinizing the map, hovering around it like a scene from an old war movie; while Amy, Laurie, Melinda and Jenny cooked for the day's travels. Matty and Georgia sat with Jules and talked of missing their new friends. Everyone seemed occupied and it almost felt normal for a few moments.

Mark looked around saying, "Where is Renee and Kimmie?"

No one could recall seeing them that morning, Mark hurried to the rooms looking for them. John asked if any of the night's sentries had seen them leaving, and no one could recall anyone leaving or even seeing them since they first arrived.

A few hours passed as they searched for them as the mood grew darker. Comments about scenarios and thoughts of kidnapping were beginning to look more plausible. Returning to regroup and look for anything that might indicate what happened to them, John and Dickie spotted them sitting on a log bench beside the porch.

John approached them, not sure if he was concerned or angry, saying, "Where have you two been? We have been searching for you for hours."

Both of them looked at him like he was crazy, Renee saying, "We've been right here wondering where everyone went."

John was becoming angry because he knew they were not there earlier said, "You were not here earlier."

Kimmie said, "Oh, we were in the attic."

John looked puzzled, but also knew they were not in the house earlier, he had called into the attic himself. He asked, "What were you doing in the attic? No one has seen you both since yesterday."

Renee said, "We were just exploring the place and I guess we fell asleep up there."

John knew that they were lying, but he could not figure out why or where they actually went. The others started returning and asking questions, Mark was just happy they were ok. No one could really understand why it was Mark tolerated some of the things they did. Mark was a helpful, hardworking, honest man; and they both were secretive, vindictive and generally up to no good. John would often tell Amy before all the problems began how he could not understand why Mark put up with it, recalling that at one time, they almost got evicted because Renee was spending all the household money on shopping trips and parties while Mark was working.

Shaking off the uneasy thoughts about these two, John announced, "We will have to stay another night here. It is too late in the day to start out. No one, and I mean No one is to leave the house without one of the guys to keep an eye out."

Laurie said to Amy, "We should use this extra time to get some of this food prepared and packed for travel. We may not be able to cook along the way."

John and Dickie prepared a watch rotation and headed out to walk the perimeter before the sun set. They walked a complete perimeter as far out as they could go and still see the building.

John was quietly walking, looking at the ground when Dickie broke the silence, asking, "What is bothering you?"

John said, "I really don't know, something is nagging me as wrong, but I can't figure out what it is."

Dickie replied, "I have felt like something is not right as well, especially after our driver was so cryptic when dropping us off."

John stopped, looking up at him like a light bulb was over his head and said, "I forgot about the note."

Dickie looked at him quizzically asking, "Note?"

John said, "Remember, the note that only you and I were to read?"

Dickie replied, "Right! Let have a look at it."

John pulled the crumpled piece of paper from his pocket and opened it so they could see what it said.

The note was short, but spoke loud and clear. *"You have a traitor in your camp. A small group of ruthless killers is following you. Someone in your group is leaving markers for them to follow."*

John looked up from the note eyes wide and said, "Do you think?"

Dickie responded, "Renee and Kimmie?"

John said, "They have been disappearing."

Dickie nodded and looked back in the direction of the others and asked, "Why do you suppose they only trusted us?"

John thought a moment and said, "I don't know, but we should keep a very close eye on everyone. I know for a fact Amy is not a problem, and pretty sure Jules is clear too."

Dickie said, "Yeah, we should get them to keep an eye out as well."

John looked down and said, "This is bad, we could be bringing a shit storm to the others."

Dickie nodded, saying, "Well, we can stop the trail of breadcrumbs by making sure everyone stays together. Maybe they will lose the trail, so to speak."

John said, "I hope so."

They continued their perimeter walk and found nothing, on the way back John looked at Dickie saying, "We don't even know what we are looking for. I don't know what kind of bread crumbs are being left."

Dickie said, "I am sure the crumbs for this stop are already planted, we will have to be very aware though. We should observe and let them be left, but pick them up. Our traitor won't know that their messages are not getting out."

John just looked at the ground, saying, "Yea, maybe."

Amy and Laurie prepared a large meal for the night and packed up the prepared food for travel. Roger and Ray examined the map and noticed that they were not at the Kentucky border, but some thirty miles into the state. This left them with a little over one hundred miles to go. It was cold that evening, which made it perfect for keeping everyone together. John had all the mattresses brought to the main living room and a fire was started in the fireplace. Initially they were worried about the smell of smoke, but after Dickie went outside and smelled fire, they knew the smell would not be an issue and once it got dark the smoke would not be seen.

When morning arrived, they packed up and made their way to the power lines which would carry them another fifty or more miles closer to their destination. On the map was marked places where supplies would be cached for them. They were to be careful to follow the map, and avoid areas shaded in red no matter what. It was impressive how in only a few months this network had been established and was working so well.

John asked one of the drivers how they managed to be so organized so soon after the collapse of things and was told that they belonged to the A.N.T.S. network before any of this happened. They had never heard of A.N.T.S. before and were told it meant Americans Networking to Survive. John wondered why he had not heard of this before and wished he had.

They traveled a number of days, on foot. There were complaints from a few, mainly Kimmie and Renee. Danny was struggling to maintain the pace of ten miles per day. His leg was healing well, but he was still weak. Jules was getting sicker by the day. Even with the fresh insulin the pregnancy was taking its toll. Amy and Laurie told John that they could not continue this way.

The pace had to slow no matter what John had hoped, he knew they could not continue as such. Another few days passed and they were only making half what they started out with now at five miles per day. He knew they would have to have a day or two of rest, his hopes were too optimistic. John wanted to push through, only another five or so days at this pace and they would be more than half way there, they were nearly to the area of the map where the power lines intersected with the railroad tracks that they would follow for a time.

At this intersection the location of the cache was an old barn long forgotten by those who built it. Inside the barn there were two men who stepped out as the group approached. Quickly they identified themselves as A.N.T.S. and told them to come inside, they had news from their friends.

One man introduced himself simply as Red, the other said nothing. Shaking hands all around, he told them that there was a hot meal ready on the other side of the barn and that they would spend the night inside.

Red said, "I need to talk to John, which one of you are John?"

John stepped forward with his hand out and said, "Right here." Taking his hand in a handshake.

Red replied, "Good to meet you, let's step outside and chat a moment."

John nodded affirmation toward Dickie and followed the man out the door.

Once outside, Red said, "I was instructed to tell you that you need to be more careful when packing up camp. You still have the group tailing you."

John nodded and said, "We were hoping we managed to lose them without the trail of breadcrumbs."

Red said, "They are struggling to follow now, but they are still on you."

John looked off a moment and said, "I will personally check the camp when leaving. Was that all?"

Red said, "No, I have news from Arthur."

John was excited asking, "Is everything ok? What is the news?"

Red laughed, saying, "Yes, everything is fine. Your friends will be moving soon, but you are to stay on course. They are part of a much larger group that will take over for us once you get closer."

John was full of questions asking all at once, "Why are they moving? Where to? Is everyone ok?"

Red put his hands up for him to calm down, saying, "Everything is fine, I have not been given any of the details. I was supposed to check on you and give you that information."

John nodded, and shaking his hand said, "I'm sorry, thank you for everything."

Red replied, "No problem, I would be excited too, sorry I didn't have more news."

John smiled, saying, "It's good to hear any news. This trip has taken far longer than I ever would have thought and it helps being reminded of our friends."

Danny and Jules were both in rough shape. Danny's wound had mostly healed, but the massive infection took its toll on his recovery. His leg was getting stronger with the help of Amy and Laurie getting him to stretch it each night, but he was becoming frustrated at his limitations. Jules was getting worse each day, at this point everyone knew there was something terribly wrong and it was making the others uncomfortable not knowing.

John looked at Dickie as he stood looking at her and said, "It is time to tell the others what is going on with her."

Dickie looked down and said, "Yeah I know."

John replied, "It might ease the burden on Amy and Laurie as well as you.

Dickie had tears he was holding back when he said, "They don't know if she is going to hold on long enough."

John looked horrified, saying, "We might lose them both?"

Dickie looked at him almost pleading for guidance and asked, "Was it wrong to let her keep the baby?"

John put a hand on his shoulder and said, "My friend, if things don't start righting themselves, you would have lost her either way. She is type one diabetic and insulin dependent, the supply would have run out eventually. No my friend I don't believe it was wrong."

Dickie, tears rolling down his cheeks said, "We talked long ago and she knew I wanted a son, the doctors told us no more children, that her body couldn't handle it. John, she knew this before she got pregnant. I don't know how I'll go on without her."

John became stern saying, "You will go on. You have a daughter to care for and God willing, a newborn. You need to get it together."

Dickie nodded and said, "Thanks mate, not only for this, but for everything you have done. We never would have made it to Dez if it were not for you."

John began to shuffle his feet, saying, "Aww shucks."

They both laughed, Dickie regained his composure and they walked over to where the food was laid out and began making a plate. John and Dickie sat with Roger and Jenny chatting about how much further they had to go, when Amy came over and sat down.

John looked at her saying, "To what do I owe the pleasure of the company of such a fine lady as you?"

Amy smiled slightly and said, "I wanted to talk to you."

John said, "What's up sweetheart?"

Amy replied, "Take a walk with me?"

John stood, saying, "a change to go walking with a beautiful lady? Sure thing."

Once they were outside the barn, John could see she was troubled about something and asked, "What's wrong?"

Amy looked troubled, saying, "We can't keep up this pace, at least not without at least a few days' rest."

John was agitated, saying, "But we are so close."

Amy scolded him, "What good is it if we can't all arrive together?"

John stopped and looked at her, brushing his hand through his longer than usual hair and said, "What do you mean?"

Amy wrung her hands and said, "Its Jules, she is too weak to go on right now. She needs some rest."

John hung his head in thought for a moment, recalling the conversation he and Dickie had only a short while ago and said, "This is a good place, we have shelter and good defensibility. We will stay here, it will be good to get our bearings and prepare things for the next leg of our journey anyway."

Amy was shocked he didn't put up more of a fight and asked, "You're not going to argue this with me?"

John looked sad and said, "No, I guess I knew we couldn't keep up that pace. How is Jules?"

Amy looked sad saying, "I don't really know, she stopped telling us what was going on with her but I know it is bad. Her color is off and she is not eating much, honestly, I don't know how she keeps going."

Amy continued, "At some point her kidneys are going to quit working all together and we are going to have to do something. I have been reading up on C-sections and I'm really worried about the baby as well. I just don't know that much about diabetic kidney failure and the implications for the baby. Eventually Jules will fall into a coma and die, there is nothing we can do about that. My concern is knowing the right time to take the baby. The longer we can wait the better she is only twenty six weeks and there is a chance this premature we will lose them both."

John looked pained as he said, "We will stay put as long as we need to." Then kissed her on her forehead and sent her back into the barn.

A few moments later Dickie came out with Roger and asked if everything was ok. John said that they would be taking a break here for a few days and that they should prepare a watch rotation and get the group settled in.

Two days they remained in the barn, by now everyone knew that Jules was not doing very well. She did not get any better with rest, but instead progressively got worse. Amy told Dickie he was off watches and all other duties because she needed him to pay constant attention to Jules right now. Amy and Laurie knew Jules was fading, but didn't know how to help her.

On the fourth day Amy awakened to Dickie shouting, "Jules, Jules…. Please baby wake up!"

Amy came over to him and placed a gentle hand on his shoulder saying, "I'll tend to her, will you please make us some coffee?"

Dickie looked quizzically at her saying, "Coffee? We haven't had coffee in weeks."

Gently Amy spoke, "There is some coffee in the duffle bag near the cart. I've been saving it for when we had snow, thinking it might lift spirits. Let's have some, shall we?"

Dickie knew today would be the worst day of his life as he walked to the cart his wife had been riding in. He found the coffee right away along with a perk coffee pot. It didn't take long for the smell of coffee to arouse everyone. Amy had Georgia and Matty read a story to Jules so the adults could talk.

She sat in the midst of everyone and sighed as she spoke, "We need to take the baby. Laurie, Melinda and I have been preparing for this, it is important that everyone knows their role here."

Dickie let out a small sob asking, "What do I need to do?"

Amy said, "For now? Be with your wife, when we are ready, I need you to stay close to Georgia. Matty will help you."

Then she began handing out assignments. John and Ray were to go to the creek and get lots of water, filling every container they had. Roger, Ray and Mark were needed to set up a perimeter to keep watch. Jenny would assist Dickie with the kids while Laurie and Melinda would assist with the C-section. Kimmie, Renee and Danny would keep the fires going to boil the water. They all agreed without any complaints and everyone hurried to their task.

Jules never moved or woke up while preparations were made. Dickie was grief stricken and nearly immobilized with sadness. Georgia and Matty did not really understand what was going on but Amy feared Dickie's grief would upset Georgia. Jenny took the kids outside to help gather firewood for the fire. They were admonished by John to stay in an area where he could see them at all times.

The preparations made, it was time to deliver the baby. Following the procedure set forth in all the readings the ladies began the terrifying task. They were not at all sure of themselves and were noticeably shaky.

Dickie reached out for Amy's hand, saying, "The best you can do is more than we hoped for."

Somewhere during his moment Dickie had found some clarity and was now the rock Amy needed to steady her hand. Following the procedure like a textbook operation, they successfully delivered the baby and stitched up Amy. She was still not awake, but the baby, a little girl, Dickie named Kayleigh, after his favorite song by Marillion back in the eighties, lay next to her. She was small and struggled to breathe, what she really needed was an incubator, but she was holding her own... for now. Dickie and Georgia spent the remainder of the day with Jules and the baby, they slept that night all cuddled up as a family.

# Chapter 24

## "Bittersweet arrival"

*"If this is victory, then our hands are too small to hold it."*
-J.R.R. Tolkien

During the night Jules quietly died, her family huddled around her. The sadness of this morning was palatable, everyone was silently going about the tasks at hand preparing for the inevitable funeral they would soon need to attend. Jenny cared for the children while others prepared a grave. Dickie was silent, never uttering a word to anyone as he stoically helped dig the hole that would become his wife's final resting place. This worried John, fearful his friend would retreat into his grief and be unable to carry on.

Amy further worried about Kayleigh, she was still struggling to breathe and she was so tiny she could practically fit in the palm of her hand. They had plenty of formula and she was being fed every hour hoping to quickly boost her weight. Only time would tell if this little miracle would survive in the new and harsh world.

They stayed another night in the barn, but knew it was time to move on. In the morning they would pack up and head for their new home. Dickie was still quiet and reserved, barely even acknowledging anyone and refusing to hold or feed Kayleigh. Jenny kept Kayleigh with her, holding the baby girl against her skin to help keep her warm, hoping her father would soon take up the task.

Georgia remained quiet but seemed more worried about her father than she was about her own feelings. Matty stuck to her side, never letting her be alone. Ever since the loss of his mother, he had become almost cold to anyone but Amy and Georgia. He seemed to have a unique understanding of her grief.

The sun rose and the barn was awakened to the smell of coffee once again. It was Dickie, he made a warm fire and some coffee and tea for himself, to start them on what they hoped was the last leg of their journey.

While everyone gathered around the fire for warmth and coffee, Dickie approached Jenny saying, "I cannot thank you enough for all you are doing to care for my Daughter."

Jenny replied, "It is my pleasure, she is such a precious little girl."

Dickie leaned over and kissed the top of his daughter's head saying, "You hang in there my sweetheart, your mom won't have no quitters in this family."

He then headed over to John, stretching out his hand said, "Cheers, mate for everything."

He then reached out to Amy squeezing her in a big bear hug.

John was happy to see his friend in better spirits, but Amy was troubled.

John asked her what was wrong, she replied, "Stick close to Dickie, he is not alright. He's not being thankful or moving on, he's saying goodbye."

John looked shocked and said, "Are you sure?"

Amy replied, "Yes! Do not let him out of your sight until he deals with Jules's death. There is yet more, Kayleigh is not out of the woods, without proper medical facilities six months along is very premature and she has at best a fifty-fifty chance."

John told her he understood and would keep him busy and make sure he was never alone. Dickie was distraught over the death of Jules and struggled to maintain his composure. Georgia fared far better with Matty at her side, they became inseparable. They had a commonality each losing their mother tragically in this, the world they now lived in.

The camp was packed and the travelers prepared to move out. A head count was taken and all were present. They paused a moment as a group to say goodbye to Jules, each either silently or openly saying a prayer or goodbye. John did not worry about leaving anything at this location as they were leaving behind a grave and were not about to leave it unmarked.

They set out along the railroad tracks that would carry them to the next junction of power lines. They needed only travel twenty-seven miles along the tracks and after only a few hours, even the kids wished for the easy trials of the power lines. The tracks were more difficult to navigate, each side was overgrown making it necessary to travel on the tracks themselves. At first the kids loved it balancing on the track and making a game of it, but soon grew tired of it. The cart was difficult to pull, each step followed by the *whump, whump,* of the hard wheels falling between the railroad ties, then climbing the next.

The sun began to sink on the horizon and it was time to start looking for a place to camp. Beside the tracks about twenty feet there was a small clump of pine trees surrounded by the thorny whips of raspberry bushes. Ray had them stop so he could check it out. Pine needles would be good bedding and the thorny protection made it a good site he said.

Ray and Roger parted the raspberries while Dickie grabbed some pine boughs to place over the newly made path into their little haven. Once they all crossed into the pines they removed the pine boughs and let the raspberries return to how they were. Camp was set up in what seemed like moments, they were all becoming very efficient in its set up and tear down. Laurie pulled out some things for dinner, which consisted of jerky, some previously boiled eggs, cold beans and precooked hot dogs. There was also PBJs on some flat bread they made the night before.

They sat eating as Ray looked over the map, John approached him asking about their position. Ray looked up from the map chomping on a piece of jerky saying, "I figure we have made it a good eight miles, judging by the overpass we crossed about a mile back."

John looked pleased, saying, "Wow, I didn't feel like we made very much progress, that is a respectable distance."

Ray replied, "If we can maintain close to that we should have no more than another day and half, maybe two of these tracks."

John nodded and turned to walk away when Ray asked, "Is Dickie alright?"

John turned back to him, saying, "I don't really know, he has been off on his own, I'm hoping he snaps out of it soon.

Ray looked down and said, "Me too."

They sat silently drinking a hot cup of... What exactly it was no one was sure, except Laurie, but it was hot and sweet with a minty taste.

While they sat staring into the woods, Roger came over and asked, "Hey, do we have a watch rotation established yet?"

Ray looked up at him with a chuckle saying, "You didn't do that yet?"

Roger shrugged and said, "It's always the grunt that has to do the shit work." He smiled and walked over to recruit Mark to help him.

The night was quiet but there was a hint of smoke in the air. They wondered if it was their followers camped nearby. Before the other campers could catch up and even the sun came into view the next morning, they were packed and back on the railroad tracks.

John carefully checked the campsite, pretending the need to relieve himself before getting onto the railroad tracks. He told them to go ahead and he would catch up. He found an arrow made from sticks on the far side of the camp. He was stunned that someone would betray them.

The arrow pointed in the direction on the tracks that they were going. John quickly rearranged the sticks to point in a direction leading off into the woods. Hoping this would at least delay their trackers for a few hours or so.

They hoped the group would make at least another seven miles this day, but they made it twelve miles, so much better than they hoped or expected, this left them only six miles to the intersection of the tracks and powerlines that they would next need to follow. At that intersection they also reached another cache location marked on the map.

Ray could not believe how much help they'd been given, saying to John, "I don't know how your friends did it, but the help we have is making this journey much more bearable."

John replied, "Matt and I have been friends for years and I would never have thought this was possible. But Dez? She is the one that has the resources."

Ray looked impressed, saying, "Sounds like a handy person to have around."

John chuckled, saying, "I'm still trying to figure out what she sees in Matt."

Ray winked saying, "Maybe some handsome devil in camo will come steal her from him." Running his hands through his hair as if slicking it back and raising his eyebrows.

They laughed a moment and then set off on the perimeter check. The location was not as secure as the previous night's camp and was easily visible from the tracks. There was a long trestle ahead that spanned between two ridges and John wanted to scout the area before getting into the open or worse yet trapped on a train trestle. The plan was to get the camp secured and then Roger and Dickie would do a little recon to see if it was safe to cross, or if they should skip it and go down into the valley. Doing so would add miles to their journey, if they felt it safe to cross it they would do so.

That evening they smelled fires again, and after dark Dickie and Roger headed to the trestle. Approaching the area where it was open to the valley they were stunned to see the number of small fires scattered through the woods. They were definitely not alone. Dickie made the gesture to have a look at something, pointing with his index and middle fingers to his eyes, then pointing to an area just below the beginning of the trestle. There just below was a small fire with a number of figures sitting around it. Silently they crept closer, trying to hear the conversation and maybe get an idea of who they were, and if they were a threat.

In the stillness a voice boomed out from beside them, saying, "We know you're there and who you are, show yourselves."

Startled, Dickie stood, pushing Roger to the ground as he did. Dickie put his hands up saying, "I was just trying to see who you were."

The voice responded, "The other one too, stand up."

Roger stood, looking around, he could see no one.

The voice said, "You know the routine, we don't want to know you nor you us. The bridge is not safe in the daytime, go get the others and cross tonight. Another team is on the far side and will lead you to a different camp spot."

Dickie looked at Roger and then into the darkness saying, "Are you with…"

The voice cut him off, "There is an update from Arthur at the intersecting point. Go now, get the others and cross. This area is not secure and you are not safe here."

They nodded and quickly returned to camp. Hurriedly entering the camp, they startled John, who hopped up asking what was wrong. They quickly explained what they'd been instructed to do and said they needed to pack up quickly and go.

After explaining that they would receive an update at the intersecting point and, how the voice told them that they were not safe. There was no question, everyone quickly stowed their things and broke camp. Within the hour they were ready to cross the trestle.

Approaching the edge of the tracks, the voice materialized. They were shocked to see it was a teen boy, he looked no older than fourteen. He instructed them to move quickly and silently. He led them out onto the trestle with two other teens that were previously sitting at the now extinguished fire following up the rear. It was obvious they did not intend to come back across as they carried their packs with them.

They were met on the other side by another group of teens that led them to a small outcropping that made a makeshift cave. They already had a weave of branches across the front of it and ushered everyone inside. They learned that this was where these teens lived and asked them about parents.

These teens ranging in age from about twelve to seventeen, seemed to be well supplied and put together.

A young girl who looked to be one of the youngest said, "When they came to put everyone in the camps my dad sent me and my brother here, the others are the same."

Ray asked, "Have you heard from your parents?"

The girl looked down, saying, "None of us have. Up on the next ridge is mister Goins, he came here a few weeks after and told us they would not be coming back."

Ray was saddened by the harshness of life now and said, "I'm sorry to hear that."

The young girl said, "We help the network now and they help us. Things are different now than they were."

Ray blankly stared at her, she was right and he knew it, nothing would be the same again. They rested and were offered some meager tidbits for breakfast, it was obviously all the group of teens had. John told them they were fine and even had some extras that was becoming too much to carry would they mind if the group slimmed down the packs and left some with them. The teens knew what he was doing, but didn't object, they were grateful for the extra food and supplies.

They headed back down the track to the intersection of the railroad tracks and power lines that would lead them into Richmond, Kentucky. Today's travels were shorter and they arrived at the cache location before sunset. It gave them a chance to set up their camp and relax a little bit. The cache was filled with food and even goodies. A note that read, *"Happy Thanksgiving, it is not a feast, but hopefully will bring you some joy in your travels. The area should be secured and there is an old well just to the north, it is covered with a steel door, the water is good."* It was signed simply A.N.T.S.

No one realized it was Thanksgiving already, there were mixed feelings, ones of joy over the feast that was left them and sadness at the Thanksgiving holidays of past and lost loved ones.

Dickie was quiet, just staring off into the woods, it startled him when John approached, saying, "Everything looking good?"

He stuttered a moment and replied, "Don't sneak up on a guy like that."

John laughed feebly saying, "Didn't mean to startle you. I just thought you were looking at something."

Dickie grimaced saying, "I'm sorry, I was just thinking of Jules and how she loved to make a huge meal on Thanksgiving."

John put his hand on his shoulder and said, "I am sorry my friend, I didn't think about how a holiday might affect your family."

Dickie looked up at him, a small tear in the corner of his eye, quickly he regained his composure and stood, saying, "My family... I've got to take care of them, Jules would toss a pan at my head if she knew how I've acted."

John smiled inwardly, and pointed over to Jenny, who was still holding Kayleigh and talking with Georgia and Matty. Dickie reached his hand out to John thanking him for being there for his family, nodded and walked over to where Jenny sat.

Approaching Jenny he asked, "How's Kayleigh doing?"

Jenny looked up at him, saying, "She's eating well finally, and seems to be breathing better. I think she was producing extra insulin for Jules and once they were separated she kind of had to re adjust"

Dickie still struggled to contain the tears as he spoke, saying, "I can't thank you enough for all you have done for my children."

Jenny stood and handed Dickie the tiny swaddled infant and said, "I am going to go fix her a bottle, have a seat and visit with your baby girl."

Dickie failed in keeping back the tears that now sat like droplets on his bottom lash, not big enough to fall but too much to pull back and hide. He sat with Matty and Georgia holding Kayleigh. He looked upward as if knowing somehow Jules were watching and said, "She's beautiful my love, I will protect them right up until my last breath."

He hugged his daughter close and openly cried mourning the loss of his wife. Matty squeezed his hand and hugged him before going to join Amy at the feast preparations.

They did not know that today was Thanksgiving and they had good reason to give thanks on this day. They made it to the last intersection and would soon be finding themselves among their friends. The A.N.T.S. network continued to see them across the state providing caches.

They were thankful for Gerald and his group for the ride clear across the lower section of Pennsylvania and the news from their friends. Each reflected on the weeks and months past and some talk of how fortunate they were to have all the help that made the journey bearable. They talked of the friends they lost and the betrayal they suffered and considered how much more difficult if not impossible the journey would have been.

The evening mood swung from one of thankfulness and gratitude to tears and sorrow. Tomorrow they would begin the journey of the last twenty miles to Richmond, they would leave the power lines there and follow some older country roads. Somehow, Richmond felt like making it to their destination even though they still had another leg of the journey to go at that point. They knew from their benefactors that Richmond was under the protection of the Militia that their friends were associated with. That gave them a feeling that this would afford them more protection.

Calling it a night they went to bed, sentries walked the perimeter and kept a keen eye. As John walked his watch he could not help but think about those that followed them. He knew they still had a tail, no one could seem to figure out who or why, but they were out there in the dark following them. Someone in their own camp was leaving clues, in their midst...a traitor.

# Chapter 25

## "Sickness"

*"Sometimes even to live is an act of courage."*
-Seneca

*November 21ˢᵗ*

The morning was cold and hazy with a light drizzle, the dampness making everything feel even colder. There was something wrong in the camp, only a few were moving about and some moaned as though in pain. Dickie walked over to Amy, who was up and asked her what was wrong.

Amy said, "I don't know, there is a sickness, I can't tell if it is food poisoning, some kind of dysentery, or my worst fears."

Dickie shuddered and asked, "Your worst fears?"

Amy explained that Ebola started with fever, vomiting and diarrhea. Telling Dickie they needed to separate everyone, sick from well.

Dickie hurried to see if Jenny was ill, she was not and the children weren't either, he settled them into the area on the far side of the camp. Setting up a tarp over them and a small fire in a Dakota pit, this would hide the flames from unwanted attention and keep them warm. Amy already had

John and Roger settled into the large tent that would now become the infirmary and quarantine area. Kimmie and Renee were fine, but Danny, Mark and Melinda were ill. Laurie wasn't sure if she was sick or just upset so she sat away from those that were not sick, but she did not go into the quarantine tent. Ray was like Laurie in that he felt slightly ill, but not like the others, so he too stayed separate but on watch across the camp. He set up a spot with some cover and a tarp to keep the rain off of him, but near the power lines, away from the others.

One tent was kept for those not at all ill, Kimmie and Renee slept in there, another for Jenny and the kids. The last of their four tents was for Laurie and Ray, who were both still feeling slightly queasy but not really ill. The girls were asked to help with watches, but Kimmie and Renee were lazy and didn't want to stay awake. Dickie, Laurie and Amy each relieved Ray in his position. Jenny put the kids down and set a watch near their tent.

Days went by with little improvement and worries of dehydration became the first order of priority, keeping those ill hydrated would be the key. Amy was sure it was not Ebola, they suffered no bleeding as can be seen in hemorrhagic fevers, but they were not out of the woods yet.

Near dawn of the third day, John called out to Amy. She hurried to the tent and found that his fever broke, he was alert and thirsty. Still weak from the fever and dehydration he tried to rise, instantly he fell back, dizzy and nauseous.

Amy said, "You need to take it easy."

John wearily replied, "Is everyone ok?"

Amy told him, "Yes, so far everyone is hanging on. I feared the worst but I think it was just a case of food poisoning."

John asked, "Why didn't you get sick."

Amy replied, "I actually think it was the honey mead. Ray and Laurie were feeling queasy for a day and they only sipped it, just to try. Dickie and the rest of us girls who didn't drink any have felt fine.

John said, "I don't understand how honey mead could have food poisoning."

Amy softly replied, "Well, I'm glad everyone is feeling better and we will be on the move again soon."

She looked to the door of the tent and leaned in to kiss John, whispering in his ear as they hugged, "I don't think it was food poisoning, and I think our traitor was trying to slow us down. You guys need to rest as much as possible, seems pretty certain we are going to have trouble soon."

John looked at her, eyes wide, he gave a slight nod, saying, "Is there anything to eat? I'm starved."

Amy laughed an uneasy laugh and said, "Let me get you some broth."

Dickie was by the fire when Amy approached, she began to spoon some broth into a cup. She nodded to him, a signal letting him know that she passed on the information to John. Dickie nodded and walked to the watch location where Ray was waiting. Knowing they could not move on yet, the chances of a confrontation became more likely by the day.

On the seventh day at this camp the illness was mostly gone and they were moving about normally. Mark was the only one still ill, but was improving every day. Dickie, with

Roger and John sat that evening around the small fire discussing moving on and having Mark ride in the cart when needed.  Renee walked up to them, hearing them talk about moving on and pretended to look upset.

Raising her hands, palms up beside her head, she began to act concerned for Mark's welfare, when in fact she only visited Mark one time, three days ago.  After her visit he was just a little sicker.  Amy thought it was because of the excitement and chaos her and Kimmie brought everywhere they went.

Again acting upset she stood in defiance towards the three saying, "He cannot be moved right now.  I forbid it."

They looked at her like she completely lost her mind.  John said to her, "We will take every precaution and Amy is taking good care of him, he would be better off if we could get him to a real doctor anyway."

She stammered and replied, "I don't like it at all, and I think he needs a few more days."

Roger stood and angrily shouted, "How would you know, you haven't even given him the time of day."

John reached out touching his arm, indicating to him to sit down, saying, "Amy will decide, she and Laurie have been caring for him.  We would never knowingly harm him."

Renee huffed off, returning to the tent that she and Kimmie shared.  Angry conversation could be heard but she did not come out of the tent for the remainder of the evening.  John knew something was up with these two, but hated to think they were the cause or the traitor.

*December 1st*

The next day found Mark feeling much better and he agreed they needed to get moving. The tents were packed up and the site cleaned to leave little trace, but after ten days in this place it was difficult to make it look untouched. They determined that leaving no trace of who had been camping was the best they could do.

Their path now returned to the power line right of ways they found themselves at less of a risk of contact with other people. The illness brought to light, a fear almost forgotten amongst the others, that of Ebola. Having no contact with anyone in the past ten days Amy said was helpful.

John asked, "Why do you say that?"

Amy replied, "Because Ebola has an incubation period of up to twenty-one days and we can't risk bringing infection to the others."

John pursed his lips in thought, saying, "You're right, I didn't consider that. We need to be more careful and remain at a safe distance from anyone from this point forward."

Amy nodded as Dickie spoke from behind her, "We should have eyes open all sides while traveling, and making sure no one approaches us."

Stopping to check on Mark and have a quick meeting for everyone to be aware of the Ebola concerns they quickly got back on the path.

That day the managed four miles, and while it wasn't their best distance, John said they had made good progress. The terrain was a little rougher as the hills continued to rise and fall and Mark was still weak.

Over the next few days they made similar progress and saw no one. There was a cache exactly as marked on their map and they were careful eating. Ray, who had not been sick volunteered to taste everything and wait to see if any illness would fall upon him. Ray was visibly nervous about eating anything, but proceeded to eat some of the bread and fruit. Anything in cans was deemed acceptable and they prepared all canned food that evening.

Trying to make Ray feel better about it, John said, "Way to get all the best food there guy."

Ray grimaced saying, "My momma didn't raise no dummy."

John knew the fears as did everyone else. Although laughing everyone knew, this was a dangerous move on his part. Ray whispered to John that he felt like a goldfish in a bowl, everyone staring at him from a distance. John laughed and told him he was just about as pretty as one too.

Ray had no ill effects from the food and the relief was almost palatable amongst the travelers. The mood bordered on joyous as they traveled alongside the right of way. Just inside the tree line, where they would be able to maintain some cover made the journey a little more difficult, but deemed necessary for safety.

Midday on this, the fifth day of their final leg, Dickie heard something strange and told everyone to take cover as he and Roger investigated. What he heard was something like a drum, but more like a hollow log being tapped. Woodpeckers abounded, but there was something rhythmic about this, it dawned on him that it was rhythmic and he recognized it.

Turning to Roger he said, "I knew this was Morse code."

Roger then recognized it, saying, "Now that you mention it, I hear it too."

Dickie said, "I'm not real good with it, can you make out what it is saying?"

Roger nodded, his eyes looking up and right as he listened. He reached out to Dickie, signing for something to write it down with. Dickie searched his pockets and finding nothing, put up one finger and ran to where John was. Making the same sign at the group, Amy reached into her pack a produced a small pad and pencil. Dickie returned to where Roger was and handed him the pad.

Roger said, "It is fast and I am rusty but I have managed to get a few words already. It is repeating so I will get it all in a few minutes as long as it continues."

They listened carefully hearing the rhythmic tapping and saying each sequence. Dot dash dash dot, dot dash, dash, dot dot dot. Dickie wrote the code out as Roger continued to listen.

Roger said, "Next word, dash dot dash dot, dot dash dot dot, dot, dot dash, dot dash dot. You get that?"

Dickie nodded and they continued until the message began to repeat. They sat down to decipher the code and Roger easily converted the dots and dashes into words.

"*Path clear camp just beyond tower painted red, message and supplies delivered. A.N.T.S.*"

Tapping on an empty water bottle in response, they sent the code for, "Understood, KY bound."

The tapping ceased and they returned to the others, explaining what they were able to decipher, the travelers looked for the red painted tower. They found the red paint on the fifth tower, nearly two miles from where they heard the Morse code. Stopping at a small pine clearing they found a pile of rocks carefully stacked.

Roger smiled, dropped his pack and said, "Home sweet home."

Within minutes of arriving to the clearing a rider appeared with a satchel. He unceremoniously tossed it in their direction, tipped his hat and rode off. Inside they found canned foods, rice and oatmeal. There was jerky and some kind of pemmican bars and a note.

The note read *"Large gang activity beyond Richmond, at blue painted tower exit power line easement. Look for blue ribbons, follow to house with blue shutters. Enter via back yard into the house through bulkhead. Inside supplies, truck will come in two days' time and carry you last leg. Do not leave the house or speak to anyone, Ebola confirmed outskirts of Richmond."*

They were excited knowing the end of the journey was near. That night they rested and talked about making it to the blue tower the next day. Everyone wanted to sleep indoors again and even if just for the feeling of normal that could be to just relax on a sofa. John talked about hanging out with Matt while Danny couldn't wait to see Toni and Jeremy.

During the midnight watch, Danny saw a figure dart across the easement in the moonlight. He snapped twice to alert John, who was on watch with him. Pointing with his index and middle finger to his eyes, then pointing to a tree where he had seen the figure crouch, he nodded to John to watch. John too saw the figure move to another tree, and another making their way into the woods.

What it was neither knew, shrugging in silence to one another. They both remained on high alert until relieved at four a.m. When Ray and Dickie appeared to relieve them they were briefed on what was seen. Dickie returned to the tent and coming back with Mark to stand his watch, he then disappeared into the woods, moving silently in the same direction the figure was seen.

Ray looked at Mark saying, "I hate it when he does that."

Mark yawned whispering, "Gotta give it to him though, he never made a sound. I'm glad he's on our side."

Ray nodded and with a little chuckle in his voice said, "You got that right."

Two hours passed before Dickie whistled his return, after arriving, he waited for to John to join in the debriefing. Telling them what he saw reminded them that they were not alone.

Dickie began, "It appears that the guy was just passing by and was unaware we were even here, but there is something else."

John looked perplexed, saying, "Well... are you gonna let us in on it?"

Dickie nodded and continued, "I found something you're not gonna like, and before I go into the details we need to get the others on breaking this camp ASAP. We need to be on the move immediately and leave NO sign or indication of where we go."

John looked stunned as did the others, he got the women started on breaking camp and instructed Amy to see to it that there was no trace of them.

Returning to the conversation John said, "Ok, we will give it the once over to check after they are done packing up."

Dickie sipped the coffee, and mumbled "All I want is a bloody cuppa Tea!" sighing, he said, "Our benefactors were right, we are being tailed, I don't know why they haven't hit us.  They are just following, watching our every move. I sought out all of their scouts watching camp and eliminated them so we should be able to slip away."

Mark gasped saying, "Someone has been watching us all this time?"

Dickie continued, "I made sure to ask a few questions of our observers.  They are under the impression we are going to a compound that is easy pickins and flowing with milk and honey, all the supplies they could ever need."

John looked puzzled saying to no one in particular, "I don't know why they would think that."

Dickie said, "Me either, until I went to check the camp and see for myself.  I found something very interesting sitting right there in front of the fire."

Ray said, "Something?"

Dickie responded, "In a manner of speaking. Ok, so I can see but not hear the camp.  I see sitting right up front and center that Morgan bitch."

They all gasped as Dickie continued, "She was busy spinning some kind of tale and they were all sitting around listening to her.  So of course I had to get a closer look so I could listen. She was telling them of the compound where

Matt and Dez are, and that they would be able to have all they need and go on raids from the secret location. I learned a few things listening, she is not alone, and that other bitch we tossed with her, is along as well."

John said, "Cindy."

Dickie pointed in his direction, saying, "That's right, her."

Roger asked, "Is there anything else?"

Dickie said, "Yeah, they don't know how we have been keeping ahead and losing them. So they don't know about our helpers. Someone in this camp is definitely feeding them information. I do know from listening, that she hates each of us in this little pow wow. This is why I know all listening right now are trustworthy, let's keep this to just us."

Dickie took a long drink of his coffee, while he gathered his thoughts and continued, "They plan to ambush us right before arrival, so this little ride we are getting should help, but not for long. She has someone on the inside at the house that has been getting CB messages relayed."

Ray showing his anger said, "There is another in the camp we are going to?"

Dickie said, "Yeah, but I don't think these guys will be able to stand up to them and us, they aren't that big. There is maybe twenty of them, including women and some children. I am worried that they could attack us so soon after arrival that no one could get prepared."

John stood and said, "Ok, let's adjourn this and get moving. Roger and Ray, will you police the site and a good twenty paces out in a perimeter, I am sure there is a note. This one we definitely have to find. Mark, get the others moving so they don't see what we are doing in the camp or realize we are looking for the note."

Dickie stood and said, "John, the bodies of their guys need to be hidden."

John agreed and he and Dickie began to collect the three bodies. They moved them to the other side of the easement where they piled them up, covering them in pine boughs and leaves.

John was right, Roger did find a note that simply said, *"Follow the blue ribbons."* John considered leaving the note and once they found the ribbons, sending them off in another direction, but he thought it was too risky to leave such a clue if he failed to get to the ribbons. It wasn't long before the area was left as though no one had been there and they caught up to the group. It seemed to take forever, but in reality it was less than five miles to the blue tower. The ribbons to the path were quickly found and the group exited the easement and struck out into the woods.

Dickie made a big show about scouting on ahead of them to check it out and took off in a trot following the ribbons. When he was out of sight, he immediately doubled back to end up behind them and just out of sight. He quietly collected the ribbons after they passed by, making sure that they were leaving no trace for their followers.

By nightfall they all arrived safely, Dickie was sitting on the back stoop when John approached saying, "Where did you take off to when we were getting here?"

Dickie grinned up at him and reached into his pocket, pulling out a handful of the blue ribbons.

John laughed and said, "I sort of figured it would be something like that.

John went up the stairs to go see if they were settled into that little house with the blue shutters. Walking into the kitchen, he saw here was food on the counter and a note that reminded them not to have contact with anyone. John thought back to the beginning of their journey and how they thought they had enough. He mused at how truly ill equipped they actually were and was thankful for their friends.

The two days passed quickly and most just took the time to catch up on some sleep or reading. In the evening of the second day there was a knock at the door. The inhabitants of the little house sprang to alert as John cracked the door open. Taped to the outside of the door was a note, again reminding them to have no contact but to prepare for transport, another knock would come when the bus arrived.

When the bus arrived, the driver was wearing a full hazmat suit including a respirator. It made the group feel strange and the children were frightened of the man. As they boarded the bus the man told the kids that there was candy in the box back there for them, his voice told them he was smiling despite his face could barely be seen.

Once everyone boarded the bus the gentleman stood to talk, He removed his mask to speak and said, "Precautions, you understand." Everyone nodded as he continued, "This is not a long trip and you will be briefed when you arrive."

# Chapter 26

## "Reality of life now"

*"We can evade reality, but we cannot evade the consequences of evading reality."*
-Ayn Rand

In less than an hour they were pulling up to a house, it was dark inside and looked like it had been abandoned for some time. The front window was boarded up and a number of bullet holes riddled the siding. John stared out the window as they pulled around the drive, wondering what place this was.

Suddenly Matty jumped up running to John's window exclaiming, "We're here!"

John looked at him asking, "Where are we?"

Matty looked at him quizzically saying, "This is my dad's house, him and Dez are here. We made it!"

The bus stopped and again the driver stood to address them, saying, "Inside you will find some items left for you, as you can see the group is no longer here. There is a Walkie talkie in one of the boxes. You need to contact Arthur with it and let him know you are here."

Questions came quickly and all at once, the man put his hands up for them to quiet and John asked, "Is this the same Arthur that we contacted from Pennsylvania?"

The man nodded and said, "Everything is fine, your journey is over, but you have to remain in quarantine until we are sure there is no threat of Ebola."

John nodded and thanked the man instructing everyone to disembark. They gathered their belongings and began to exit the bus.

The man spoke to John again, saying, "Contact Arthur immediately, he has the ability to contact your friends. He will get a hold of Ryan, the local militia leader, this will get the ball rolling for getting you to your friends."

He then put his gloved hand out for John to shake which John said, "Thank you for everything, I hope you don't think I'm rude if I don't shake but, I think it is important that we maintain the quarantine. We have had no contact with anyone in over two weeks."

The man laughed tossing him a haphazard salute, saying, "Excellent, I'll let them know as well. Good luck and welcome."

John mimicked the haphazard salute and nodded as he entered the house. Matty already made himself at home, knowing the house from all his visits. He brought Georgia to his room saying, "Some of my stuff is still here, come on, let's go in my room and see what we can do." Georgia happily followed and the two of them sat playing dominos.

John found the walkie and contacted Arthur, he told them he would contact Ryan and get word to Matt and Dez about their arrival.

John acknowledged him, saying, "10-4"

Arthur came back saying, "Ryan will stop by tomorrow to chat with you, till then just relax. If you look out the front door you will see one of the militia vehicles sent to keep watch, take a break y'all deserve it."

John thanked him and went back inside to find a quiet corner to gather his thoughts. Their trip had been a cake walk in comparison to what it could have been, and it was hard. They lost friends and family. He put his head in his hands and silently wept, he wept for Jules, for those the cannibals killed and even for Rita. If it was not for the network that they found he wondered if they'd have made it at all.

Dickie walked up to him and sat next to him, not saying a word. He placed his hand on his shoulder and gave it a good squeeze. Putting his head back against the wall he sat on that floor, knees up and his hands in his lap.

He stayed there next to John a while in silence before saying, "You know it ain't over yet, right?"

John raised his head and looking right at him said, "What do you mean?"

Dickie sighed before speaking and said, "You forgot our followers? We may have slowed them down, but they have someone inside Matt and Dez's group. They also have this address, they will come."

John sat dumbfounded saying, "I was so elated, I never gave it another thought."

Dickie nudged him and said, "You ready for the kicker?"

John said, "What is that?"

Dickie replied, "Whoever their insider is has got to be family to someone here."

John looked around the room at his fellow group mates and said, "That just seems crazy."

Dickie said, "I've thought about this and there is more. Who is Morgan associated with?"

John looked up aghast, saying, "Matt, why?"

Dickie replied, "Think about it, and this. Remember when we tossed Morgan and Cindy out of the group how certain Matty was that Dez needed protecting, and that she was in danger?"

John had a look like he had just had a revelation and said, "No, can't be."

Dickie said, "Probably not, but the only one I want to say anything to is Dez. Remember, we have a traitor as well."

John agreed and they settled in for what they hoped would be a week of rest.

December 11th

Near midday a shout came from the front of the house, a man stood and identified himself as Ryan. Dickie and John exited the front door, closing it behind them. They approached Ryan to be able to talk without shouting what they had to share they did not want everyone to hear.

They shared all they knew about the traitors and the gang that followed them with Ryan, asking that he not share it with anyone but be on heightened alert. Knowing there was a traitor also in Matt and Dez's group meant many secrets about their militia and community resources as well as other information might be compromised. Ryan agreed to keep it between them for now. He also added extra men to guard the house and sent another ten to Dez and Matt.

The seven days passed without incident, Dickie or John spoke with Arthur daily for updates and Ryan stopped in every couple of days.

On the seventh day Ryan knocked on the door, when Dickie opened it Ryan eagerly shook his hand saying, "You're all clear. The bus will arrive for you after lunch."

Over his shoulder he waved at someone to come over, a small group of four vehicles pulled up and exiting them were people carrying dishes of all shapes and sizes.

Ryan said, "Guess it is about time we celebrated your arrival. Sorry about all the cloak and dagger stuff, we just had to be sure."

Dickie chuckled and said, "It's a pleasure to finally chat face to face."

Ryan escorted him and John over to an older gentleman introducing him as Arthur.

John reached out for his hand, saying, "I have a feeling we owe you everything kind sir."

Arthur took his hand and said, "It's been a pleasure tracking your journey on my map."

John asked, "You knew?"

Arthur said, "Of course, after Gerald's group got you to Kentucky, I contacted my nephew, who is head of the Kentucky A.N.T.S. They could not transport you like Gerald's network could, but they do supply caches and drops all the time, it is what they were organized to do before the shit hit the fan."

Dickie standing there said, "This was a massive undertaking getting us half way across the state. The level of organization for both groups was impressive."

Arthur replied, "It had its challenges, but you made it."

Dickie looked down, saying, "Well, most of us anyway."

Arthur looked saddened saying, "The diabetic, Yes, I heard about her. I am so sorry, how is the child?"

Dickie said, "She is small, but a fighter, she is hanging in there."

Arthur replied, "We do have a doctor in town, I will tell Ryan to have him make a visit to the farm to check him out."

Ryan came over carrying four beers, Budweiser's. Handing them out to each of them said, "I bet you could use one of these."

John took a long drink, saying, "Mmmmmm, never tasted better."

They all laughed and continued chatting while others made acquaintances with people from town. Soon the bus arrived and they boarded it waving goodbye to their new friends. Assured they would see one another again all were excited to get to the farm, as Arthur referred to it.

Looking around the bus Dickie noticed Jenny was not on the bus, nor were the children. He called out, "Hold up we are missing someone."

He got off the bus to search for her, he and John both searching the whole house, found nothing.

In a panic Dickie called out, "Georgia... Georgia where are you?"

A faint cry could be heard from the woods behind the house, Ryan instructed his men to flank either side as he, John and Dickie made their way to the rear of the house. Moving out by the barn they heard it again. Dickie took off running full sprint in the direction of the cries. He could see about a hundred yards into the woods Jenny dragging Georgia who was holding Kayleigh. Rage could be seen in his face as he called out moving toward the girls. Jenny looked around, as if looking for help and let go of Georgia.

Georgia began to run full speed toward her father, when Dickie noticed a smile emerge on Jenny's face. Horrified, he knew Georgia was the target. He ran in her direction, calling out to her to take cover, but she could not hear him. A shot rang out and he watched his daughter's steps falter and her slump into the forest floor. Cries from Kayleigh echoed across the hillside. By now all of the men from the bus were in the woods and Roger looked at Jenny horrified that he had not seen her ever leaving notes or anything that would give her away as the traitor.

He stopped looking at her as she smugly looked over her shoulder at him, still brandishing the grin across her lips. Dickie reached Georgia and seeing the blood un-holstered his M9, aimed and fired before Ryan could get to him. Striking Jenny in the upper chest near her shoulder, she dropped to the ground.

Looking up the hill she reached out and cried, "Help me you fools."

No one came for her, she looked around with panic in her eyes as Dickie approached her, murder apparent in his eyes.

Ryan grabbed Dickie by the arm, saying, "She's alive, we need to get her to the infirmary right now."

Dickie raised his hand with the gun in it and backhanded her, knocking her out. Two of the men with Ryan dragged her into one of their vehicles to be taken to their jail. Amy hurried in and took Kayleigh from the arms of his sister while Dickie picked her up, carrying her lifeless form to Ryan's truck. Ryan instructed the bus to meet them at the infirmary and hopped into his truck speeding off towards town.

They arrived and carried Georgia inside, where the doctor and his nurse immediately began working on her. They asked Dickie her blood type, but he didn't know. They said she needed blood, she had lost a lot. Working feverishly to get her stabilized, they barely noticed Dickie slump to a heap on the floor. Ryan helped him off the floor and ushered him to the outer area.

Seating him in a chair he said, "Doctor Burman is a good doctor, a surgeon before all this. She is in good hands."

Dickie shook his head saying, "Hasn't my family suffered enough?"

Ryan put his hand on his shoulder saying, "Do you want to get those bastards?"

Dickie looked up at him, fire in his eyes and between gritted teeth said, "I'm gonna kill every last one of them and everyone they ever cared about."

Ryan sat beside him and began to speak in a softer tone, "Listen, you can't fall apart right now. Only you and John know what is going on, Dez is in danger and we don't know who is leaking the information."

Dickie gasped, "These are my children, and they're all I have left in this world. My Jules is gone and it is my job to keep them safe."

Ryan said, "Exactly, so let's get these bastards and make a safe home for them."

Dickie looked at him like he was asking him to donate his leg and asked, "What do you want me to do?"

Ryan said, "When the bus gets here, get on it. Go and watch over Dez. I am going to go get Sara, she is the kindest woman on earth I swear to sit with the kids while they are being treated. Kayleigh needs some time as well, she is weak."

Dickie said, "You want me to leave my kids?"

Ryan nodded, saying, "Yes, yes I do. I'm asking you to trust me and I know that is difficult, but they really are in the safest place they could be and we need you.'"

The bus arrived and the driver talked to Ryan a moment, Ryan returned to Dickie and said, "Change of plans, we are taking the jeep and two trucks. Let's load them up. Oh, and Dickie?"

Dickie said, "Yeah?"

Ryan looked at him squinting his eyes and said, "If anyone asks, Jenny is dead. We don't want it to get out that we could get info from her, I am not sure she was acting alone."

Dickie agreed and they all climbed into the vehicles. The trip was short to the farm and upon arrival they found that their friends had prepared a feast for their arrival. Everyone exited the vehicles and sought out their loved ones.

John and Dickie gave each other knowing looks as they each exited.

The evening was going well, Danny was showing off his scar from the near death infection while Melinda and Laurie regaled Toni with stories of the journey. Kimmie and Renee never left the food table while Matty couldn't be pried from his father's leg. Mark, Amy and John sat chatting with Matt about Matty's struggles over losing his mom.

Roger and Ray were engaged in serious conversations about defense with Sam and Tawny when Dickie noticed Matty go with Dez into the barn.

Jeremy caught sight of Dickie standing alone watching the going on's and asked him, "Whatcha thinkin theah guy?"

This caught Dickie off guard, but he always loved the way Jeremy would talk like that. Laying on the strongest accent he could muster he said, "Just can't Adam n' Eve all the bollock's we've gone through."

Jeremy taking a more serious tone said, "Yeah brother, I heard about Jules and the kids, how are you holding up?"

Dickie looked dead into Jeremy's eyes and said, "My kids are in the hospital, I don't even know if they are still alive. I am here for your momma."

Jeremy looked shocked and said, "What do you mean my momma?"

Dickie said, "Listen mate, I know you are an ok guy, so I can talk to you. Let's take a walk."

They walked over to where the outhouses were, trying to look like Jeremy was showing him around.

Dickie began, "Pay attention, your momma is in danger. We don't know all the details, but someone needs to stick to her at all times. There is a traitor amongst you, we caught ours and now we need to flush out yours."

Jeremy looked shocked, asking, "Woah, what is going on?"

Dickie said, "Morgan a friend of Matt's is with a gang that has been tailing us. She has information from this group and Dez is her target. They wanna take over the farm and kill her."

Jeremy flushed with anger as his voice raised, "What?"

Dickie touched his arm hushing him, saying, "Tell no one but never let your mom be without someone by her side and most of all don't tell Matt."

Jeremy looked shocked, saying, "Don't tell Matt? Why?"

Dickie said, "Rita told Amy that Matt was having an affair with her."

Jeremy looked disgusted, saying, "Are you serious? Matt was cheating on my mom with that scum bag? Dude, seriously, that chick is nasty."

Seeing Dez come out of the barn they started walking back, Dickie made some disgusting comments as they returned to the party making Jeremy laugh.

The sun began to set and feeling relieved that everyone would soon go inside, Dickie walked with John to the food table. Dez and Amy headed for the outhouses when a shot rang out, echoing across the hills. A scream coming from the outhouse direction drew all attention there. Dez lay half in and half out of the outhouse, blood rushing from her side.

Amy could be seen struggling with someone and took off up the hill after a woman. Jeremy followed chasing the women into the woods. Ray rushed in with his shirt applying pressure to try and stop the stream of thick red fluid. Dickie stepped in and scooped her up placing her in Ryan's jeep and sending Ray along for protection.

Matty hopped into the jeep crying, saying, "I was supposed to protect her."

Dickie scooped Ariel from Charleigh and said, "Take them with you."

Charleigh objected, but another shot rang out sending them for cover, this one from further in the distance.

Dickie turned to her saying, "My kids are also where they are going, and it's the safest place for them. I know you can shoot Charleigh we need all the guns we can get."

Ryan's men were already positioned on the ridge above the attackers and began to create a crossfire as the occupants of the farm fired from below.

John crawled to Dickie and pointed to Matt. They noticed he wasn't even paying attention to the battle, but watching a figure dart across the other ridge with two others following.

Dickie gasped, "That is Amy and Jeremy chasing the shooter."

John was horrified as he looked, he saw Matt taking aim, and he was not aiming for the shooter but for Amy and Jeremy. John and Dickie both sprinted reaching Matt just as he pulled the trigger. Amy faltered and fell to the ground at the same time John tackled Matt.

What was left of the gang slipped away, including the shooter. They counted five dead from the gang, one of which was Cindy. This confirmed it was the same ones that were following them.

Jeremy came down the hillside with Amy hanging on to his arm limping. The bullet passing clean through her right calf.

John and Dickie still had Matt held down as Amy approached saying, "What? Are you blind or something?"

She kicked dirt at him as she headed for the barn to get bandaged. John went to the barn with her to check on the wound. While Dickie stared Matt down.

Matt looked at him and said, "I didn't know it was her, I was just trying to get one."

Dickie knew something was wrong but couldn't prove it... Yet. He shoved Matt at Jeremy and went to check on the others and get a vehicle to take them to the infirmary. Jeremy looked at him shaking his head. Everyone knew Matt was an exceptional shot and it was clear to everyone as well who was who on that hillside. John was sure he was giving the shooter the chance to get away.

Most wounds were superficial, Amy was the only one with a gunshot wound. Sarah made some coffee while they waited for the ok to go check on Dez.

A crackle came over the CB, "Militia leader to farm, do you read?"

Jeremy grabbed the mike responding. "We read you, how's my mom?"

Ryan came over the air saying, "Status unknown on that. I have a person requesting admittance to the farm at the infirmary."

Jeremy replied, "Who is it?"

Ryan said, "She says her name is Rita and she has information about the gang and has proof of who had Dez shot."

Everyone gasped, and John shook his head no. Jeremy replied, "Negative we will come to you."

John and Amy sent Dickie, with Charleigh and Jeremy to town to meet with Rita.

John looked to Mark saying, "We have dark days ahead I                                                            fear."

# Note from the Author

Many of the inventions or ways that the persons in this book choose to improvise are derived from various sources and things learned over the years.

In an effort to share some of these things with my readers following I have compiled a few resources to assist in the application of these techniques.

While I do not personally endorse untrained persons in attempting some things they are not trained to do. I always encourage others to learn so you and your families can be prepared in the event of any unforeseen "dystopian" moments.

Preparedness, is an age old means by which people for generations made it through tough times. Many prepare for eventualities such as described in this book. Being prepared is a mindset. It is sometimes as simple as keeping a months' worth of cash in the bank for something like time off work.

Those in hurricane prone areas might keep water stored or wood on hand to board windows. Persons in Tornado prone areas might have a storm shelter. But the greatest preparedness tool you can have is Knowledge.

Many of us have had, "One of those days." You wake up late to find the pipes are frozen and you can't take a shower. You fluff yourself up enough to not look like you're a wrinkled mass that just rolled out of bed. To find that the car won't start and when it does and you finally get there. Someone dumps a cup of coffee all over you. The day continues this way until you finally fall into bed completely spent.

These days happen… In this book this day happens but on a larger scale. How many of us keep a spare shirt at work in case of coffee? Or have a battery pack to jump the car? This is an example of being prepared.

Many have the view of a person who tries to keep these bad days from being much more than an inconvenience that is possibly not positive. The connotations of the media and other places sets people with an eye on the horizon and the forethought to consider the inevitable as some kind of disturbed human.

Realistically the things in this book could happen and have, possibly not to some of us. But world over many things happen that will carry us from our comfort zone.

If we are spent at the end of, "One of those" days, where will we stand on, "One of THOSE days?"

This book is without a doubt an *idealized* view of how things could go, they find many resources along the way and have help from other like-minded individuals. Ideally we could all live a life free from the constraints and needs of the big cities, but often this is not the case.

Our group in this book must travel over nine hundred miles, not just a small band of wanderers but friends and family of the group in the first book. Many drawing on the knowledge of others and sharing.

In book three Dystopia: The Dark Days, we get to look into the darker side of human nature when no one can be trusted and betrayal is commonplace. At the end of the resource section find a preview of Dystopia: The Dark Days.

Following are a few websites, books and videos I have enjoyed while writing this book. Included are the prior book's resources as well. I hope you find them useful as well.

DJ Cooper

# Resources

## More from DJ Cooper

www.djcooper.co
www.prepperbroadcasting.com/surviving-dystopia
www.survivingdystopia.com
http://survivalblog.com/planning_for_extra_mouths_to_f/

## Composting

Composting is the art of recycling organic matter into excellent fertilizer and garden material. Adding compost to your garden can enhance the nutrients plants need.

Basics of composting
http://eartheasy.com/grow_compost.html
http://www.planetnatural.com/composting-101/
Book: Composting secrets by David Isaac Yoder

# Rain Water

Collection of rain water has been a viable source of water for many in the Midwestern states and continues to be used today.  Please check local ordinances and laws for your area as some areas regulate rain water catchment systems.

A basic article about catching and storing your own rain water
http://www.wikihow.com/Build-a-Rainwater-Collection-System

I love mother earth news, there is always tons of information for the homesteader in this magazine
http://www.motherearthnews.com/homesteading-and-livestock/rainwater-harvesting-system-zmaz03aszgoe.aspx

This one is good because it also touches on the grey water usage
http://www.ext.colostate.edu/pubs/natres/06702.html

# Solar Hot Water

The sun shines on us a tremendous amount of energy. This energy can be harnessed in many ways.

https://www.youtube.com/watch?v=6DKJ4AkxJr0

This site actually has lots of good information
http://rimstar.org/renewnrg/diy_pex_solar_hot_water_thermal_dn.htm

# Wood Fired Hot Water

Those who burn wood for heat could easily heat their water using some of these techniques.

http://www.motherearthnews.com/diy/wood-stove-water-heater-zmaz76ndztak.aspx

# Solar Panels

http://www.mdpub.com/SolarPanel/

http://www.instructables.com/id/DIY-Solar-Panel/

# Batteries

The use of batteries can make a solar, wind or hydroelectric system provide them with enough stored energy to run an entire home.

http://www.instructables.com/id/DIY-Solar-Setup/

http://www.altenergymag.com/emagazine/2010/12/the-diy-guide-to-off-grid-solar-electricity/1650

# Solar Window Heaters

http://www.motherearthnews.com/diy/diy-solar-heating-zmaz77sozgoe.aspx

http://www.thediyworld.com/DIY-Passive-Solar-Heating-Projects.php

http://stonehavenlife.com/7-diy-pop-can-solar-heaters/

# Morse Code

*Noun:* an alphabet or code in which letters are represented by combination of long and short signals of light or sound.

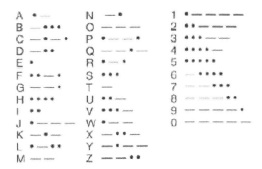

www.learnmorsecode.com

www.morsecode.io

# Bug out bags aka the BOB

www.survivingdystopia.com/how-to-build-your-ultimate-bug-out-bag-aka-the-bob

Book: Bug out Bag by Roger Clark

www.Survivalsullivan.com/154-bug-out-bag-essentials-open-list was fairly comprehensive an in list form

# A.N.T.S

Americans Networking to Survive…I highly recommend you check out this site as an excellent resource for finding like-minded individuals and excellent educational resource.

www.americansnetworkingtosurvive.org

# Cache

A cache or survival cache is a small established hidden supply location. Like with your computer cache, this can be temporary and should be emptied and restocked often. Some good sites for this info can be found below.

www.survivalcache.com

www.survivalistprepper.net/a-preppers-survival-cache-from-building-to-burying

## Canning and preserving

Canning is the process of saving food for later by processing into jars. There is a specific method for doing this to ensure the food safety. My go to book for is the Ball Blue Book of Preserving published by Alltrista Consumer Products.

www.freshpreserving.com

www.homecanning.com

## Dakota pit or fire hole

The Dakota Pit is a means to build a fire for heat or cooking with limited light and smoke signature. A means to remain stealthy from prying eyes in situations when you may wish to remain hidden

www.graywolfsurvival.com/2430/how-to-make-a-dataoka-fire

# Ham Radios

The ham radio is an excellent means of communication worldwide. There are specific rules and regulations for Ham operators and licensure to operate.

www.wireless.fcc.gov will explain the regulations

www.arrl.org this site is full of great information for Hams

# Videos

Youtube channels with lots of great information, be sure and follow their channel so you can get updates whenever they put out a new video

John Milandred, well known for his experience and survival expertise has some great how to videos.
https://www.youtube.com/channel/UCcU9nITkSdxeEbZ2Wo92Gfw

Eric ware, this channel has some very good information about a wide variety of topics
https://www.youtube.com/user/eware421

## About the Author

DJ Cooper is the author of the Dystopia series and other short works. Currently she is a student at Southern New Hampshire University studying for her Bachelor's Degree in Creative Writing/English. Working on a double major in fiction and media

Often writing humor, or research articles for her blog titled surviving dystopia and others, she keeps up on things for her post-apocalyptic fiction. She can be found in front of a computer somewhere, favoring the outdoors when writing. When asked about what kind of writer she is, she says, "The starving kind. Believing that writing is an ART, often times one must sacrifice to maintain the artistic integrity of the works."

She works in and around the Cincinnati, Ohio area flipping houses and spends much of her time in the areas of Kentucky she writes about in the Dystopia books.

### Works by the Author

Dystopia : Beginning of the End

Dystopia : The Long Road

Dystopia : The Dark Days

Surviving Dystopia.com

| Contact the Author | | |
| --- | --- | --- |
| Email : | DJCooper.Author@gmail.com | |
| On the Web: | www.djcooper.co | |
| | www.survivingdystopia.com | |
| Social Media: | Twitter | Djcooper2015 |
| | Skype | DJcooper2015 |
| | Facebook | AuthorDJCooper |

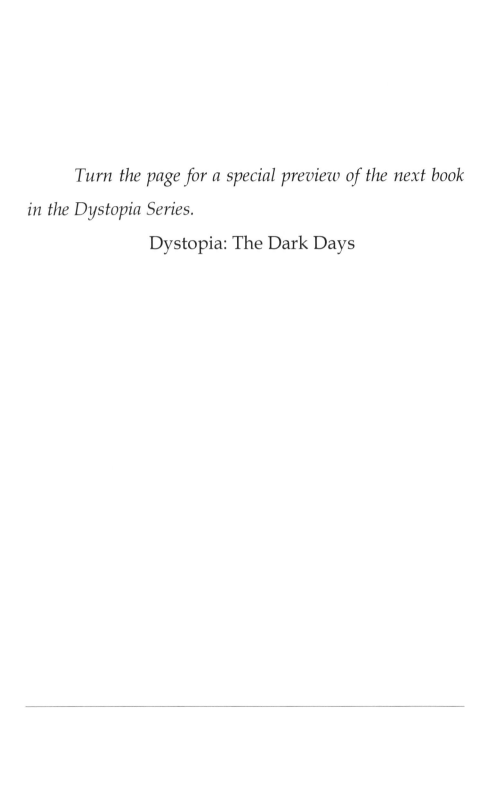

*Turn the page for a special preview of the next book* in the Dystopia Series.

Dystopia: The Dark Days

# Dystopia

## The Dark Days

# Chapter 1

## "Dark days loom ominous"

*"We are fast approaching the stage of the ultimate inversion: the stage where the government is free to do anything it pleases, while the citizens may act only by permission; which is the stage of the darkest periods of human history, the stage of rule by brute force."*
-Ayn Rand

Racing into town with Ryan in the jeep, Dickie sat shotgun while Jeremy and Charleigh sat silently in the back. All were worried about the fate of those at the infirmary. No one knew if Dez was even alive, Dickie worried about Georgia and the fate of those at the farm was as yet, still unsure. Though the battle brief, each knew it would not be the last. Morgan had a vendetta and now Matt's loyalty was in question. Dickie sat wondering if he intended to shoot Amy to save Morgan or if it truly was an accident. Jeremy's face showed an anger while Charleigh was sheer worry. Each in their own thoughts that were clearly shown in their facial expression, silently they rode into town.

Back at the farm Laurie and Sarah patched up Amy and the others not badly wounded. John asked some of the others to sit and discuss defenses. Tawny and Sam volunteered to work on that for a meeting in an hour. The children were settled into a movie in the barn with Janice keeping an eye while she made some coffee. Most worried it would be a long night. Toni recruited Lynn and Rebecca for the task of settling in the new additions to their group. Everyone seemingly had a task... Except Matt.

John sat with Matt across the picnic table outside, staring into his friend's eyes, a look questioning if he had indeed seen what he thought he saw. Asking him the simple question garnered a response he was not prepared for.

John asked Matt, "What is up with you and Morgan, and don't lie because I have already heard a lot."

Matt stoically replied, "She is none of your concern."

John said, "The hell it isn't, we have been through hell. She and another woman killed Kevin and Rita. Following us here she just shot Dez... remember? Your girlfriend? I'd say she is everyone's concern right now."

Matt sat resolute in his refusal to discuss Morgan saying, "I'm not going to discuss her."

John sneered, saying, "We know more than you realize and your own son saw what she did. I'll kill you with my bare hands if I find that you intentionally shot Amy to save that piece of shit."

John got up, leaving Matt at the table, he paused to talk to Connor, and stormed into the barn to check on Amy.

Connor sat staring at Matt with a look of contempt, the word had already gotten around the farm that it was Matt that shot Amy and the uncomfortable stares in his direction made Matt fidget. The farm was busy like a bee hive working on security, triage and preparations for the defense of their homestead. All were involved, some carrying in supplies and food, others digging trenches into the hillside. All determined they would not be caught unaware and off guard again

Arriving at the infirmary Dickie leapt from the jeep before it was even stopped and sprinted into the building. Finding a nurse asked about the condition of his daughter and Dez. To his relief Georgia would be fine, although, she would still need to spend some time there recovering. They were all told that Dez was in surgery and there was no word yet. Quickly they were ushered to the area near the room being used for the nursery, they found that Kayleigh was fussy. She had an IV for fluids and lying in an incubator the nurses were having a difficult time getting her to eat.

Dickie explained, her mother Jules had been an insulin dependent diabetic. The nurse looked at him with a nod saying, "That explains a lot, it seems that Kayleigh had been producing insulin for her mother while inside her. It will likely take a week or so for her little body to adapt from this beautiful symbiotic relationship between mother and baby."

She explained that what happened was, that after the delivery Jules likely slipped into a diabetic coma and died. Noting that it would have been peaceful and how calm it would have been in the arms of her family. Noting that Kayleigh would have to be forced to take formula even just a little until she adjusts.

Charleigh having found Ariel already, volunteered to take care of feeding Kayleigh. Cooing at her she gently picked up the tiny infant and she immediately began to quiet. Offering her the bottle of formula she readily rooted looking for the nipple.  The nurse explained that the doctors felt optimistic about her chances in spite of all the adversity.

They all sat waiting for word on Dez, except Jeremy, who could not stop pacing.  He would sit a moment, then something would trigger him to stand and walk about.

Dickie asked, "Ants in ya pants?"

Jeremy said, "I'm gonna kill that bitch myself."

Dickie nodding, said, "You'll have to take a number mate."

Jeremy looked at Dickie, asked, "Do you believe Matt shot Amy on purpose?"

Dickie said, "I dunno, but I do know there is a lot of things that aren't feeling right."

Jeremy changed his look to one of confusion, saying, "I can't believe he would have anything to do with that skank."

Dickie looked at him hard, saying, "Whoever this spy is at the farm, I will kill them.  We didn't kill Morgan after she killed her husband and what they did to Rita, I won't make the same mistake twice."

Jeremy looked up with realization, and said, "Rita? She is here.  Where is she?"

Dickie looked back and forth and spotting a nurse rose to ask her about Rita. Walking over to the nurse, who was talking to a man in camo.

Dickie said, "Excuse me, sweetheart?" In his best English Accent,

Looking at him, she said, "I heard you talking, and yes she is here. She is being treated for some minor injuries and you will be allowed to see her very shortly."

Dickie nodded and said "Cheers love". As he walked back to Jeremy, the man in camouflage followed and approached them.

Reaching out to shake hands, he asked, "You're friends of Rita?"

Dickie responded, "Yes, we thought she was dead. You know her?"

The man put his handout to Dickie, saying, "I'm her husband, my name is Rich Davidson."

Shocked, Dickie looked at the man asking, "Husband eh?"

The man stammered saying, "Yes, It is a long story and one I'll leave up to her to tell you."

Dickie shook his hand, inviting him to join them waiting for word on their friends and family. Sitting he introduced himself to Jeremy and asked if he was waiting to see Rita also.

Jeremy said, "Yes, I am but I am also waiting to find out if my mom is ok."

Rich asked, "Did she get hurt?"

Jeremy said, "She was shot."

Rich, raising his eyebrows asked, "What happened? I hope she is going to be ok."

Jeremy and Dickie began to tell him, about Morgan, who knew Matt, who was incidentally Rita's ex and her son's father, explaining all the details of how it all worked.

After the long explanation, Dickie blurted out, "She shot her."

Rich stood exclaiming, "Morgan? She is who we followed here to find her son Matty. She shot your mom?"

Jeremy sitting silently, nodded in affirmation.


Coming soon Dystopia: The Dark Days

61831774R00173

Made in the USA
Lexington, KY
22 March 2017